D0231414

CITY OF THE DEAD

An exciting new medieval mystery series

Down on his luck in the Crimea, Venetian entrepreneur Nick Zuliani is dragged out of the gutter by Friar Alberoni. The priest wants him to be his bodyguard for an amazing journey to the court of the Mongol overlord, Kubla Khan, in the fabled city of Xanadu. Zuliani jumps at the chance, but he regrets his decision when he becomes embroiled in solving the murder of the very man Alberoni was seeking…

CITY OF THE DEAD

A Niccolò Zuliani Mystery

Ian Morson

Severn House Large Print
London & New York

This first large print edition published 2010
in Great Britain and the USA by
SEVERN HOUSE PUBLISHERS LTD of
9-15 High Street, Sutton, Surrey, SM1 1DF.
First world regular print edition published 2008 by
Severn House Publishers Ltd., London and New York.

British Library Cataloguing in Publication Data

Morson, Ian.
    City of the dead. -- (A Niccolo Zuliani mystery)
    1. Explorers--Fiction. 2. Bodyguards--Fiction.
    3. Civilization, Medieval--13th century--Fiction.
    4. Mongolia--History--Fiction. 5. Detective and mystery
    stories. 6. Large type books.
    I. Title II. Series
    823.9'14-dc22

ISBN-13: 978-0-7278-7870-0

Severn House Publishers support The Forest Stewardship Council
[FSC], the leading international forest certification organisation. All
our titles that are printed on Greenpeace-approved FSC-certified paper
carry the FSC logo.

 **Mixed Sources**
Product group from well-managed
forests and other controlled sources
www.fsc.org Cert no. SA-COC-1565
© 1996 Forest Stewardship Council
FSC

Printed and bound in Great Britain by the
MPG Books Group, Bodmin, Cornwall.

If there is light in the soul, there will be beauty in the person.
If there is beauty in the person, there will be harmony in the house.
If there is harmony in the house, there will be order in the nation.
If there is order in the nation, there will be peace in the world.

Chinese proverb

In Xanadu did Kubla Khan
A stately pleasure-dome decree;
Where Alph, the sacred river, ran
Through caverns measureless to man
Down to a sunless sea

'Kubla Khan' – S.T. Coleridge

Thanks for the emergence of this novel go to the two women in my life – Lynda, my long-suffering wife, and Dorothy Lumley, my ever-optimistic agent.

Preface to the original text of
The Life and Travels of
Messer Niccolò Zuliani

Let me tell you about the extraordinary life of
the Venetian traveller and explorer, Niccolò
Zuliani. Much of what I have written down in
this book you will not believe. But it is the
God's truth, copied by me from the lips of
Messer Zuliani in the last years of his long and
varied life. There is another Venetian, whose
name I shall not mention here, whose claims
are so unusual that he has truly earned the
soubriquet Il Milione – Teller of a Thousand
Lies. Most are unbelievable, and those that
have an element of truth were stolen from his
contemporary, and infinite superior, Messer
Niccolò Zuliani, who was not able to recall all
the events of his full and perfect life. So I have
drawn on the recollections of those he lived
and worked with, even in some cases his
enemies, of which he had many, it must be
said. For he was a man of deep convictions,
and implacable will, which did not suit those

7

he sought to overcome. I have interwoven others' stories in the overall narrative, and relate this extraordinary life to you as a story, but believe in its very truth. For every word is accurate.

Xian Lin, 1299

An Ending

The butcher is amazed. How can there be so much blood in one small body? Why does he struggle so much? Beasts usually give up their life so easily.

It fountains up from the slashes, befouling the golden creatures surrounding the two struggling figures. Fabulous beasts from a long and venerable past look on in amazement at the scene, crouching low in horror, and cowering at the sight of so much blood. Ancient dragons hiss as the crimson spout spatters them with its flow. Fantastical beasts with lions' heads, their heavily maned upper bodies ending in scaly serpents' tails, flee before the rivers of blood that run across the beaten floor. Not that such fearsome beasts are afraid of such a noisome sight. Oh, no. It is because of the violation perpetrated in such an ancient sanctuary that they shrink back from the stinking flow that threatens to soak their padded paws, and fishy extremities.

As the bloodletting rends a gaping hole in the stillness of the place, gentler, plainer creatures

9

continue to forage in the undergrowth outside. Until even they catch wind of the scent of death, and raise their horny heads. With nostrils quivering, hart, doe and roebuck trot prudently away from the killing ground not knowing, or caring, that on this occasion they are safe.

It is human preying upon human.

It is a cold butchery of cutting and slashing that the victim endures, even though he is quickly beyond pain – beyond recall. One slicing cut follows another, carving up the shocked and dying victim. Soon, he is barely offering any resistance as his life oozes away. His feet slither this way and that in the wet pools of his own life's blood on the floor beneath him. His breath bubbles one last time through the new mouth in his neck, and his body becomes a dead weight.

His slayer gasps for breath, realizing the task is done, and lets the body fall. Tired lungs inhale deeply, filling their cavities with the cloying scent of death. The butcher is shocked at the suddenness of the action, and wonders what to do next. This has been so unexpected, in a life that has managed to eliminate the unexpected in the long journey to this point. Yet it has been a necessary task. The feelings should have been of satisfaction, fulfilment, but there is just ... emptiness. A great void in the greater emptiness that is contained by the Great Khan's hollow world. If generation after generation has striven merely to end up at this point, what is the purpose of it all? The butcher's thought is, *Might as well finish it here too.*

But somewhere in the butcher there is a small instinct for self-preservation, a small spark that inhalation still nurtures, kindled into fire by a breath. The fatal lethargy is shaken off, and surveying the surroundings, plans are made. The blood is impossible to wash completely away from the gilded walls, the floor, and the staring beasts. But discovery of this murderous act might still be delayed, if first the body can be hidden. Delay is all that the butcher needs. And it merely involves grabbing the lifeless legs, and dragging the body away.

1. YI

If you must play, decide on three things at the start: the rules of the game, the stakes, and the quitting time

It was the tenth year of the Pig in the current celestial cycle – Guihai, the end of the great cycle of sixty years. And this morning wasn't so bad – at least I knew where I was, and something of what I had done last night. I could not have drunk all that much at the Great Khan's banquet. But then, maybe I had, bearing in mind what I did remember. Had I really volunteered to track down a murderer like some plodding Venetian lawyer? Surely not. I laughed at the idea, though the sound that actually emerged from my lips was more of a hacking cough, wrapped in spittle.

Then I saw the bundle in the corner of the room, and knew that the nightmare was true. I noticed that the cloth covering the body had been pulled back, and the face left exposed. Also, a bluish arm flopped lifelessly out of the wrappings. The disturbance of the parcel could only have been caused by our Tartar servant,

Khadakh, poking his nose in, and satisfying his eternal curiosity. He had attached himself to the household like some faithful hound. No doubt to keep an eye on us for someone.

As if on cue, Khadakh appeared in the doorway, and looked over questioningly into my eyes. I didn't feel up to taxing what little command of the Tartar language I had in order to explain. I ignored him. He just shrugged, and dragged himself over to the body. He poked the offending arm with the toe of his boot, and was just about to cover the man's face, when Friar Alberoni emerged from his chamber.

He was holding the most precious of his gifts for Kubilai Khan. It was a small vial that contained oil from the lamp in the Sepulchre of God in Jerusalem. Precious it may be, but he almost dropped it when he saw the dead man's face properly for the first time. Up to now, he had studiously avoided the gruesome remains, but now he looked more closely. He seemed not sure at first, but I could see that a closer examination convinced him. He turned to me, his face drained of all colour.

'This is the man we've been looking for. This is Francesco Pisano.'

'You're sure?'

The friar nodded.

'Look at his black robe. Francesco Pisano is ... well, was ... a Dominican friar. And though he looks much older than I remember, it is after all a few years since I met him in Rome. It was

14

during a mass audience with Pope Alexander the Fourth. At the time of the promulgation of the Pope's warning about the umm...' He glanced nervously over to where Khadakh was busy boiling up some brick tea, and lowered his voice. 'The Tartar invasion. You remember His Holiness's *"Clamat in auribus"* warning us all of the "scourge of Heaven's wrath in the hands of the inhuman Tartars".'

Alberoni spoke like that, sort of pompous and righteous all in one. He was especially fond of quoting the Pope. He went to carry on but I silenced him with a look. I didn't have time for all that flowery talk.

'Still, it has been a few years. And the face is mutilated.' I wanted him to be sure of his identification. A lot depended on it.

'Yes, it must be over two years since Francesco disappeared off the face of the known Earth. But I would know him anywhere. No, this is him – the man we have come all this way to find.' The friar groaned. 'A wasted journey, it seems. Though at least we now know he did find his way to the centre of the Tartar Empire. But what he has done here in the last two years will now remain a mystery.'

I bent over the figure and gently lifted the wrapping back over the face.

'A mystery? Maybe not. As for our journey being wasted, let's wait and see.'

2. ER

*One never needs their humour as much as
when they argue with a fool*

Right, back to the beginning. The quirk of fate
that had brought me to Shang-tu happened
because of my enforced flight from Venice. I
had done ... no, it was claimed that I had done
... well, something that needn't bother you
now. Suffice to say, I was suddenly persona
non grata in the Serene Republic, and only
escaped death by the skin of my teeth. Since
then I had had a poor time of it scratching a
living on the margins of Venice's trading empire. With my true name a dangerous invitation
to imprisonment and death, I had adopted
many over the months, until I had almost
forgotten my real identity myself.

In Sudak I had toiled as middleman in deals
that earned me nothing. And worked my arse
off as a bodyguard for merchants afraid of the
evil reputation of those they traded with, but
too greedy to pass up the opportunity for profit.

Sudak is in Gothia – some call it Crimea – on
the northern side of the Black Sea close to Rus.

And it was there I had my first brush with the Tartar Empire. An experience that now stood me in good stead. I learned to sup with a long spoon when dealing with those particular devils.

The trouble was the money poured out of my pockets as fast as it was going in. I seemed to have lost the golden touch that had secured my reputation in Venice. But then, the margins were wafer-thin in Sudak, and the wine expensive. It was soon after my final spectacular trading failure in Sudak that I began to drown my disappointing existence in good wine. Until I could afford the good stuff no longer. I was so poor eventually, that I could only buy the harshest gut-rot alcohol to numb my memories of the good times in Venice. And the lovely Caterina Dolfin. I had been drunk and near to starving, when the friar had pulled me out of the gutter. I had no idea then how Friar Giovanni Alberoni – for years the Zuliani family priest – had even found me. I had been so addled, I had not even quibbled over the friar's reinstatement of my real name.

'Niccolò Zuliani? Is it really you? I can hardly recognize you.'

'No, not Zuliani. My name's ... Carrara, Francesco Carrara.'

'Nonsense. I know Francesco Carrara. He's at least twenty years older than you, and considerably larger in girth.'

This conversation wasn't going well, but my

drink-soaked brain wasn't able to come up with a different line, so I let the priest take me back to his lodgings. I knew who he was, even if he had difficulty recognizing me. His piety had bored my father stiff but, as the family priest, he had the ear, albeit reluctantly, of all the Zuliani brothers. Particularly my uncle Matteo, whom I suspect now of sending the friar to save my soul. I was soon to learn that Alberoni had his own reasons for appearing in this arse-end of the crumbling Venetian Empire.

Let me explain.

My name is Niccolò Zuliani, once of Venice and more lately of Shang-tu, the summer home of Kubilai Khan, the Great Khan of all the Mongols. Shang-tu is better known as Xanadu, the fabled city of wealth and opulence. How I came to be there is the story I am trying to tell. Which is why I have to go back to Sudak to start the tale, and to the year of our Lord 1262.

If you saw me now, you would see a tall, red-haired man, thickly bearded in that manly way that the Chinee would consider shockingly animalistic and foreign. Any observer would guess I was in my thirties, despite the fine tracery of lines at the corners of my eyes and mouth. My cheekbones are high and deeply tanned in the way of sailors. My green eye, too, had the faraway look of a sailor. Though some fancied they could also see in them the distant

18

stare of a man with deep pains buried in his soul.

When Friar Alberoni dragged me out of that gutter outside the drinking den in Sudak's harbour area, I was not at all like that. I was at what you might call a low ebb. The lowest, in fact, since I had slunk out of Venice under cover of darkness, and at low tide. At low tide you could still cross the Lagoon on foot and unnoticed. And I had needed my exit to be unnoticed. Now, I just wanted to die, and didn't thank the friar for saving me.

Until he uttered one word in my ear.

At first I had not listened much to the friar's explanation of how he had found me. As I suspected, Uncle Matteo came into it somewhere. But I was too busy working out how I was going to screw some money out of Alberoni to continue my dive into oblivion. I reckoned I could call upon the priest's sense of duty as the Zuliani family priest to give me enough cash for a square meal. Yes, I would try that on. Priests liked being charitable, after all.

'Are you listening to me, Niccolò?'

'Of course I am, Friar Giovanni. You were saying how much you owed my family.'

'I was saying that I owe it to your uncle to offer you the position of my personal body-guard. Though, God knows, you are unfit to take care of yourself, let alone another, on such a perilous journey.'

'Perilous...?' Befuddled as I was, I couldn't

recall what the friar had been talking about, but I didn't like the thought of that word peril. A risk-taker I might be, and a chancer. But not with my own life. I suddenly felt sick to my stomach, and vomited down the front of the priest's robe. I passed it off as the raw sewage that I had inhaled in the gutter. And I must have looked a sight then, so I was surprised that Alberoni wanted me to look after him. I must have given the impression I couldn't look after myself, let alone a man of God who proposed to travel to God knows where. I was filthy, emaciated, covered in the scabs of numerous falls and beatings, and my hair was a mass of lice. But then, Alberoni told me he could not afford the price of a sober bodyguard for such a speculative odyssey. I looked into his eyes, assuming he was making a joke at my expense. There was no humour in them. And as he dabbed fastidiously at my noisome exhalations, Alberoni pressed on.

'It will be a journey to fulfil the mission that the Pope himself has charged me with. To go to Tartary. To Xanadu.'

That was the word that changed it all. I instinctively felt the itch of ducats passing across my palm, and pulled myself together. The heart of every Venetian beats a little faster at the thought of profit, and trade with the Far East – silks, precious stones, salamander cloth, impervious to flames – means big profits. In fact, a Venetian would sell his grandmother to the devil for a profit, and to damn with the fact that successive popes had condemned the Tartars as hell's spawn. I suddenly reckoned I might even be able to buy myself back into favour in Venice with such riches. I agreed to the commission with alacrity. I had no further left to fall anyway.

'Of course, the place is really called Shang-tu, which merely means Upper Capital in the heathen tongue they speak there.'

I ignored the friar's droning catechism, and dreamed of Xanadu. Already it was known as a place of enormous wealth, and I wanted to have some of that wealth rub off on me. After all, it couldn't be that dangerous, could it?

'And you need a bodyguard, you say?'

Alberoni nodded, recalling the stories that went round the friary in his youth.

'It is said that the Tartars are anthropophagi – dog-headed cannibals – who eat their victims, and ravish their virgin captives, then cut off their breasts afterwards as dainties for their chiefs.'

The stories apparently had been told with relish by some of his monastic fellows – especially the part about ravished virgins and violated breasts. And I didn't doubt they had been the instigation of nocturnal private gropings and moanings under the bedclothes in the dormitory afterwards. But I could tell that for the young Giovanni Alberoni they had been shocking. They had clearly made a lasting impression on him, changing the course of his life. Before then, he told me he had been unsure of his vocation, and had struggled with his studies. After hearing of the Tartars, and their Godless ways, he knew what he had to do.

'I am resolved to carry out God's will, and have read every report on the Tartars to reach us in the West. I know what they are capable of. The devil comes in many pleasing disguises, and seduces the unwary with alluring and complaisant visages.'

I tried to stop him going off on one of his rants again.

'And your mission from the Pope?'

The friar turned his face away from me, grubby and bearded as I was.

'The Pope always seeks converts.'

I had been too busy thinking of the riches of Xanadu to bother with the friar's equivocal statement then. The whole truth only came out later. However, he did offer me one clue.

'We are to seek out a Dominican by the name of Pisano. He left for the court of the Great Khan almost four years ago. The Khan would have been Kubilai's elder brother Mongu then. He died. But not a word has been heard from Pisano since.'

My answer, occasioned by a murderous headache and a sickness in the gut, was scathing.

'So we are to travel to the ends of the earth, and hunt down a man who may never have got there. And if he did, he may already be dead.'

Alberoni glared at me.

I did not know then how prophetic my words were to become. I mean, the last thing I had wanted was to be embroiled in a murder again. Hadn't I fled Venice because of one? Oh, didn't I mention that? Well, I promise I will tell you about it some time. Set the records straight, like. For now, I was left wondering if they were following me around – murders, I mean. Maybe it was a result of the bad luck that had dogged me of late. How could I have guessed then I was to get mixed up in the death of Friar Pisano – the very man we had come all the way to Xanadu to track down. And all because of some mad idea that obsessed both him and Alberoni.

3. SAN

Great souls have wills, feeble ones have only wishes

I first had an inkling of what this was all about towards the end of our journey from Sudak to the Khan's residence. After we had travelled on our own through the mountains, Friar Alberoni and I had been met by a small band of Tartars. It was more than a little scary at first, to see these legendary warriors galloping out of the dust of their own horses' heels. Like demons appearing from the mists. But apparently, they were there to escort us from the shores of the Ghelan Sea to Kubilai's court. It was the first indication I had had which Alberoni was anticipated.

We had long since passed through the almost mythical Iron Gates. A narrow defile between lowering cliffs, which formed the barrier that Alexander the Great had closed to separate the tribes of Gog and Magog in the east from our civilization in the west. Once beyond them, the land we passed through had become more and more unfamiliar. Until I had realized we were

24

lost, knowing neither north from south until the sun arose each morning, and reassured us of our direction. But that was all we knew – the direction of our travels. In truth we were blundering in the dark with no knowledge of even our return passage. Then the Tartars had picked us up, and at last led us unerringly beyond the Alanian mountains and the Ghelan Sea, and across the empty wastes of the East.

Day followed day as we had passed through lush pastures, and scattered fruit groves, until we hit the edge of the Tartars' homeland. Vast mountain ranges loomed in the distance, at first trimmed with sparse groves of pine. Then, day by day, the vegetation got sparser again and more stunted, until it ceased to exist at all. The land had become a strange wilderness to the eyes of us two inhabitants of the soggy Adriatic coast. The wagons moved through a succession of broad valleys, with here and there frost-shattered rocks breaking through the thin soil. The only signs of life in this vast emptiness were the distant shapes of falcons and eagles soaring and circling in the intense blue of the sky. Used to the heavy thickness of sea breezes, I marvelled at the thin dryness of the air, guessing we were as far from the sea as a human being could ever get.

At first, the savage Tartar warriors had been taciturn and uncommunicative, and I felt uncertain for our future. They sat on the hard wooden saddles of their little ponies for hours

25

on end, occasionally relieving their back-breaking journey by standing in the stirrups with their legs flexing like a steel blade. Their faces revealed nothing of their inner thoughts.

But, when we began to cross the Great Desert of Lop in the cart, the oppressive solitude had somehow pulled us together. I picked up more of their words, and turning it back on them, broke through their reticence. Their leader's name turned out to be Khadakh. He was a grizzled bundle of pent-up energy. But once I had softened him with a few stumbling words in his own tongue, we forged a sort of bond like travellers on a long sea voyage together. And it was a vast sea of sand, formed into great static waves, undulating into the distance with neither sight of real land nor hope of fresh water.

Suddenly the cart felt like a great ship, and I abruptly came into my own, adapting my natural sea legs to the pitch and sway of the wheels. Friar Giovanni, on the other hand, had turned ashen, and vomited over the side. Matters were made worse for his good Christian soul, when we gathered from our Tartar guides' gruntings that, if you travelled Lop alone, the spirits that roamed its great silence ended up getting into your head. They started calling out your name, and taking you off course to your doom. Of course, I had heard it all before, and began to feel at home. I told the nervous priest to take heart.

'These rumours are just like sailors' drunken talk that I heard as a boy, when I used to hide, wide-eyed, under my father's table. Every time a ship came into Venice, I would hear tales of seductive sirens who lured the unwary on to the jagged spurs along a distant, rocky coastline. Just an excuse for careless seamanship really. Now it looks as though these landlocked Tartars have the same tall tales for this sea of sand.'

Alberoni had been silenced – reassured for a while at least. Later, he had resumed his grumblings, and I had yearned once again for the great silence of the desert. The Franciscan's objections to the heat of the day, and the freezing cold of the night, the jolt of the cart, and the hardness of his bed, drove me to distraction. But finally we had cleared the wasteland, and found sweet water again. To celebrate, the Tartars had broken into their last skin of kumiss. And told us the tale of Genghis Khan.

Khadakh told the story. It was all about Kubilai's grandfather, who was known to them as Chinghis Khan. However you pronounced his name, it seems he had had another name as a youth. Temujin.

This was how Khadakh began his story.

'When Temujin was eight, his father Yesugei took him to his mother's people the Olkhunu'ut to marry. On Yesugei's return journey, he had no choice but to sojourn with the Tartars

27

even though he had fought against them years earlier.'

I stopped him. 'Wasn't this Temujin a Tartar?'

Khadakh's face creased in amusement at my interruption of his story. He knew what we called him and his fellows.

'No. We are of the great nation of Mongols, who had been wrongly named Tartar by you foreigners. What I speak of is a little tribe within the Mongol nation who had the misfortune to make Temujin their enemy. It is only this little clan that are called Tartars by us.'

I translated this news for the friar.

'Hmmph. I shall still think of them all as Tartars, because they are well named as devils from Tartarus.'

Khadakh smiled, not comprehending Alberoni, and continued his story.

'One of the Tartars saw through Yesugei's disguise, and poisoned him. His wife Ho'elun and her four boys were made outcasts, and it was only through Temujin's extraordinary will that, as an adult, he finally gathered the tribes around him and became Khan, taking the name Chinghis. But he never forgot what the Tartar clan did to his father. It was when Chinghis was in his prime that Wang Khan joined forces with him, and slaughtered the Tartar tribe at their camp on the Ulkhui River. Chinghis' decree that all Tartars who stood higher than the lynchpin of a cart should be killed was

28

bloodily carried out. The survivors lived only to be driven into slavery.'

Khadakh's comrades nodded in approval at the bloody revenge of Chinghis Khan, and the mood in the tent made me shiver. Little did I know I was to become embroiled in just such a vengeful deed in Xanadu. Now it was as if an icy blast had blown in through the flap.

In a Tartar tent, there is barely room in the roof for the smoke of the central fireplace to escape, and Friar Alberoni – far taller than the tallest Tartar – spent the time stoop-shouldered with his head in the stinging fumes. He refused to prostrate himself on the threadbare rugs as I soon had, after discovering the easiest way to adapt to life in a tent was to squat or lie down. He also did not touch the goat-skins of foul, yeasty brew that were passed round after the daily meal. I adapted easily to that also, in a hungry way that I could see had Alberoni worried. He had kept me away from wine for several weeks, and I could tell he thought his catechism on the perils of self-indulgence had stuck.

My first night of kumiss drinking had soon set him right. He might have hoped that the fermented brew of mare's milk would be too foul to tempt me. And a year or so earlier in Venice, I would have agreed. But I was not the same man. Now I was used to gut-rot wine and tempted still by the vision of oblivion that drink offered. So I drank more and more

29

eagerly as the evening progressed. Then the drinking session led to a bout of gambling, and I won some new clothes from our escort. No amount of drinking affected my sleight of hand, which could tip any game of chance, Venetian or Tartar, in my favour. With my new garb, Alberoni reckoned he could hardly tell me apart from the swinish Tartars. And estimated that I would soon be taking several wives next if he didn't control me. I must say, the thought was tempting, but I could stand his cant no longer.

'It's been ten months since we started out from Sudak, and you've done nothing but moan and complain all the way. It was your choice that we should finish this journey by ox-cart, when we could have halved the time riding on horseback.'

'On horseback! Since when has a Venetian travelled happily on anything other than a boat? Give you a horse and you would complain that it didn't float when you threw it in the Lagoon.'

I bridled at the insult. To my mind, the lanky family priest hovering over me was in no position to mock the ways of a Venetian. Didn't his own family come from that god-forsaken strip of shingle that edged the Lagoon? It hardly made him Venetian, and I gave back as good as I got.

'And when we crossed the Desert of Lop, who was landsick, and seeing demons in every heat haze?'

That shut him up, and then the evening suddenly improved when another wagon loomed out of the weary dark. Like ships that pass in the night, our encampment was curious about the new arrivals, crowding together at the tent flap. Khadakh invited their leader, who turned out to be a wizened old woman, to pitch her camp next to ours.

'Come, old mother, join us. You and yours are welcome.'

Khadakh's leathery face split in a cheery grin. The kumiss had already taken its effect on his normally reserved nature. The rotund old woman eased herself down from beside the driver of her cart, and gave us all a suspicious look.

'I think not, *bahadur*,' she rasped, speaking from the darkness. She grudgingly gave him the respectful title that is more appropriate to the leader of a full regiment of Tartars. But that was all the leeway she offered. 'I carry precious goods for the Great Khan, and I wouldn't want them spoiled.'

As she moved into the flickering light cast by the open tent flap, I could see the look in her eyes. It spoke of power and swift retribution if she were crossed. I was still half sober, but Khadakh had swallowed deep of the goat-skin already. Throwing caution to the wind, he reeled over to the old woman. He stuck his moon face into hers, breathing out kumiss fumes.

31

'And we are the Great Khan's most trusted soldiers. So let's see what is so precious, little mother.'

The old woman stepped back in disgust, and crooked her finger as though Khadakh was some recalcitrant child. He turned to grin at his fellows round the tent's entrance, and followed the old woman to the back of her wagon. She lifted the flap, and as she did so whispered something into Khadakh's ear. His eyes widened at the contents of the wagon, at the same time as his face blanched at what she said. He came scurrying back to us, horror showing in his eyes.

'It's the witch-woman herself, and she has the Kungurat tribute in the back.'

My understanding of the Tartar language was still poor, even though I had spent a year trading with them in Sudak, and learned some words from Khadakh.

'That old bird is a witch, you say? And what's the ... Kungurat tribute anyway?'

I admit I sensed the possibility of a treasure trove to plunder. Khadakh looked fearfully over his shoulder to make sure the old woman was not within earshot.

'She is Bolgana, some sort of relative of the Great Khan's *obok* – his clan – come to Kubilai's court for the first time. And she is bringing the tribute of thirty virgins sent every few years by the Kungurat people to the Khan.'

'Virgins?' My ears pricked at the word.

'There are girls in the back of that wagon?' I grinned at Alberoni, and spoke to him in our own tongue. 'No wonder this Bolgana wants to keep them separate from this desperate, drunken crew. Still and all, virgins!'

'Zuliani! Don't even think it. The woman would have your hide.'

I grinned at Khadakh and his compatriots, expecting ribaldry. But their faces were made of stone. I could feel an air of tension as we sat back round the fire blazing in the centre of the tent. If I hadn't known better, I would have said these Tartar warriors were scared. And of an old woman. For her part, Bolgana eventually settled her charges in a separate tent pitched safely away from our encampment. Then she joined us, preferring no doubt to keep an eye on the men, and thereby make sure her virgins were safe. I sat opposite her, and had an opportunity to assess this woman whose reputation struck fear into the hearts of our Tartar escort.

When she had first arrived, I had taken her to be in her late fifties, as her face was deeply lined and weather-beaten. In fact, by the light of the fire, I could now see that Bolgana was much older, her skin a little looser than at first appeared. Her face reminded me of the yellow and deeply rutted, tilled earth of the Northern plains of Lombardy. Her body was a series of generous undulations that gave her a motherly and comforting look, all wrapped up in a sturdy Mongol jacket. Around her neck hung a long, thin leather packet I took to be a talisman. Her legs were like two bowed tree stumps, and her tiny feet pointed outwards like little arrowheads. Despite her ferocity though, I had the curious impression that, if she did but open her arms, I would feel a strange inclination to run straight into them, whimpering for comfort. But in other circumstances, I knew her hands and short stubby fingers could deliver a fearfully hard slap across the face if I ever displeased her.

Maybe it was the tense atmosphere, or the kumiss brew that affected me. But I distractedly took a coin out of my pocket, and began rotating it through my fingers. Sleight of hand had stood me in good stead at many a gaming table, and though it had also contributed to my downfall I still practised. I liked to keep my hands supple. The coin sparkled in the light of the campfire as it twisted through my fingers, and I soon became aware that Khadakh was watching closely, his eyes wide open. Without thinking much of it, I palmed the glittering coin, so that it apparently disappeared from my hand, and leaned casually over to Khadakh. By this time, the others, including Bolgana, were drawn into the game. Kneeling before the wary Khadakh, I reached behind his ear, and made it look as though the palmed coin had been plucked from the Tartar's grizzled locks. If there was one thing I had learned on my interminable journey by cart from the shores of the Ghelan, it was that the Mongols were fascinated by magic. And sights that baffled the mind drew them like a magnet.

The other Tartars guffawed at my simple trick, and even Khadakh eventually grinned in embarrassed pleasure at being the centre of attention. A fresh goat-skin of kumiss was produced, and passed around. I performed another trick, which was followed by another guzzling round of the heady brew. I made sure that the old woman joined in the festivities too, until all the Tartars, including Bolgana, slumped in a drunken stupor. Alberoni of course had retired to his own tent in disgust as soon as he saw the way the evening was progressing. All of which finally left me free to explore the camp made by our new arrivals.

4. SI

*If you wish to know the mind of a man,
listen to his words*

Morning. Someone spoke, and threw the blanket and animal skins back. The cold air struck me hard, like a blow in the pit of my stomach, and my uncovered balls shrivelled. The friar turned away, embarrassed by my nakedness, and stared out at the brightness of the dawn. I pushed myself up from the low couch, feeling the warm spot where the girl had been when I fell asleep. With some relief, I saw that she had gone. My belly was suddenly eager to throw back up the kumiss which I had drunk last night. I swallowed hard against the stale, sour taste, quelling the queasiness, and longed for a good red wine. Belching acidly, I pulled on my patched drawers, and threadbare hose that lay at the bottom of the couch. Then I began hunting for the rest of my clothes, discarded in the throes of the previous night's lust.

I laced up the front of my thick leather boots, enjoying the frustrated sighs of Friar Giovanni

Alberoni as I dragged out the completion of my dressing. The boots were a Tartar pair I had won off Khadakh last night, my old buskins being quite worn through. As were most of the clothes I had bought years ago now from the little tailor in the San Silvestro district of Venice. Old times, good times.

Once dressed, I followed Alberoni out of the tent. The cool, crispness of the early morning gave me a renewed seizure of coughing. I could have cheerfully murdered the friar. His long, skinny frame stood a few yards before me, stubbornly outlined against the morning light. He spoke again.

'Did you hear me? They say we will see the palace today.'

The palace. Those words were enough to clear my head. Alberoni was talking of the home of the Great Khan.

'Xanadu.'

The friar turned back to look at me as I spoke the word. I spotted my chance to clear up a riddle that had been puzzling me for some time.

'Alberoni, don't you think it's time you told me why you are really here? You know why I am. After all, you are paying me to act as your bodyguard. But what is it that really draws you?'

Alberoni turned away, and tried to divert my enquiry. 'No doubt *you* are dreaming of some of the Khan's fabled wealth rubbing off on you.'

I ignored the pointed, if pertinent, remark.

'Oh, I know all you priests dream of bringing the Tartars to God. But you also know that others have tried, and failed. I don't think you are that starry-eyed. So what do you truly hope to achieve?'

'Others? Oh, you mean Carpini. That was twenty years ago, and we understood so little then. We know so much more now. As for that Flemish man – William Rubruck, wasn't he called? – he just preached hellfire and damnation like all Flemings. No finesse. No, I am not here to convert the Khan.'

'No? What, then?'

He leaned close to me, and spoke into my ear with air of a conspirator.

'Remember that story Khadakh told you last night?'

'About Chinghis Khan? Of course I remember it – I had to translate the whole damn thing for you. What's so interesting about Kubilai's bloody family history?'

'It contains the answer to a puzzle of vital importance to Christendom.'

I frowned. 'If you say so. What puzzle?'

Alberoni suddenly would say no more. 'Come, they are waiting for us.'

He strode off, and I watched with impatience as the tents were dismantled. They were called yurts in the Tartar tongue – a noise that sounded like a drunken belch to me. Like the wine-sodden exhalations of my decline from tavern to gutter. I belched experimentally. *Yurt.* It did, it sounded like the word. I grinned, and watched the striking of the encampment. I confess the girl was filling my mind with stray thoughts, and I didn't concentrate on what Alberoni was telling me. I wished later I had.

Layers of black, tarry felt were being stripped from the roof, and bundled up along with the padded curtains that hung around the sides of the tent, and kept the night-time chill away. What was then exposed was the skeleton of a tent; long roof poles slotted into a central wheel, and walls that were a latticework of slender saplings bound with rawhide. I stood, and marvelled again at how the walls came down, and concertinaed into a manageable bundle of sticks. In no time at all, the yurts were struck, and loaded on both carts.

The little group of Kungurat girls stood uncertainly in a shy huddle on the now bare plain. Their chaperone, the redoubtable Bolgana, looked a little worse for wear. Maybe she was unaccustomed to drinking kumiss. Irritably, she hustled them up to sit in the wagon on top of the dismantled yurt. She failed to see one girl giving me a secretive wave. For myself, I was glad that the one who waved was presentable. In my kumiss-sodden state last night, I had conceived a healthy lust for any of the dark-haired girls. One had responded to my whispered blandishments at the tent opening.

She had dared to sneak out of her tent under cover of darkness without being detected. But for the life of me, in the morning, I failed to recall her face.

I winked surreptitiously at the girl, assuming it was the one I had seduced, and reluctantly turned away as the wagon flap was lowered. At least one of the Khan's treasures would not be arriving in the condition expected. Then Alberoni, already on the second cart, impatiently gave me his hand, and pulled me up. The Tartar escort mounted their shaggy, short-limbed steeds, and the wagon train was under way.

The final day of our journey lengthened in much the same way that the days had before it. Soon the scenery, once fascinating, but now monotonous and repetitive, and the regular sway of the cart, lulled my senses. I dreamed again of Venice, and though my mind was half on the girl in the other cart, I wondered what fair Caterina Dolfin, my foxy lady, was doing now. I resigned myself to the thought that she was probably no longer fair, but fat, matronly, and being harassed by a brood of little brats provided by another man. I grimaced at the thought.

'Look!'

Alberoni was shaking my arm, and pointing out ahead. I couldn't make out what he saw until the dust around the cart began to settle. The driver had stopped, and was pointing in the same direction as Alberoni with his leather whip. We were on the top of a small rise, poised to descend into a lush valley. It was now evening, and the rays of the sinking sun behind us threw our shadows out long before us on the grassy plain. Suddenly, it was as if our little band of travellers could not wait to get to the great city that was Kubilai Khan's summer residence, and our shadows were hastening before us.

Right to the walls of Xanadu.

The sun was bathing the elevated roofs in a glow that turned them golden. But the most impressive sight was the defensive wall that enclosed the Khan's palace and the homes of his subjects. Though a simple earthen wall, it extended across the horizon as though barring the way completely. Our driver whipped up his oxen, and the cart began its careering descent towards the city, with the outriders galloping far ahead in their exhilaration. The other cart driver did the same, and the girls shrieked out loud as the cumbersome conveyance swayed and bounced, almost throwing them out. The wall rose ever higher as we got ever closer to it, until it seemed to blank out the sky. At the last minute, just as I feared we might career into it, the driver swung the cart to run parallel with the wall. Our Tartar escorts, exhilaration now exhausted, now led the way at a more sedate pace. And for what seemed like an endless span of time, we skirted along the forbid-

41

ding ramparts, until at last I spotted a narrow gate that would let us pass inside.

Once through the gate, the teeming city behind the walls was a shock after the vast emptiness of our months of travel. Everywhere there were people and noise. Especially noise – as the sound of thousands of souls exchanging greetings, bartering for food, and crying out to sell their wares assaulted our ears. The sounds and the smells of thousands of strangers were disconcerting, rankling in my nostrils. So many bodies pressed together, shoulder to shoulder, within these extensive walls, would take some getting used to after the void we had crossed. Dizzy with the excess of impressions, I had to press my hands over my ears to still the din.

At my side, Friar Alberoni closed his eyes, and I heard him offer up a short prayer of thanks for our safe arrival. I wondered if the prayer was premature. For I suddenly felt more vulnerable and exposed than I had done for years. In Sudak at least I had found ways to hide. Under false names, and in the arms of drink. Here, there was no retreat for me any more – no familiar landmarks. And almost no chance that I might revive the dream of return- ing to Venice. I was further away from my home than ever before. And, after the vast open spaces of our journey, I also felt hemmed in. A feeling underlined by the sense of being watched rapaciously by a hundred thousand eyes. My hands trembled, and I was not sure if it was the shock of the city, or the need for a drink.

The cart jerked, and I saw a Tartar of military bearing step out of the crowd near the gateway. He grasped the harness of the lumbering oxen that had stolidly pulled us halfway across the world. The driver hauled on the reins, and the cart ground to a halt. I watched as the wagon in front of us containing the Kungurat girls rattled away, and was swallowed by the crowd. I caught one final glimpse of the raven-haired girl staring back towards me. Was it my imagination, or were her eyes wide with regret? Then she too was gone, like all my other fleeting couplings of the last few years. Incomplete, failing in commitment, and endurance.

Just as I liked them.

The soldier motioned for us passengers to get down, and, stretching my stiffened limbs, I set foot on the earth of Xanadu. Alberoni appeared to have cramp, and I had to assist him to take his first step. The short, stocky Tartar stepped up to me, and scrutinized me closely. I returned the stare as coldly as I could, pretending not to be afraid. Then I ostentatiously yawned. The short sword thrust through his belt, and the javelins held in one horny hand showed him to be a light cavalryman. That much I had learned from our Tartar escort. The soldier beat his chest, and uttered a guttural grunt that I took to be his name – it sounded something like Zianipe to my Venetian ears. Then he held out his hand; not in a gesture of welcome, but palm up as though expecting to receive something.

'What do you think he wants?' Alberoni was at my elbow, hissing in my ear.

Now, if I had been anywhere in civilization – by which I meant anywhere within the sphere of influence that was the Venetian Republic – I would have reckoned to slip the man a few coins. Border guards were the same the civilized world over. But this wasn't the civilized world. Here, I was all at sea, unfamiliar with the rules, and didn't wish to make a serious error so early on. There was an awkward hiatus, until the problem was solved by the intervention of Khadakh. He bowled up to the soldier, produced a long, flat token from the folds of his furry jacket, and waved it importantly under the man's nose. It flashed gold in the setting sun.

Apparently, it impressed Zianipe, and he stared at me and the friar with renewed curiosity. Then he beckoned to us, and turning away, stalked off. Khadakh grinned, then returned the magical token to his jacket, and waved at us to follow. He pointed at the man's black tunic, trimmed in red, under black leather armour, and the black shield slung over his back.

'Imperial bodyguard,' Khadakh said impressively. 'Go.'

Alberoni started to follow immediately, but I surprised the old Tartar with an emotional embrace, hugging his sweat-stained body close to mine. Then I too turned away, and hurried after Zianipe. The golden token had been too alluring to resist. It now resided in the folds of my sleeve.

As we walked behind our Tartar escort, heads popped out of the ramshackle houses that formed the Outer City. It was a hot, dusty summer's evening, and the packed earth of the narrow streets rose in a cloud at our feet as we passed the staring faces. Many foreigners attended the Great Khan's court but few were Westerners like Friar Alberoni and myself. The remnants of my old clothes were threadbare, but my hair and beard glowed flame red in the lowering light of the setting sun. It was a tint that was not uncommon amongst Venetians, but so rare in Shang-tu as to warrant wondering looks in this Tartar city. Besides, I was head and shoulders taller than any Tartar, and walked with a seaman's rolling gait. Quite unlike the stiff-legged stomp of the guard who preceded us. Alberoni, no shorter than me, was skeletally thin next to my bulk.

Zianipe – or Dzhanibeg as I later learned to truly call him – led us through the Outer City briskly. Here, the native population lived their lives; traded, argued, drank, killed each other in drunken brawls, and generally carried on just like pagans do. Or so I imagined. The houses were low structures with sweeping, curved roofs of red tiles, held up by a sturdy framework of wooden beams. The streets themselves were long straight thoroughfares, and were filled with carts, men on horseback, beggars on foot, and exotic figures being transported behind closed curtains in sedan chairs.

I was bewildered by the hordes of people, barely able to tell them apart. Strange banners with indecipherable symbols hung on the front of some of the buildings, which I took for shops, though what they sold was uncertain. And I could hardly yet stop to venture inside one to find out. Then I saw a more impressive sight than all the bustle of activity around us.

Our escort's route had brought us out from the streets lined with thatched huts, and past a gateway set in another vast wall, itself inside the outer ramparts. This internal brick wall just had to be the one that separated the Khan from his subjects. It was the height of three men, but the gateway soared even above that. Pillars painted a vivid red stood like sentries either side of the great portal over which ranged an aisled gallery also painted red and etched in gold, which was itself surmounted by a sloping roof of ochre tiles. It defined an opening that was not one but actually three doors. The central one was so grand it had to be for the Great Khan only. Lesser mortals clearly had to use the smaller outer doors. I had stood before these portals in my dreams over the last few months. Now Alberoni and I were a stone's throw from our goal.

But we were not going to find it easy to gain

entrance. Our escort spoke briefly to one of the guards at the gate, who was dressed the same as himself, and was answered with a shake of the head. It seemed the Great Khan was not at home. At least not for us. I lingered a moment by the tempting doorway, then followed Dzhanibeg as he strode on towards more humble portals. It was getting dark by the time he left us in front of the house that was to be our home in Shang-tu for the foreseeable future. The low timber-frame structure had a tiled roof, and looked to me depressingly like one of those fishermen's refuges on the outlying mudflats in the Venetian Lagoon. I suspected it might stink as strongly too.

With a cry of anguish, Alberoni leapt towards our baggage that had been tossed in a heap in the lane. Obviously, we had been given the guided tour of Shang-tu to impress us, and our possessions had been brought directly. I had no desire to carry it indoors that night. Any thief was welcome to all that remained of my belongings after two years on the run. All I craved was a bed. Preferably one occupied by the Kungurat girl, but I guessed she was almost certainly Kubilai's property by now. Anyway, even if she had by some miracle been in my bed, I was so exhausted that I feared I would not have been up to the challenge. Dizzy with fatigue, drink and the pace of events, I left the friar fussing over the bundles, assuring himself that his gifts for Kubilai had not been purloined, and entered the hut.

As I slid open the creaky wooden door, I smelled neither the aroma of fish as I had imagined, nor the sweet scent of the nameless girl's hair. It was the bitter smell of the familiar foul brew the Tartars, or as I should now be calling them, the Mongols, called brick tea. I peered round the door, and saw a figure hidden beneath a bulky jacket, heating a kettle over a blazing fire. For a moment, my weary mind imagined it was the girl, and I wondered how she had escaped her chaperone and avoided becoming one of Kubilai's concubines. Then the figure turned round, and gave me a grin with a mouth full of rotten teeth. It was Khadakh. He of the token that had so impressed Dzhanibeg. The one I had stolen.

I groaned. All I wanted was to sleep, and here was the victim of my theft, intent on celebrating our arrival in the heart of the Mongol empire with strong tea. I went to push past him. But Khadakh bared his rotten teeth in another eager grin, and offered me a bowl of the steaming brew. Wearily, I returned the smile, and patiently took the offering. Meanwhile, the gold token burned a hole in my sleeve.

5. WU

If you are patient in a moment of anger,
you will escape a hundred days of sorrow

The following day, Alberoni complained that a fever had laid him low. He seemed set to spend the time abed, though the ague seemed not to affect his appetite. Meanwhile, I was not allowed to be idle. Over the next few days he sent me off to scour the foreigners' enclave of Shang-tu for any sign of Pisano.

As I wandered through the dingy streets lined with mud and board huts, I felt dejected. The place bore no resemblance to the legends already circulating Christendom about Xanadu. There were no streets of gold here. Instead, the foreign quarter was low, dirty and mean. The Frankish traders, religiosi and artisans lived, breathed and traded in an area of the Outer City that was no bigger than one of the six *sestiere* in Venice. And like each district of La Serenissima, everybody knew everybody else's business – or, if they didn't, thought they had a right to. There were stories aplenty to be had about Pisano, but none that led me to him.

49

I needed to spread my search wider if I was to find Alberoni's contact.

After a fruitless few hours, I ended up at a crossing of the ways I thought I had encountered before. I was uncertain which way to go. A few sallow-skinned locals with little to do eyed me with curiosity from the verandah of a large building. When I stared back, some of them looked the other way, and made gestures that were clearly charms to protect themselves. The sun angled down hotly on my head, and I shrugged, tossing my last remaining ducat in the air. Let fate decide the direction of my search this day. After all, I had gambled on more risky matters than the hunt for the abode of a friar on the flip of a coin before now. I caught the tumbling coin, and slapped it on the back of my hand. The noble visage of Doge Zeno stared obliquely up. Heads.

I turned right, and was soon in a network of busy streets that were new to me. I elbowed my way through streams of men and women intent on their business. Unlike the idlers at the crossing, they scarcely gave me another glance. One or two passed on horseback, forcing me back against the walls of the houses. The riders' leather cuirasses and fur-edged jackets marked them out as Mongols. Most of the people on foot, men and women alike, were native Chinee. They were dressed in loose-fitting robes that were, by and large, of drab brown cotton. At one corner, my eyes strayed on to a small gathering of three women dressed in tight-fitting long-sleeved jackets, decorated with bird-like shapes, from under which flowed a pale skirt that dragged on the ground. They giggled like courtesans behind their hands as I passed.

Further along the thoroughfare, a few more of those who hurried past were Westerners like myself. I wanted to stop them, but they looked away when I called out. The sun was frazzling my brains. I stopped, feeling dizzy and disorientated. The noise and commotion was so unlike the stillness of the plains through which we had recently travelled. Then, it had been easy to find solitude by walking a few hundreds yards from the encampment. Then, I could stare into the distance, and imagine myself on board a ship in the Adriatic with only the horizon as my boundary. Here there was bustle, noise, sweat and close confining walls everywhere. I grimaced, standing stock-still while the tide of humanity flowed around me. A horse's sweating flank nudged past me, the animal's muscles straining. My senses reeled, and I knew I needed a drink to settle my throbbing brain. I saw I was on a street lined with little workshops. From every doorway came a ringing sound like the tinkling of tiny bells. I knew the sound – I had heard it last in Venice. It was the sound of silversmiths at work, beating their metal into fanciful shapes and designs. Someone here had to be a Westerner who would help. I simply chose the first door I came to, and poked my head inside.

A little man with grey hair, and a bald patch on the top of his head, sat hunched over a bench on which sparkled a silver dish. He was busy tapping a design into the surface, and at first did not hear me enter. I coughed, and the man looked up. He was a European, and bearded. But the left side of his face was marked with a long, livid red patch on which no beard grew. It gave him a curiously lopsided look, but obviously did not embarrass the man. I tried him with some Italian. He stared at me, his eyes wide open in silent enquiry. Then I essayed some English, which the man also failed to understand, responding in some tongue I had not heard before. I shrugged my shoulders, and was about to leave, when the man spoke again.

'I speak some Austrian,' he said, mangling the accent of an inhabitant of the city of Vienna. It was a language of which I also had a smattering. I dredged the words up from the depths of my brain, and begged a drink. The man poured something from a pitcher set in the shade at his side, and offered me the beaker. He continued to speak as I drank the weak beer in great, thirst-quenching gulps. It turned out the little man was a Silesian Pole from Breslau, where he had used his skills as a silversmith to build up a nice little business. Then the Tartar hordes had arrived out of the blue and taken him into slavery. There was an involuntary movement of the silversmith's horny fingers to the scar on his face when he spoke of the invasion. I could guess how he came by the disfigurement.

'But that must have been more than twenty years ago!' I couldn't believe it. This man – Tadeusz Pyka by name – had been enslaved for a lifetime. Hadn't he tried to escape? I couldn't bear the thought that I might be separated from Venice for so long. Tadeusz explained that at first he had been filled with fear – the Tartars had descended like the Hand of God destroying everything and everyone in their path. He had witnessed the slaughter of his friends and neighbours all around him. Bodies had been piled in the streets of Breslau like the plague had struck. And the Tartars had been like a plague, selecting victims at random, sweeping them off and passing on, leaving devastation in their wake. Only a handful of the men of Breslau had been spared, and taken away in chains – a pitiful half-dozen left from a once thriving town. At first Tadeusz hadn't known why, of all people, his life had been given back to him. Then the little band of men, comparing notes, realized they had one thing in common. They were artisans, possessed of skills their captors valued. They had been dragged back to the Tartar homeland, on more or less the same journey I had voluntarily taken more recently. My journey had numbered in months

53

– Tadeusz Pyka's meandering trip with the marauding Tartars had taken four years.

'And you are still a prisoner?'

'Oh, no. I am here of my own free will now.' The little man eased back on his high stool, and explained that his skills were so well regarded by the Mongols that he hardly felt a slave. 'I make a good living here, better even than I did in Breslau.'

'But don't you want to go back? To go home?' As soon as I said it, I knew I was only expressing my own deep-seated yearnings. Venice seemed a pleasant place to be in, looking from such a distance.

Tadeusz sighed. 'To what? Everything I knew was destroyed, the buildings, the people. What is there still for me in Breslau? If it even still exists.' He shrugged his shoulders in resignation to his fate. 'Now tell me why you are here.'

I explained something of how I now needed to find where a Dominican friar by the name of Francesco Pisano lived. The Pole's eyes lit up at the name, but then he shook his head sadly.

'I can tell you where he was living. But no one has seen him for weeks. He has disappeared. Mind you, I'm not surprised.' He tapped his head with a horny finger in the universal sign of madness.

When I asked him to explain, Tadeusz willingly imparted all the gossip at his disposal. He explained that the friar had been on the fringe of Kubilai's court for a number of years, yet had not made many allies because of his obsession with silly old tales and mysteries. When I asked Tadeusz to amplify, the silversmith waved his hands in embarrassment, and did not explain.

'He did recently seem to be getting along with one of your countrymen, though. Someone who already had access to the Inner City.'

'A countryman of mine? Perhaps he can not only lead me to the friar, but help me get into the Inner City too. Do you know his name?'

Tadeusz smiled lopsidedly. 'Yes. He is called Azzo Sabattine.'

That was not good news. With a name like that I knew the man had to be a Genoan. Genoa and Venice were at war. No help getting into the Inner City from him, then. I thanked my new friend nevertheless, handing back the cup from which I had drunk, and went back out into the crowded street.

The description of the quarters where the friar lived, given by Tadeusz Pyka, was reasonably precise, but that didn't mean much in the anthill that was the city of Shang-tu. At first I kept going round in circles – not even sure if where I was at any one time, was somewhere where I had stood before. If it had been Venice, I would have been intimately familiar with each *calle*, *corte*, and twisting canal. I could have named each house and *palazzo*. But here, the houses were laid out on a grid, and their

55

monotonous similarity, one to the other, was bewildering. So much for the seasoned voyager, travelling thousands of miles from home – I was lost in an area a few hundred yards square.

Eventually I stood at yet another intersection of lanes and scratched my head. It looked much like the last crossways, where I had turned right. Had the Pole said left or right here? I would have to make my mind up, as it was getting dark. Then I saw it. A little way down the lane to my left stood a wooden door with a Christian cross crudely inscribed on it. This had to be the residence of the missing friar. I walked towards it, then instinctively began to ease my poniard in its sheath. The door was ajar, and I could hear sounds from inside.

Afterwards, I blamed the lack of a kumiss stiffener for being caught out as I was a moment later. Alberoni would have blamed it on an excess of the brew. Maybe I was simply a little lacking in exercise after a long land journey. Reflexes not properly honed. Whatever, I was taken completely off guard when the door was yanked open as I approached it. The curly-headed man with heavy features who confronted me looked almost as startled as I must have done. But he reacted more quickly, stooping to slide his blade out of his boot. At last, I responded like the street fighter I had descended to being in Sudak. I kicked out with my foot, catching my opponent on his shin.

Taken off-balance, the man yelled in pain, and went down.

'Good Christ, that hurt.'

The man looked bewildered by my assault, and I thought that I had maybe misjudged him. To rectify my mistake, I incautiously bent over the prostrate figure to help him up. But as I held my hand out, the man on the floor grabbed it, and yanked me over, jagging a judicious knee into the side of my head as I fell.

My ears rang and I saw stars.

When I had picked myself up off the ground, spitting dirt, the other man had gone, disappearing into the maze that was the Outer City.

6. LIU

*When you want to test the depths of a stream,
don't use both feet*

I think that was the moment my luck changed. Not that I thought so at the time, as I had just been stiffed. At the time, I had a sore head, inflicted by an underhand Genoan. The curly-headed bastard had to be Azzo Sabattine. Nobody but a citizen of Genoa could be so duplicitous, and I had lost him. Doubly annoying because when I ventured into Pisano's hovel, calling his name, it was obvious I wasn't going to find him there. The only room was sparsely furnished, and totally deserted. What personal belongings Pisano did have had been looted. Shards of broken pots and old papers lay scattered on the floor. And his little truckle bed had been torn apart. Azzo Sabattine must have been looking for something powerfully important. My only hope was that I had disturbed him before he had laid his hands on it. The trouble was I had no idea what I was looking for, and for the first time felt a need for Alberoni to be here to guide me. But, even without him, I had to look anyway, even though there was no point in looking where Sabattine had wreaked havoc.

On the other hand, there were precious few other places in the spartan accommodation. So I poked around for a while, turning over the papers that were strewn on the floor. They seemed to be some sort of record of Pisano's time in Xanadu, and may have afforded me some idea of the priest's whereabouts. But Sabattine's rough search had created complete disorder of the separate sheets. I picked some up at random, and read of a meeting with Saracens on the day before Ascension. Then there was a tale of some lady at court giving Pisano a tunic and trousers of grey samite at Quinquagesima. But that would have been months earlier than the other entry. For all I knew it may not even have been in the same year. The only recent reference was to a possible meeting in the Inner City for the eve of the Assumption, but it did not say with whom. God forgive me, but I was not even sure that the Assumption had not yet come and gone.

I kept this single sheet and threw the remainder aside. In my frustration I accidentally knocked a stoppered jar from the end of the bed; it pitched on to the floor, and shattered. A little embarrassed at my own clumsiness, I scooped up the contents that had spilled out. Not jewels or precious metals, merely a bundle of old letters. I rubbed the coarse and ancient paper through my fingers. The letters crackled, threatening to fall into dust, and I absent-mindedly stuffed them into my purse. I thought Alberoni might be interested in them. I stood amidst the debris, and wondered what to do next. Going by Pisano's own accounts, to find out what had happened to him, I would have to find some way into the Inner City. As my only local contact was the little silversmith, I made my way back to Tadeusz Pyka's shop in the hope he might have some idea how I could get past the forbidding gates of Kubilai's palace.

Then one of those fortunate accidents happened to me that had once littered my gilded life. As I said, my luck changed for the better. Just as I was about to step over his threshold, I saw he was in conversation with some young Chinee. The boy was short, but his chest and arms were sturdy. A peasant build, not that of a court official. The boy's insolent, dark eyes stared at Pyka from his smooth-skinned, almost innocent face. The cheeks glowed a healthy red, and his hair was just that sort of spiky shock that a doting grandmother would love to try and tame. Only his eyes gave the lie to his ingenuous visage – those shifty, untrusting eyes that even now I saw boring into Pyka. When they weren't darting round the shop, and surveying the bustling street outside. I had no doubt what they were on the lookout for. Officers of the law, or prying government

60

officials, had the same effect on me. Those ever-shifting eyes made me pull back into the shadow of the roof overhang.

Tadeusz was putting on his most obsequious smile, and speaking rapidly in the Mongol tongue. The boy clearly understood him, but spoke in another tongue I could not follow. However his gestures were clear enough for me to get the drift.

'Well now, young Zhou. Do you have something for me?'

A sly grin creased Zhou's face, spoiling the cherubic appearance for good. His words obviously meant – 'I think you will like this, silversmith.'

He cast one last look over his shoulder, to ensure he was not being observed, and dipped a hand inside his jerkin. The boy pulled out a goblet that sparkled in the rays of light from the front of the shop, and held it out for Pyka's inspection. I saw Tadeusz gasp. And I could see why. It was a beautiful object – far finer than I had ever seen before, even in the West. The silversmith took it from the boy's reluctant grasp, and turned it over in his fingers.

'It is a shame that one side of the rim is dented. It does detract from its value considerably, of course. It's only good for melting down.'

The boy scowled. I could see he was unsure if he was being cheated by Pyka. The silversmith continued to bargain.

'Of course, I could rework it, but the silver may split. And that would reduce its value even further.'

Even I could see that the goblet was so exquisitely wrought that it would be a crime to destroy it. In fact, it was so exquisite, of such high quality, that I knew it could have only come from one place. The Inner City. An idea began to form in my head. The boy looked again at Pyka, and thrust his head forwards and down into his shoulders at the same time in a gesture of stubbornness. He thrust out his hand, and said something that had Tadeusz worried, for the silversmith responded with shock.

'What? You will find someone else who will melt it down!'

Tadeusz knew he had been outsmarted, and made his decision. He could not bear to see the work of art destroyed. Despite the dangers of taking it, he nodded, and quickly agreed on a price that even I knew was far lower than its true value. That confirmed for me that the chalice was stolen.

Once the deal had been struck, Pyka gladly saw the boy to the door.

'It's beautiful.'

My voice startled them both, and Pyka nearly dropped the chalice. He turned and scuttled across the workshop on his stubby legs, and held my arms in a vice-like grip.

'You must never tell anyone what you have seen here. It could spell the death of all of us.

Understand?'

My eyes fell to the object in Pyka's left hand, and I nodded. He let go of me, and picked up a dirty rag from his bench. It was the sort he would have used to buff up his own work after he had burnished it with his fat, padded thumb. The cloth was blackened and old, and he wrapped it round and round the beautiful chalice, hiding away the glorious craftsmanship. Then he stored the inconspicuous bundle high on a shelf. He saw the Chinee boy still staring at it, as he stretched to push it to the back of the shelf. I knew he would have to find a more secure hiding place for the stolen chalice after the boy and I had left.

'Now,' I said, 'introduce me to your friend. I need to get into the Inner City.'

There are thirty-two doors leading out on to the vast courtyard within the Inner City, and every one of them guards a room that houses items belonging to the Great Khan. But the three men who guided me around the edge of the square under the shadow of the colonnade were only interested in what was behind some of them. They saw little value in the rooms that contained Kubilai's accoutrements of war: vast arrays of ornate wooden saddles studded with metal where the riders' thighs would press, or rank upon rank of sharp metal spears, or stacks of honed-edged swords. No, their goal lay in the rooms that held more negotiable treasures –

the gems and precious metals that fed men's greed. They did not even care about the worth created by the craftsmen who had worked on the cups and salvers of gold and silver. All they saw was the intrinsic value of the metal or the stones. Cups and dishes that an artisan had worked on for weeks or months would be melted down in minutes to provide an amorphous and entirely untraceable lump of precious metal. Gems artfully inserted in settings fit for a king would be gouged out and re-cut if necessary. Everything had to be untraceable because the stakes were high. Very high indeed.

Anyone who was caught stealing from the Khan of Khans would, if he were lucky, be strung up between two stallions, who would then be encouraged in opposite directions by the judicious application of a switch on their flanks. The thief would be ripped asunder, and the pieces of his shattered body left for the carrion crows. That was if he was lucky. If he was unlucky, he would be attached to one skittish horse, and dragged for miles over the stony ground of the plains outside Shang-tu with everyone watching in fascinated horror. The first end was a swift death, the second a lingering, painful one that stripped skin from flesh, and raw flesh from shattered bones. And that was why the skinny official who had met Zhou, his father Da and me was trembling like a dry leaf on a cherry tree.

Earlier, in Pyka's workshop with a scared Zhou held by his arm, I found that my poor Mongol tongue was not clear enough for the thief. Tadeusz Pyka had to act as my interpreter. When I told the boy he had to get me inside the Inner City or I would hand him over to the authorities, he had begged and pleaded. Pyka was sweating as he translated. His life depended on my actions too. I had to suffer Zhou's miserable sob story before he gave in.

Apparently, his path in life had not proved promising, for his father had coveted his neighbour's chattels. In this case the neighbour's wife. The husband had found the two in bed together, and beaten Da badly. Da had gone off to get drunk, and on returning home, found his own wife had disappeared with the niggardly savings of ten years of marriage. All she had left behind for him was their son, who was already proving as lazy as his father. Resentful of his beating and the ensuing collapse of his life, the father had sneaked out at night with his boy in tow, and stolen his neighbour's chickens. They both had then fled, selling the chickens further down the valley to set in motion the course of their future life. In their wake, they left a trail of petty thefts, always moving on before they were caught. They also left behind their family names, becoming known merely as Da and Zhou – Big Man and Son. Until arriving in Shang-tu, their thievery had been petty, sustaining them only from one week to the next. Finding the weakness of a greedy official at court had changed all that.

The boy had finally agreed to take me to see his father. And now we were gathered under cover of the grey of dusk at one of the side gates that led into the forbidden areas of Shang-tu. The corrupt official had balked when he opened the side gate, and saw me with the thieving father and son. He hid his face from me, and tried to get out of doing what he had agreed to do for the thieves. Especially when we were almost spotted by an old woman servant bundled up against the cool of the night. The woman looked like an old Mongol crone, wrapped as she was in a heavy jacket and with her felt hat pulled down over her head. She was hurrying out of the palace area, and had made to cross the centre of the great square that stood beyond the gate.

The bigger and elder of the two thieves had gripped the skinny official's arm, and dragged him into the shadows of a doorway. It was the entrance to what I later learned was the Hall of Great Harmony. I pressed behind one of the pillars, watching the woman cross the court-yard and make for the Meridian Gate. Fortu-nately, she seemed as skittish as we all were, and in a hurry to get to the Outer City. When she passed I smelled a sweet scent that didn't suit the hag. It had me thinking of mutton made out to be lamb.

The younger thief sniggered as he felt the

shaking of the Chinee's body against his own. But it was no laughing matter to the older man, Da, or to myself. We knew the weak-willed bureaucrat could place us all in danger if he couldn't let us out again. Da and he bandied words. Even standing apart at a distance, I could imagine the exchange between the thief and the official.

'It's too risky,' the Chinee would be saying, his voice high-pitched with fear.

The older man waved a big, raw fist in his face. 'Not if you get a grip of yourself. You told us there was a feast on tonight. We'll give it a little more time. When it's dark enough, even the gods won't see us.'

The Chinee drew in a breath at the words from the big, burly man, but took a little courage from the strong grip on his arm. He nodded his head, but kept a silk scarf wrapped firmly round his features. We waited for what seemed like an eternity to me, but what was only time enough for the darkness to sink on the courtyard like a blanket, and for the Inner City to settle down again.

The official led the way to the fifth door down on the eastern side of the courtyard. He was still so afraid that he almost dropped the keys out of his nervous fingers. They jangled, and a beefy fist closed over them and the Chinee's own slender fingers, crushing them painfully. The official did not dare squeal though. The father looked round, and then nodded for the Chinee to continue when he was satisfied no one had heard. Like someone who had drunk too much rice wine, and sought to control his errant limbs, he slid the key in the lock with exaggerated care, and turned it. The bolt slid open silently and easily. He had taken care to grease it that very morning. He eased the door open a crack, and we all slipped inside. The boy waited and only lit the lantern he carried with him when the door was firmly closed behind us.

It illuminated a sparkling cave of delights the like of which I had never seen before. Row upon row of gold and silver chalices stood on shelves, glittering in the yellow beam of the lantern. Stacked at the far end of the room were piles of dishes, ewers and serving bowls. Everything was ornately chased with dragons and other imaginary beasts, which curled their tails round the rims of cups, and intertwined their furry limbs across the surfaces of dishes. Zhou pulled out the sack that had been tucked in his belt and, licking his lips, began to pick up objects at random. The Chinee squeaked in horror, and jabbered some warning.

I could guess the nature of the scam. I had come across such a scheme elsewhere – it is better that I do not say exactly where. Suffice it to say that I was involved. The little bureaucrat had probably spent weeks scratching out certain items from the meticulous inventories he was responsible for keeping of Kubilai's vast wealth. Only those items that were never used, that Kubilai never requested be produced, could be appropriated. Once removed from the inventories, it was as if they never existed. Now by grabbing at random, these two stupid thieves were going to destroy his careful work. Emboldened, he slapped Zhou's fingers, making him drop the cup he had picked up. The boy snarled, and the Chinee official grovelled in fear at his own temerity.

Da took the sack from his son's grasp and, following the other man round, began dropping the treasures that the bureaucrat pointed out into the gaping top. Each clanged softly as it dropped in. Soon they were finished, and the sack was bulging and heavy. The Chinee went nervously round rearranging the items left so as not to show any gaps, while the two others stood waiting at the door. Unlike his brainless son, Da obviously knew why they had to be careful. The scheme was to skim off the cream of Kubilai's riches without being discovered. Carried out in that way, the thefts could go on for years.

I had seen enough. My desire had been simply to get into the Inner City. The bonus of viewing Kubilai's riches had just been too much to resist. But, much as the sight of the treasure made my Venetian palms itch, I had other business. The treasure-house door was locked behind us, and I stood and watched as the lantern was doused, and the three men made their escape into the night. I was abandoned to my own devices.

It was not long before I realized how foolish I had been. Despite the prediction by Zhou that everyone would be feasting elsewhere, as I penetrated deeper into the palace, there were more and more servants bustling about. And everyone I walked past stared at me. I was an unescorted foreigner in the inner sanctum of the Great Khan of all the Mongols. I walked purposefully, as if at home in the palace. But eventually I was confronted by a cool and shady small courtyard with several exits. I clearly had no right to be here, and everyone seemed to know it. All I could do was to appear to know where I was going, and cross the square with some authority.

Luckily all I passed were garishly robed Chinee officials like the one who had let the thieves into the treasure house. They seemed inquisitive but lacking in initiative. Still, I felt very conspicuous, at every moment expecting the heavy hand of a Mongol guard to fall on my shoulder. I bowed my head, and hunched my shoulders in the hope I might become invisible. But I was not happy until I reached the comparative shelter of another maze of corridors. But I still didn't know where I would even begin to search for Friar Pisano.

I strode down the glittering passageways, seeming to turn purposefully at each intersection. My brain raced feverishly as I peered in every direction for a sign of a Dominican friar. On several occasions I passed more men, whose eyes I felt boring into my back after I had gone by. I dared not turn round though, and betray my lack of assurance. Deep in the heart of the palace complex, I finally hesitated at a cross-passage that offered me the choice of four ways. I knew I was hopelessly lost.

And I could hear the pad of footsteps approaching.

7. QI

There are two perfect men –
one dead, the other unborn

I didn't have a chance to toss a coin this time. I chose a corridor at random, and headed away from whoever was approaching. As I rushed through a bewildering maze of small halls and dark passages, I became aware of a strange sound. To Alberoni's ears it would probably have sounded like the rustling of heavy robes in the passages of the Holy City, mingled with the hiss of conspiracies whispered in dark passageways. I thought it more like the crash of heavy seas breaking on a shingle beach. It was neither, of course. As I was drawn inexorably towards the source of the sound, it became clear it was the buzz of numerous voices. For a fantastic moment I thought it must be the sound of a thousand people, or even more. Then I laughed at my own stupidity – such numbers could not be imagined in one place, especially not on this godforsaken edge of the barbarian world.

I turned a corner and stopped. Before me

stood a set of heavy, double doors painted bright red and bracketed by two rows of stern-faced Tartars garbed in what I recognized as the uniform of the Khan's personal bodyguards – the *Keshikten*. My steps faltered. I wanted to turn back and leg it, but I could once again hear someone approaching from behind. Besides, the guards had seen me already. My mouth went dry. There was nothing for it but to brazen it out. Hadn't I been in many such fixes before in Venice?

Actually, no I hadn't – the Doge was severe, but he wouldn't have resorted to having a pair of horses drag me apart. I gulped at the thought as it invaded my panic-stricken head. I made my trembling legs work somehow, and walked arrogantly up to the suspicious-looking sentries. It's funny how your mind works, but I suddenly thought of Khadakh's admonition about not stepping on thresholds of their yurts.

'Do not step on the threshold – it is a grave offence to a Mongol. And you will be punished severely.'

As I approached them, I could see the guards' grip tighten on their spears. I saw the whiteness of their knuckles. I got ready to turn and run, and take my chances with whoever was coming up behind me. Instinctively, I dropped my right arm towards where my knife would have been, if only I had been carrying it. But, of course, I had left it behind. I hadn't wanted to be skewered in the Inner City merely for bearing arms. Bad decision. It looked as though I was going to be skewered anyway. Something slipped from my sleeve, and clattered on to the wooden floor. It was the golden token I had stolen. Now I was going to be skewered for trespassing in the Great Khan's palace *and* pulled apart by horses for theft. It was no consolation to think that I would feel nothing of the second punishment.

I bent down to pick up the token, wasting time while my mind buzzed trying to figure out how to get out of this fix. For once, I couldn't think of a thing. My mind was a blank. Maybe they would give the condemned man a last drink of kumiss. Or maybe as a special treat, they wouldn't. When I looked up again in resignation of my fate, I could not believe my eyes. The guards were standing rigidly to attention, their gaze fixed firmly on the gold bar in my hand. It slowly dawned on my feeble brain that this must be some powerful token. Damn me, I probably could have breezed into the Inner City with it, without the collusion of the Chinee thieves.

With a flourish, the guards simultaneously pulled open the double doors, and the roar of voices overwhelmed me like a tidal wave. For a long moment, I stood transfixed at the threshold to the maelstrom – a whirlpool of activity which made me dizzy as it sought to suck me into its maw. Truthfully, there had to be more than a thousand souls gathered here.

In the foreground Tartar men and women sprawled on carpets, their laughter barking out so that they actually did resemble Alberoni's feared dogs of war. The women were barely distinguishable from the men by virtue of the similarity of their clothing, their shapeliness muffled by the large jackets. It was clearly Tartar custom that the women were all arrayed on one side of the hall and the men on the other. The men on the floor were the lowest ranking nobles, who had to be content with the carpet as their banqueting table. They were already delving into the communal pots of steaming stew that lay between them. I was reminded of the endless fare of boiled meat Alberoni and I had been presented with on our long journey to Kubilai's court. It seemed the food was just as unspeakable here.

I watched in horror as a grizzled Tartar to my left pulled something greasy and stringy from a pot and devoured it with relish. The man continued to speak volubly to one of his companions as he ate, and spat shreds of his meal over the rugs as he spoke. Servants wandered around bearing large pitchers, which they used to refill the wine goblets clutched in the diners' hands. When the pitchers were emptied, their bearers returned to a large, gilded chest with finely wrought figures carved on it that stood glittering in the centre of the room. At each corner of the golden chest there was a spigot from which the Tartar servants freely filled the pitchers that then circulated round the hall again. The heat that emanated from the throngs of men and women, their red faces, and the babble of loud conversation, intertwined with voices raised in anger, spoke of the volume of wine and kumiss that had already been consumed.

I tore my yearning eyes from the vat of wine, and started taking in the dimensions of the Hall of Great Harmony. Sizing it up with a mariner's eye, I reckoned it must be a full two hundred yards long, and almost as wide. But it was difficult to perceive the full dimensions because the walls receded into the dimness left by the handful of blazing torches that illuminated the scene before me. The ceiling disappeared in a pall of smoke thrown off by the same torches.

The main source of light concentrated my gaze at the further end of the hall on to a raised dais surrounded by tables at two or three levels stepping down from it. Those who sat at these tables wore clothes more subtly refined than those nearest to me, and they picked at their food more daintily. The tables were so arranged that those who sat at the lower levels had their heads no higher than the feet of the occupants of the highest table. At this table, were just two people – a man and a woman. But what a pair they were.

The woman was swathed in ornate brocades that fell in straight lines from her shoulders, so

76

it was impossible for me to assess her shape. But I could guess at her portliness from her face, which was bland and rounded like a full moon, her cheeks full, and her lips a painted red gash in a sea of white. On her head perched a crown of sorts made of blue, shimmering feathers.

The man was equally rotund, but his face bore an outdoor, robust complexion, and his nose was broad and flat, squashed centrally in the bulging features. A wisp of moustache and beard outlined his sensuous lips, wet from the wine he was draining from a huge goblet. His eyes were like two dark raisins in his head, but I could see they took in shrewdly all that they surveyed. He too wore an ornate robe, but where the pattern on the woman's gown was too far away to discern, I could clearly make out the dragons that twined over the man's shoulders, their faces looking out at the assembled throng. Their staring eyes matched the man's own, adding to the feeling of being examined.

Awe-struck as I was by the brutish alien nature of the scene, I could see the one constant. Wherever you were in the world, rulers set themselves apart from those they ruled. The aura around the man, and the fawning of those at his feet told me this was Kubilai Khan. At last I had my goal in sight.

'There is no chance you will get to speak with him. I have been waiting for weeks, and still the monkeys surrounding him fend me off.'

I looked round at the man who had appeared at my elbow, and spoken in execrable Italian. He was a heavily bearded man with a dark complexion wearing a fur-trimmed, but rather travel-stained, greasy long robe of a fellow from the cold lands of Rus. This Russian looked disdainfully at my motley garb, taking in the patched Venetian hose and Tartar jacket, and sniffed. He clearly thought I had descended to the level of the Khan's entourage.

Looking around me, I now saw that, around the edge of the carousing Tartars, was a milling throng of people. Some in Western dress, some in the ornate robes such as the thieving Chinee official had worn. Along with the Westerners, this other group were clearly not welcome to participate fully in the banquet. In fact, I could now begin to tell that in mannerisms as well as dress, they were quite different from their masters, the Tartars. I was getting my first inkling of the subservient nature of these Chinee, whose vast land the Tartars had taken by force. Just as the devils had done in the land of Rus in the north-west. Here, all these disenfranchised peoples merely hovered on the fringe of power like supplicants.

Which is exactly the position men like Alberoni and myself were in, eager simply to catch the crumbs from the rich lord's table. The Chinee were there to serve their Tartar overlords, and the Westerners to seek favour and advantage. I turned to the Russian.

'And the reason for the feast?'

The stranger grinned lewdly.

'Chabi, his concubine – that's her sitting next to him with the self-satisfied look on her face – has provided him with a son and heir. And look, there's his aunty with the little beast.'

I followed the man's pointing finger, and saw a familiar old woman standing behind the regal pair, nursemaiding a small, well-wrapped bundle. It was the witch Bolgana, now relieved of her virgin charges. I hoped she hadn't discovered my tamperings with her little treasures. For a moment her eyes strayed from the baby in her arms, and scanned the throng. I ducked behind the bearded Russian until her gaze had passed. Then Aunty Bolgana looked away again, and began rocking the child in her all-encompassing arms. I wanted to know more about Kubilai and his brood, and this bewildering, alien world I found myself floundering in. But before I could ask my new friend anything else, I saw Sabattine.

He was across the other side of the hall talking to a group of Chinee. We were separated by a milling mass of bodies, but I began to edge my way towards him. As he spoke he was responded to by a shaking of heads. He then moved on to another group, only to apparently receive the same reply. For a moment he was obscured from my sight as I elbowed aside some swarthy Easterners. When I looked again for the Genoan, he was gone. I had lost him in the crowd.

I looked again at the group of Chinee that Sabattine had been speaking to originally. I had half a mind to try and find out what the Genoan had been asking them. Had he too been here to ask about Pisano? I watched as they bowed deferentially when they were joined by a tall, thin man with a long plait of hair down his back, and a curious design like a unicorn on his robe. When he saw me looking at him, the man returned my gaze coldly and impassively. For some reason, a shiver ran down my spine. I felt as though he knew I was trespassing, and decided not to approach to ask about Sabattine just yet.

So I stood on the fringe of the roaring maelstrom to await another chance. Then a drunken Tartar slumped over in a stupor at my feet, and I seized the opportunity. I grabbed the slumbering man's half-full goblet which, along with drunks all over the world, he had managed to save as he collapsed. I swallowed the contents greedily, and beckoned to one of the servants prowling the hall with pitchers. The man hesitated for a moment, unsure whether he should serve a lowly foreigner. But I waved the goblet with such authority that the man came over, and filled it to the brim. It was a good red wine, and I gulped it down with a gasp of pleasure. I got another refill, and sidled through the crowd until I found a corner where I could wedge myself upright for the night of drinking ahead. I always thought better once I'd had a skinful. And from this vantage point, I could not only see everything that was going on at Kubilai's high table, but stood no chance of having my drinking arm joggled. Slowly the drink drowned out the thunderous noise of the hall, reducing it to a dull roar.

Suddenly, a clashing of cymbals announced the beginning of the entertainment, and the arrival of a troupe of half-naked men with long, oily locks. The show was about to begin. I had heard about these swarthy men, clad only in dirty loincloths. They were called *bakhshi* – Indian mystics who performed all sorts of amazing tricks. The assembled throng groaned in pleasure as four of them bore in a heavily carved chest made of cedar wood on top of which sat a young, loose-limbed boy. They placed the chest on the carpet at the foot of Kubilai's dais. One man – the elder of the group, as was apparent by the skeins of grey that ran through his dark locks – produced a coiled rope. He bowed low to Kubilai, his hair tumbling around him. The Khan gave the slightest of nods, and the dark-skinned man suddenly threw the rope in the air. It hissed upwards, and to my amazement stayed there. I tried to focus my bleary eyes on the top of the rope, but the rigid cord disappeared into the gloom above the wondering crowd. The hall

81

was suddenly as silent as it had been a hubbub of noise a moment before.

In the oppressive pall of silence, the little boy scrambled lithely up the rope, which somehow bore his weight until he disappeared from sight. I could not believe my eyes when the old *bakhshi* then scrambled after him. He was climbing more slowly only because his limbs were not as flexible as the boy. But he too disappeared into the gloom above everyone's heads. I was as transfixed as everyone else in the hall.

Then I heard an inhuman wail from the gloom, and the hairs on the back of my neck stood up. First a small naked limb fell from above everyone, then another, then two legs fell from the apparent carnage above, a small torso thudded on to the carpet near a Tartar noblewoman who shrieked in fear, much to the amusement of her companions. Then finally the boy's head, his hair streaming, dropped from above. During this rain of dismembered body parts, the remaining *bakhshi* had scampered around collecting up the pieces of their unfortunate companion, and loading his remains into the chest. I could now hear a low buzzing in the hall – the sound of thousands of voices anticipating what miracle was to come. I looked over at the Russian, who was now standing close to my shoulder. He was ghostly pale, and his breathing was shallow and fast.

With an unearthly shriek, the old *bakhshi* slid

down the rope, and yanked on it, causing the coils to fall at his feet. He was covered in gore, a bloody sword was clenched in his teeth, and his eyes gleamed in madness. One of his assistants gripped the boy's head by the hair, swung it around mercilessly like a trophy, and then flung it along with the rest of the brutalized body into the chest. The old man slammed the lid, and cast his maniacal gaze over the expectant crowd, as though looking for his next victim. Triumphantly, he banged the pommel of the sword on the top of the chest, and called out some strange invocation.

From that point on, everything went wrong.

There was a hiatus in the flow of events, and the old *bakhshi*'s performance faltered a little, the gleam in his eyes changing to puzzlement. He banged loudly on the lid again, repeating his invocation. This time he was rewarded with a very human squeal of horror, and the boy who had been dismembered at the top of the magic rope, scurried out from somewhere behind the chest. He was undoubtedly whole again, but I was sure this was not how the miracle was supposed to have been concluded. He should have sprung from the interior of the chest, where his dismembered body had been thrown. Not from the secret compartment in the rear. But something had scared him out of his wits. He was pale, and his big, round eyes showed utter terror, as he threw himself into the arms of the old man. His cry of fear hung in the air, and everyone was transfixed, including myself. No one seemed to know what to do.

Then I did something I had never done before in my life. I volunteered.

Maybe it was the drink getting to my brain, making me do such a stupid thing. Later, I preferred to think it was sound instinct – a trader's eye for an opportunity. Whatever it was, I found myself pushing through the silent crowd, a purpose to my step that I had not felt in a long time. Certainly not for the last two years. I felt naked without a weapon, and with a thousand pairs of eyes falling on me. But I had to carry it through. One pair of eyes in particular, resembling two dark raisins stuck in a lump of dough, scrutinized my passage through the throng with calculation and curiosity. I had hooked Kubilai like a fish.

I lifted the lid of the chest, and peered inside. I reached in, discarded the faked limbs and torso, that a short time ago had seemed so real, and began delving in the bottom of the chest. I lifted a false bottom to reveal the secret compartment where the boy had squeezed himself prior to coming back to life. I could now see why the boy had been so terrified, and I wished I hadn't drunk so much. The compartment was already full, and its occupant was in no position to spring to life in front of anyone except his Maker.

8. BA

Shed no tears until seeing the coffin

Everything happened very fast after that. Kubilai and Chabi were ushered from the hall surrounded by his *Keshikten* guard. And a chubby-faced Chinee took charge of the chest, which disappeared into the gloom. Meanwhile, yours truly – Niccolò Zuliani – was led from the stunned assembly by four stony-visaged Tartars.

I was led into a dark and sepulchral room. A room with no open aspect, the only light filtering in from the passages that surrounded it through the pierced, dark-wood screens that made up the walls. There was, it had to be said, an imposing chair at one end, ornately carved, and backed by a yellow brocade screen. I might have been put here to meet Kubilai, but the chair was too small to be called a throne. And there I waited. And waited. I wondered if I had been forgotten. Or worse still under arrest for murder.

When at last I heard a commotion in the corridor, I was glad that at least my uncertainty would be resolved. But it was only Alberoni, who was shoved into the room by a bandy-legged Tartar, who then disappeared. The friar looked pasty-faced, and scared. He glanced warily round the room.

'Zuliani! What have you done? Why have they brought me here? Are we going to be murdered or have you gained access to the Great Khan? Which is it? The second one I pray. Tell me this is the Great Khan's throne room, and we are to be granted an audience.'

I snorted in derision. 'I have seen grander reception rooms in unsuccessful merchants' *palazzi* in Venice. And you have to agree it has nothing to compare with the opulence that is Rome. No, we are here because of the murder.'

'Murder!' screeched Alberoni. 'Then you have killed someone, and we are both to die.'

'No, no, no. I was witness to a murder. Or rather to the discovery of the body. Mind you, so were about a thousand other people. But I was the one to come to my senses first.'

Alberoni sniffed my breath. 'You have been drinking.'

'Not enough, in the circumstances. No, this isn't the Khan's chamber. It's a pretty room, but not grand enough. I have seen more scroll-work in Madame Vegliano's bordello by the Rialto.'

I felt an itch in my crotch, and absent-mindedly scratched at my balls. I hoped it was the grime of travel, still not washed from my body.

86

And not something that I had caught from the girl I had had the night before arriving at Shang-tu. Maybe she hadn't been a virgin after all. I hoped not – I was already beginning to yearn for her company again. I had been dreaming of how she had swabbed me down, and cleansed my naked body after we had made love. She had given particular attention to my groin, and the thought almost caused my prick to rise again.

But suddenly, it was the hairs on the back of my neck that were rising. I felt we were being observed. At first I dismissed it as a drunk's sense of constantly being watched, and censured by the sober. With my mouth dry and yearning for some sweet wine, I peered through the latticework of the wall-screens. I thought I heard the rustle of silk, but there was no one in sight, so I slumped down in the only place available to rest my tired limbs. The friar's voice squeaked in shock.

'You can't sit there.'

'Why not?' I grumbled, reluctantly rising from the soft brocade cushion set on the un-throne-like chair. 'If they could only treat us with a little respect, then I would do the same to them. As it is...'

I did not have time to finish my threat. Into the room bustled a fat, young man with sleek dark hair hidden under a black lacquered cap with wings, and a self-important mien. It was the chubby Chinee who had taken charge at the banquet. The long robe he wore, heavily stitched in gold thread, did nothing to conceal his propensity to fatness. His face too was a little puffy as though he took little exercise. A bureaucrat, not a fighter, I decided with a feeling of contempt. Probably the third junior secretary to the deputy minister at the Directorate for Imperial Accessories. I grinned wolfishly at my own private joke. The man frowned at me, and crossed immediately to the carved chair. I had the feeling that someone had been spying on us after all. And that it was this man. The Chinee cast a disapproving look at the dent in the throne's cushion created by my arse, and plumped it back up. Then, without speaking, he ushered us from this ante-room into a more functional area that must have served as his office. There was a window to a darkened exterior, and the sweet scent of blooms hung in the air.

The man spoke.

Alberoni and I looked at each other a little puzzled by the strange sounds, and the man frowned and spoke again, slower this time. It suddenly dawned on me what it was he had said.

'He's speaking in English, I think. Well, a sort of English.'

With Alberoni knowing no English, I had to speak for both of us. I left the friar standing frustrated on the sidelines as I spoke with our first proper contact in the Inner City. I had assumed we would somehow converse in Turkish, a tongue that the Western world and the Tartars sometimes shared. And which I, being a mercenary Venetian, could speak. But English? That was very curious indeed.

The Chinee essayed the barbaric tongue a third time.

'Do you come from Effar?' Well, the last word sounded like 'Effar', anyway. And I wracked my brain to think of such a location in the Christian world. And then I realized. He was using a quaint old English word I had not heard in years. I cleared my dry throat, and tried to concentrate on not thinking about a goat-skin of kumiss brew.

'Indeed, Great Lord, from afar. From those lands even beyond the edge of the Great Khan's empire. Beyond the Iron Gates.' I can get a little flowery myself at times. 'My companion is a representative of the head of the Christian church, who is called Pope.' I knew that when starting bargaining with a stranger it did no harm to compliment him. Nor to exaggerate one's own authority.

'I myself am an emissary of the Doge, Lord of Venice,' I decided to add, for good measure. My tongue was planted firmly in my cheek.

The Chinee frowned a little as he strove to understand the words that poured from my mouth. This was going to be more difficult than I thought. He obviously pretended a familiarity with the English language greater than he really had. Now he had to struggle to follow my response. I knew he would guess that I was over-exaggerating our importance. He would have done the same in our position. The trick was that he didn't know how much was exaggeration, and how much was reality.

I could see him hastily reviewing my short speech. If there was an iota of truth in it, he could use us to his advantage. He turned to give Alberoni a slight nod, and the friar returned the acknowledgement with a deep bow. So the friar didn't see what I saw. The Chinee's nose had wrinkled at the sour smell that emanated from the friar's heavy, grey robe. Suddenly, even I could see the grime ingrained in every line on Alberoni's face, emphasizing the strain there was on the man. He looked no better than one of those magicians whose trick had been ruined by the body in their chest. At least I, threadbare though I was, was relatively clean, if a little dusty from my walk through the streets. I had, after all, been bathed by hand only a couple of weeks before. I struggled to avoid scratching a renewed tickle in my crotch.

The Chinee was about to speak, when Alberoni obtruded his bad odour on him again. And his Italian tongue.

'Will the Great Khan see me now? I bring gifts from the Holy Father in Rome.'

The Chinee turned back to me with a quizzical look on his face. I tried to explain in simple English that the friar was anxious to be presented to the Great Khan. On listening to the translation of the priest's demand, the Chinee's brow darkened. I could see that the gross abruptness of the enquiry, asked in far too unsubtle a way for the functionary, almost dissuaded him from doing anything for us. I would have to be careful – form and protocol mattered here.

Ignoring Alberoni, the man spoke directly to me.

'I am sure your wishes will be granted ... in time.'

'Of course, Lord. I know how busy the Great Khan must be. And how much this interruption to his celebrations must have made him angry. We are in no hurry to leave Shang-tu. We will await his pleasure.'

As I said, I can be quite silver-tongued when it suits. And it gave me a petty pleasure so see how the frustrated friar could only fume as I conversed with the Chinee official in English. I didn't even give him the courtesy of a translation as I went along.

'How did you learn to speak English so well?' I was curious about the other man's linguistic skills. His chubby face broke into a grin of pleasure.

'I speak it well?'

'At least as well as I do.' Which was no great compliment in truth, but the man was not to know that.

'There was once an Englishman who served

the Khan's grandfather. A ... Templar?' He looked at me quizzically to see if he had the title correct. I nodded, for I had heard tell of the renegade English Templar. The man continued. 'He taught his tongue to the man who taught me. I have long wished to make use of my knowledge. So when I was told you might be English...'

I winced. 'That would be construed as an insult to a Venetian.'

The Chinee did not understand this aside. 'If you are not an Englishman, then where did you learn to speak their language?'

'On my mother's knee, actually.'

I had never discovered how my father, Agostino, had met the dark-haired Rosamund. But little Niccolò had been a sure and certain product of their union, inheriting Agostino's Venetian characteristics of red hair and a flair for trade, and his mother's blue-green eyes, English stubbornness and persistence. I had been christened Niccolò, and all my Venetian relatives called me by that name. It was only when alone with my mother that I answered to a different name. It was a pet name we shared, and it made me feel strangely exotic on those occasions when it tripped from her tongue.

So, when the Chinee asked my name, I responded automatically not with Niccolò, but blurted out the English name that had popped into my brain. Perhaps it was just the language we were sharing at the time that made it come naturally to my lips.

'Nick. Nick Zuliani.' I thrust my hand out, and after a momentary incomprehension, the fat man took it, and self-consciously allowed me to shake his hand. It was so odd a gesture – so intimate – that his normal reserve broke down, and he found himself offering his own name. He saw me struggle to understand. He spoke more slowly for me, repeating it. 'Lin Chu-Tsai. Lin. Chu-Tsai.'

There was a moment when we made eye contact, then the *bakhshi*'s chest was heaved in, and we got down to business.

It took four men to carry in the chest, which was elaborately carved. It was obviously heavy, and the four scrawny bearers staggered under the weight. The lid of the chest was firmly closed, but the brass hasp hung open. We could immediately smell the aromatic odours of the material from which the chest was made. I could also detect an odour not entirely concealed by the cedar-wood scent. A queasy, unpleasant aroma that seeped through the chest's walls.

Lin Chu-Tsai was obviously chafing to be free from this unholy mess. But with me dramatically taking control of events, some official had had to oversee the foreigner. It looked like Lin Chu-Tsai had been lumbered.

I bent over the chest, scanning the exterior for anything of significance. I could smell the underlying odour more strongly now. At the banquet in the Hall of Great Harmony the odour had been masked by that of a thousand bodies, sweating out the drink that had been imbibed. Here, in the empty chamber, it was rank and all-pervading. There was a smear of something dark and sticky on the lock. I might have assumed it to be oil in any other circumstance, but when I absently rubbed it with my finger and sniffed, I knew it was blood. Lin Chu-Tsai, still nervous about the contents, ran his fingers along the edge of the lid too. The friar stood apart, sickened and refusing to participate. I took a deep breath, and pulled back the hasp, lifting the lid.

The cloud of buzzing flies made us jerk back instinctively. Lin Chu-Tsai waved his arms in disgust. The friar clutched at his mouth and began to heave, turning away before he got a clear view of what was in the chest. Lin Chu-Tsai recovered quickly, peering in with awakening curiosity. He almost wished he hadn't, turning away from the horrific sight. My head swam, and not entirely because of the wine I had consumed. I just managed to hold my gaze on the contents of the chest. Only the widening of my eyes could have betrayed my feelings. I forced myself to kneel, and began to examine what was in the chest more closely. Getting momentarily over his nausea, Lin Chu-Tsai too knelt at my side.

Inside the massive chest, half-hidden under the false bottom that aided the *bakhshi* to

94

perform their 'miracle', lay a bloated body. The man had obviously been dead for a while. And the glassy, fish eyes that stared up at us had no comprehension behind them. Besides, a fly was walking over the left orb. The chest bottom, designed to accommodate the slender boy, had not been big enough to contain properly the frame of the dead man, who had been stuffed unceremoniously into its confines. His knees were tucked under his chin forcing his head backwards and upwards, to stare unseeingly out at us. His jaw was open and we could see a full array of rotting teeth. His tongue, now wooden and stiff, had sunk back to fill his greyish, dry throat. Lin Chu-Tsai did not dare look too close. Like me, he had already glimpsed the maggots seething around the base of the tongue. The left arm had clearly been shoved in after the body had settled. It lay awkwardly across the chin of the dead man, the hand tucked down the side of one knee. There was blood all over the man's robe, making the folds hard and stiff when we tried to lift the body out. Lin Chu-Tsai and I had to do it ourselves as the porters refused to approach. Instead they muttered amongst themselves, making signs to ward off evil.

Whoever it was, he had been dead some time – perhaps up to three or four days – because the rigor mortis had passed, and the body was once again limp. Not to mention the presence of the flies and the gases of putrefaction. We laid the body out on the tiled floor. Immediately we could see more clearly the great slashing cuts that had caused such a significant loss of blood as to drench the robes the man wore and leave his body grey and marbly. His features were Western, not Asiatic, and he wore a friar's habit.

'A black priest's garb,' I observed. 'See how the rents in his habit show where the blade has cut through the cloth and deeply into the flesh below. And the hideous slash across his left cheek and deep into the cartilage of his nose. But it's this cut across his neck, nearly severing his head from his body, which must have killed him.'

I knew enough of battle wounds to see that this slash alone would have been enough to cause the friar to die from loss of blood. The other blows had been landed unnecessarily, or during a ferocious struggle.

Lin Chu-Tsai had gone back to look in the chest.

'Look here. There are some smears of blood, and a little dried pool at the bottom of the chest, but not enough to be the whole body's content. So this man had bled to death some time before he was ever put inside.'

The Chinee man's accent was strange, and he spoke in a low whisper, but I just about understood his English and what he was saying.

'Then we must find out where he was killed, for that may lead us to who killed him.'

96

'We?' He sighed. 'I am the Khan's Clerk to the Minister for Justice. I regret it is my sole responsibility.'

I shrugged, not sure if clerk was the same lowly position as in Venice. He had seemed more authoritative. I hunkered down over the body again, wondering if it were true that the image of a man's killer was fixed in his eyes. If so, I could not make him out in this case. The orbs were like those of a stinking fish long out of water – clouded and glassy. I didn't know what to say to this clerk, who was maybe someone of importance, or maybe not. I wasn't too sure why I wanted to include myself in the hunt for this man's murderer. I was certainly no policeman. In fact, most of my experience of the law had been on the other side of the fence. But, on the other hand, that would perhaps now stand me in good stead. And if I could solve the mystery, it would do me no harm in my desire to build bridges with those who mattered at Kubilai's court. Perhaps even with the Big Man – the Sheikh of the Mountains – the Great Khan himself. So I offered my services.

'The dead man is a Westerner. I can make enquiries in the Westerners' Quarter, if you will do so amongst those in the Inner City.'

He smiled wanly.

'As you wish. On your own head be it.'

I wasn't too surprised he seemed actually glad of my willingness to take control. The death of a foreigner must have been a minor matter to him. Maybe as Clerk to the Minister of Justice, Lin Chu-Tsai had much bigger fish to fry. If that's what they did here – I had heard the Chinee ate them raw. Besides, I had some inkling what the reward of failure would be. I thought of the rampaging horses again, and shivered. By the look in his eyes, I knew he could see that working with me – Niccolò Zuliani – could be very advantageous. And vice versa, I thought – as long as I kept my wits about me. After all, I knew nothing about the man, and could not yet trust him fully. I had no doubt that trust was as rare a commodity in Shang-tu as it was in the civilized world. I just hoped I wouldn't end up a scapegoat, if things went wrong. He had one proviso when I offered to bury the body.

'Very well, I will arrange for the body to be transferred to your quarters. But I insist that a doctor examine it before burial.'

I nodded acquiescence, though I was not sure what use a doctor would be to a dead man. What I didn't know then was that Lin Chu-Tsai worked within the crippling burden of bureaucracy that was Kubilai's great and complex empire. He just had to keep the records straight. Lin Chu-Tsai also had one further requirement, couched in his peculiar version of the English tongue.

'You will update me on your inquiries regularly. For I must report higher up in my turn.'

I nodded, adding a request of my own.

'For your part, I would be grateful if you could discover where the friar was murdered. It must have been in the Inner City somewhere.'

Lin Chu-Tsai spoke reassuringly. 'Agreed. I will scour the whole palace.'

Of course, I could see that he had no intention of so doing. He wasn't going to waste more of his own precious time on the murder than he had to. But if some information should come his way, I wanted to know about it.

'We will need a go-between to keep us in touch with each other.'

'A...?' He looked puzzled.

My communication skills were obviously beginning to let me down. I tried some other words from our shared tongues.

'An intermediary. A messenger.'

He smiled in understanding. 'Then I shall find us one. Someone we can trust.'

I laughed. 'That must be difficult in this place.'

For an instant, the dark look on Chu-Tsai's face suggested he was offended by my remark. Then he too burst into laughter – a peculiarly feminine, high-pitched laugh. And for once, when he spoke, he spoke out loud, not in his normal whisper. His voice was reedy and piping.

'Then it will be someone we both know to *dis*trust.'

The subtlety of his suggestion was clear

despite the communication problems, and I nodded again to signify my understanding. My head was going to fall off if I didn't master the Chinee language soon. Nodding wouldn't get me far carrying out a murder investigation.

On our arrival, the Mongol Empire had seemed enclosed and inward-looking, secure and sound. A monolithic structure that stood solid under the weight of its own ancient edifices. Now I was already beginning to wonder. I had the sudden thought that if I could understand this overweight man, then I might begin to peer through a gap in those Iron Gates of Alexander's, and see into the obscure recesses of the society in which I now found myself. Besides, Lin Chu-Tsai would make a good ally, if only I could trust him to be as greedy as the next man. Greed broke down the barriers created by walls.

Lin Chu-Tsai had one other comment to make as we parted. He spoke with a boyish grin on his face.

'By the way, you can keep the gold tablet you stole. It will give you the authority you need to poke your nose into other people's affairs. It's called a *paizah*, and is given to trusted servants by the Khan himself.'

9. JIU

Take a second look – it costs nothing

So here I am where you found me at the beginning. Sharing my quarters with a dead body, a Mongol soldier whose tablet of authority from the Khan himself I stole, and a Franciscan friar who had just identified the body as Pisano, the man we had travelled to the ends of the earth to find. And I, a complete stranger in a foreign land with a limited ability to communicate with the local inhabitants, and little understanding of their ways, was going to find the murderer. I must be mad. But if I didn't, I had no doubt I stood to lose my own life as a substitute for the real murderer. But then the rewards were great. In fact, when I thought about it, it was only like trading in Venice. My reputation as a high risk-taker had been widespread, and all my *colleganzas* – my investment deals – had come good at first. My image as someone who came up smelling of roses always converted greedy people into eager investors. I needed the same luck now.

I covered the ravaged face of Francesco

Pisano again. Friar Alberoni was in a panic.

'Look, if Pisano was killed in the Inner City where few Westerners are ever allowed, isn't it obvious he was killed by ... one of them?'

He nodded towards Khadakh again, leaning closer to whisper in my ear. I don't know why as the Tartar didn't understand our language.

'I told you before, they are the devil in disguise. Surely, such a vicious attack as was meted out to Pisano could only have been carried out by a Tartar, and not have been perpetrated by someone from the West?'

I didn't need Alberoni advising me of possible Mongol complicity in the murder. But I was equally sure the Khan didn't care about the truth or about punishing the real murderer. His only concern was to reassert the power of his rule, which had been smeared by someone daring to kill within the walls of his own palace. If I looked at this sensibly, I would find someone to accuse, and have done with it.

'Of course it occurred to me that a Mongol may have been the killer. But that is not what I have been asked to find. Isn't it obvious? They want me to point the finger of guilt at one of our own. That would be the most convenient solution for them, after all.'

The friar thought about this for a moment, and then a satisfied smile spread across his gaunt features. 'Then that is what you will discover. And when you have reported your findings, perhaps we will be rewarded with an

102

audience with the Khan.'

I took due note of the inclusive 'we' in Alberoni's statement. If anyone was going to be rewarded for providing a murderer, it was going to be me, and me alone. 'And what of the man I accuse? He would be executed. Gruesomely.'

There went those thundering hooves again, and the rending of limbs. Alberoni waved his hand in the air, dismissing my objection to his plan. 'Then choose someone who is unimportant. Or someone you dislike – that Genoan, maybe.'

Funny how his thoughts mirrored my own. I supped on the tea that Khadakh had provided me with. For a long moment, I relished the idea of accusing Sabattine, but I decided I would sleep on it. I may stand accused of being a rogue and cheat, especially when it came to achieving my own ends, but I didn't want to subject even Azzo Sabattine to Mongol justice. I had heard what they did to people who transgressed their laws. It was strange to find I had scruples: maybe I would have to find out what had really happened here, after all. I was quite amused at having to think like an *avogadore* – the sort of Venetian judge who had once been the bane of my life.

The life I had lost.

First, I reckoned I would have to find out who the friar's friends were, and his enemies. From my own experience, both were equally likely to be responsible for his death. And as yet, I didn't know into which camp Azzo Sabattine fell. It would also be interesting to see who turned up at his interment. In fact, this last matter was getting urgent, because the body was already stinking.

Within the hour, I had begun to organize matters a little. Khadakh had been sent off to sort out a burial plot, and Alberoni had been despatched to persuade Tadeusz Pyka to apply his language skills and local knowledge to discovering who had frequented the dead friar's lodgings. Alberoni also seemed keen to examine Pisano's quarters. I couldn't see any point in it.

'Why? There is nothing there. Sabattine probably stole anything of value. I told you that.'

'Yes, but he may not have known what was valuable and what was not.'

'Well, if you think broken pots and old papers are valuable, you are welcome to them.'

Alberoni gave me a smile as inscrutable as old Khadakh, and departed on his useless task. At least I was now free to pursue my own investigations. I was beginning to relish the thought of being on the other end of the iron fist of the law. I straightened my threadbare clothes, and slid my heavy dagger into my belt. Big enough to be a short sword, it felt good pressing against my side again. It was time to hunt the Genoan down.

Then I heard a scratching at the door of our quarters, and strode over to pull it open. Before me stood a slight man dressed in a robe and headdress more suited to Crusader Outremer in the Middle East than Tartary. The cloth that was draped over his head shaded his face, which seemed almost invisible except for two glittering eyes. A straggly, pointed beard outlined his jutting chin. He held an ornate box in front of him, cradled in both hands as though it housed something both precious and fragile.

'*Merhaba*. You are Master Nick?'

The man spoke in Turkish, and my secret family name sounded odd with such an inflection, and from the mouth of a stranger. I was a little taken aback, retorting in the same tongue.

'My name is Zuliani – who wants me?'

The Arab looked puzzled. 'I was told your name was Nick. Have I the wrong man?'

Then I remembered my exchange of names with Lin Chu-Tsai, and his declaration he would send a medical man to examine the body. I coughed to clear the gravel of a sound night's sleep from my throat. 'You are a doctor?'

'I practice healing, yes.' He continued speaking in Turkish. '*Adim Masudi al-Din'dir* – my name is Masudi al-Din – and I am from Yazd.'

I had heard of the place – it was in the heart

105

of Persia. 'Then we are both far from home. Come in.'

Masudi gave me a slight nod of the head, and ducked to enter the gloomy hovel. The light through the tiny window barely illuminated the dusty corners. In one of those corners, the body of Friar Francesco Pisano still lay half-wrapped on the floor, his face and torso revealed. I waved a hand at the body, inviting the doctor to help himself, though I did not know what he expected to find. All he would see was a body mutilated by slashing cuts.

Masudi laid down the casket he had brought on the low table in the corner of the room, and moved over to the partially revealed body.

'It is a formality merely. The paperwork will be simple in this case, and the bureaucracy not heavily troublesome.'

He leaned over the body to look closer, and felt on the neck where the strongest pulse lay for a living person.

'He is dead,' he said, with a dark smile.

I grinned, amused by the doctor's sense of humour. 'I wondered why he wasn't snoring last night. Can you tell me how he died?'

Without speaking, the Persian looked pointedly at the gaping wounds on the body. I smiled again, and tried to explain.

'Where I come from, if the Doge, our ... chieftain – ' I could not think of a more suitable word for the elected leader of Venice – 'dies unexpectedly, the *Signoria* – those in power –

106

call for doctors to examine the body to ensure they know why he died. That is, unless the *Signoria* were responsible for his death in the first place.'

'In which case they tell the doctors what unfortunate illness they are to declare that he died of.'

I chuckled. 'You understand well the workings of the Council of Six.'

'Powerful men are the same the world over,' said Masudi, shrugging. 'So you wish me to verify if the wounds are the true cause of his death?'

I nodded, and Masudi's smile broadened. His skills were required after all.

'Help me uncover him completely, will you?'

I bent down, and helped the little man unwind the cloth that had been wrapped round the body. Once this had been done, the Arab began to pull at the friar's black habit. I looked on in surprise.

'What are you doing?'

'I need to disrobe him if I am to examine the body properly.'

'I had thought a more ... superficial examination might be all that was necessary.'

'I don't know, and I will not know, if you don't help me take his clothes off. And it would help if you could lift him on to that table.' He looked around, surveying the gloomy cell. 'Is there a courtyard here?'

'A courtyard? You are not in the Inner City

now.' I was becoming more and more impatient, wondering what Lin Chu-Tsai had started. But I helped Masudi remove the slashed and bloodied habit. The stench of death could not hide the more mundane bodily aromas of sweat that clung to the underarm areas of the heavy robe. I dropped the stinking habit to the floor with distaste. Then between us we lifted the naked friar on to the low table, Masudi taking the legs at the lighter end of the body.

'No courtyard – what a nuisance. Then help me get the table out into the street.' I looked at the doctor as though he were mad, so he explained. 'It is too dark in here to see the wounds properly. I need daylight. Now get on the other end of the table.'

Between us we manoeuvred the table through the doorway and out into the street. Already it was crowded with people going about their business. The street was narrow, and the buildings were low – single storey mainly – with tiled roofs that swept down in curves almost to the height of a man's head. The walls were all of wood, or of timber frames with daubed mud panels.

Masudi went back in through the door, leaving me standing guard over the body, and feeling awkward as a crowd of gawping spectators began to gather. A peddler with his wares hung from either end of a pole scurried by, scarcely giving the body a glance. But several draymen stopped rolling barrels into the house down the street, and ambled over. A shopkeeper paused from his task of laying out wooden bowls and woven baskets, and came over too. A sedan chair borne by four wiry servants hurried by, the curtains of the side window scarcely twitching at the strange sight.

Masudi returned with his precious box, and placed it on the table next to the dead friar's head. Soon the crowd pushed forward to Masudi's shoulder, curious to know why a man should be examining a naked corpse on a public highway. I was embarrassed by the whole exhibition, but the doctor seemed oblivious to the stir he was causing. A cart loaded with squalling chickens tried to negotiate the narrow roadway towards us, but had to give up as the crowd refused to budge. The driver of the cart whipped his team of horses, then shrugged fatalistically, and joined the onlookers. Masudi went about his business meticulously, blithely unaware of being the cause of the street being blocked to traffic.

With my assistance, he rolled the corpse on its side, first one way, then the other, and examined the skin of the back. He poked and prodded the blotches of livid colour on the otherwise bluish skin. Only then, when the body once more lay on its back, staring sightlessly up at the clear blue sky, did Masudi examine the gaping cuts. Each cut that scarred the skin was long, and the dead flesh now gaped, the edges hard and inflexible to the touch. They were concentrated on the chest and upper torso. One had clearly sliced open the big vein in the neck that I knew, from experience of regular sea-battles with Genoan ships and Adriatic pirates, would have resulted in fatal blood loss by itself. And caused a nasty mess wherever the killing had occurred. I wondered if Lin Chu-Tsai was even trying to find a bloodied room in the maze that made up the Inner City.

'Good,' muttered the Arab, easing his stiff back as he stood up from his examination.

I looked at him quizzically, my eyebrows raised.

Masudi knew I wanted an explanation, but he had obviously not finished yet. He was a cautious man, who didn't commit himself easily. He lifted the lid of the box, and produced a thin, short blade on a long handle that glittered in the sunlight. The crowd edged back nervously. Masudi drew a line down the skin of the corpse's torso from neck to navel, and the slender blade cut easily. He began to peel back the already shredded skin. Someone in the crowd groaned, but generally there was a movement closer to the gruesome sight. Once through the outer layer, the doctor pulled and manoeuvred the mess of greyish offal that filled the body cavity. By now there were more than a few green faces at the front of the crowd of onlookers, and one of the draymen began to sidle gently backwards through the press to escape the horrific sight. The shopkeeper too had had enough. Their places were taken, however, by those still curious enough to watch. There was a uniform intake of breath from the crowd, when Masudi plucked out the heart, lifted it up like a trophy, and peered at it with evident interest. Even I paled at the sight.

'Excellent,' was the doctor's only comment.

Swallowing the bitter taste of bile in my throat, I asked him what he had concluded. Was his patient dead? Masudi ignored the evident sarcasm.

'There is no evidence of penetrating wounds to the body, and no tears in the heart. See it is whole and unpunctured.' He thrust the bloody vessel at me, a malicious grin on his otherwise serene features.

I did not rise to the provocation, and began to feel I could like this man. He had the same sort of gruesome humour that tickled many Venetians. Besides, I was sure the doctor had something of significance to offer now.

'Go on.'

'There is no vomit or froth on the man's mouth, nor unusual discolouring to his lips other than the blueness of death. So unless he has been washed – which I believe is unlikely – he has not ingested something that might have poisoned him. He is almost entirely exsanguinated...' He saw me frown. 'There is very little blood left, so he was alive when the wounds were made. If he had been dead before the cuts were made, the blood would have been still and less would have flowed out of the wounds – even these wounds. No, the man died of the slashing wounds. No wounds on the back – so our killer was not attempting murder by stealth. Nor was he being cold and deliberate. Look at the cuts on the arms.' He lifted one of the friar's limp arms and showed the underside. 'The typical result of throwing your arms up to defend yourself from a frontal attack. Like this.' He threw both his arms up in front of his face, his palms and forearms facing out. He struck the pose for a few seconds, and then lowered his arms again. His dark brown eyes glittered.

'An unprovoked attack, then,' I murmured.

'Unprovoked? Who is to know? One could say with some certainty that it was unplanned.'

I frowned. 'Oh? How?'

With a self-satisfied smile Masudi waved a hand over the corpse. 'Because of the marks on the body. Someone planning to kill him, would have lain in wait, and taken his life from behind, surely? And I was told he was discovered stuffed into a chest, on his side, is that so?' I nodded, recalling Lin Chu-Tsai's and my surprise when the chest lid was opened. 'What blood was left in his body would have pooled in one side of his buttocks if he had been put in there straight away. There were some marks there, but the main stains were all across his

112

back. He had lain flat on the floor for some time after death, before being hidden in the chest.'

'Meaning?'

'Meaning the body had been left for some time, while the killer sought out a way of hiding it. He took the chance that someone might come upon the body in the meantime and uncover the deed immediately. Not the actions of someone who had planned the murder beforehand.'

'Hmmm.' This was all very interesting, but I still had no idea where it might lead me.

'Oh, and another thing. Look at this.' Masudi turned the friar's head gently to one side, and pointed with his slender fingers at the side of the neck. I peered closely, and made out an oval ring of bruising and broken skin.

'What's that?'

'Teeth marks. Clearly his attacker tried to take a bite out of his neck.'

I grimaced – perhaps Alberoni's tales of the cannibalism of the Tartars wasn't so far from the truth after all. I would have to be careful if I ever met the killer.

10. SHI

A closed mind is like a closed book –
just a block of wood

If I had hoped for the murderer to turn up at Pisano's burial, I was cruelly disappointed. A Franciscan friar, a Venetian fugitive, and a heathen Tartar was the strange combination that made up Pisano's funeral procession. The three of us stood by the banks of a turbid stream that issued from underneath the forbidding walls of Shang-tu, and ran away on to the endless plain. Around us were scattered the handful of wooden crosses that defined this place as a Christians' burial ground. Khadakh, who had helped me dig the grave, explained that the stream fed the Great Khan's pleasure grounds inside the Inner City. There, the ground was fertile, and game populated the slopes and thickets. That was why, once outside the walls, the stream had lost its potency, and its will to feed the surrounding earth.

Dry rushes rustled at the stream's margin, and the water ran sluggishly away to the south. The plain was dusty, and the grass no more

114

than dry stubble, grazed to the parched earth by the flocks of goats belonging to the Mongol herdsmen who preferred to live in their tents pitched outside the walls, away from the anthill that was Shang-tu.

'The city of the dead,' grunted Khadakh.

I thought he was referring to the graveyard.

'It will do for Pisano,' I replied.

'No, no. That.' He hooked his thumb at the city hidden behind the walls. 'It is what the old ones call this city. Any city. Settle in a house, rooted to one spot, and you might as well be dead, they say.'

I could see the long look in his own eyes. The distant stare of the nomad always searching beyond the horizon.

'City of the dead,' he muttered with finality. I guess it had been for Pisano.

We lowered Friar Francesco down into the earth. His last resting place was a hole that was nothing more than a scrape in this arid ground at the ends of the earth.

As Alberoni muttered a prayer that seemed to blow away on the stiff breeze that buffeted us, my mind wandered. I stared off into the west at the distant mountains glowing purple in the afternoon sun's rays that stretched across the open prairie. Somewhere beyond there, if you looked far enough, was Venice. For the first time since my arrival at Shang-tu, I felt unrestricted, as though freed from prison. I longed to just up and go, but I knew it wasn't possible. I was a captive. Just as enslaved as surely Tadeusz Pyka had been all those years ago.

And I would have to buy my release.

I wondered if I could adjust to the claustrophobia of the Khan's great court, and whether the effort was worth it in the end. Look at what had happened to Pisano. Years of dancing attendance on this exotic creature and his minions had resulted in a brutal death and a patch of dry earth. Never in the last few years had I longed so much for ... what? Venice – certainly. Sexy Caterina – most assuredly. I longed for her soft limbs, and the velvety feel of her ivory skin. My tumble with the dark-skinned Kungurat girl ironically had reminded me more strongly than ever of Caterina's fairness. For the millionth time, I rued our last meeting, the look of betrayal on her pallid face, and how I had left without reconciling her to me.

Beside me, the old Mongol raised his eyes to heaven, and offered his own prayer up to the sky. Knowing that one clan of the Mongols held belief in a sort of Christianity, I whispered in his ear. 'Do you pray to God too?'

The old man spat, and raised his hands sky-wards, motioning at the endless blue canopy.

'To Tengri, the Sky God.'

Alberoni looked angrily round on hearing Khadakh's words, and crossed himself against the idolatrous act. I ignored him. Khadakh

116

picked up the wooden shovel he had used to shape Friar Francesco's grave, and began moving the dusty earth back over the shrouded body. Alberoni pushed past us in grim silence, and strode back towards the western gate of the city. He seemed anxious to get away from us.

In fact, since returning from his errand to obtain a promise of assistance from Tadeusz Pyka, Alberoni had been unusually quiet. The friar had closeted himself away in his little room, only emerging to carry out Pisano's burial. This new behaviour was a mystery to me. Until now, Alberoni had insisted on having me at his heel like some faithful dog. Since searching Pisano's home, the friar had become unusually secretive. But I did not have time now to wonder on the friar's change in demeanour, for I had other pressing matters on my mind.

I needed to return to the Inner City, and continue my search for Azzo Sabattine. He was the only one I knew for sure who had had recent contact with Pisano. And I wanted to know what he had been searching for in the friar's lodgings. I also wanted to talk to Lin Chu-Tsai. Though it was still early, I reckoned he would already be up and about.

Court officials in Venice did not rise from their beds before noon, and spurned any formal appointment earlier than the evening. Somehow, I could not believe that of Lin, though. He struck me as a man who would tirelessly

117

pursue his own ends until he triumphed. And he would be resistant to rushes of blood to the head. I wished I was equally immune to the dangers of an impetuous nature. Perhaps I would not have had to flee Venice all those years ago. But neither was I a man to mope for long, and leaving Khadakh to complete his melancholy task, I strode back to the teeming city.

It was not long before I realized how futile my present approach to the task of hunting a murderer was. The gold token – the *paizah* – had got me through the gates of the Inner City without a problem. And it afforded me free passage in the rooms and halls that made up most of the Inner City. But there were so many of them. Where was I going to find Sabattine? Using my new official status, I even penetrated the fringes of Kubilai's Mongol entourage. The quarters of the minor princelings and attendant concubines were a mess – stinking animal skins thrown hither and thither, and greasy stains on the floor from careless meals of boiled mutton. But that seemed normal for most of the little barbarians. They apparently liked to pretend they still lived the nomadic lives of their ancestors. Showing that they had not been corrupted, as they saw it, by the seductive elegance of the Chin dynasty they had usurped and half-destroyed. But though there was plenty of barbarian untidiness, there were no signs of blood on the sparkling walls of gold and silver ornament. No telltale stains on the intricately woven tapestries of chrysanthemums and dragons. None of the Mongols would talk to me. And the only other people I encountered were court officials. I couldn't ask any of them about Sabattine, because I couldn't speak their language. I was blundering round like a dog in an anthill. And wasting my time just as effectively. What I needed was a strategy. Moreover I needed an understanding of how this particular anthill worked.

I went in search of Lin Chu-Tsai.

I knew his office was somewhere in the heart of the maze of rooms. And I remembered a distinct smell of blossoms when Alberoni and I had first been taken there. I followed my nose, and when I could smell the scent of flowers, I suddenly recognized where I was. The gloomy ante-chamber led to his office through an archway, but there was no sign of Lin.

The room was as austere as I remembered it, though the table was now scattered with papers and scrolls. I crossed over to the heap of documents, and began sifting through them. I was hoping they might hold some clue as to what investigations Lin had in hand, and whether he was holding anything back from me. I was disappointed. Much of the paperwork was written in a spidery script that meant nothing to me. Mongol or Chinee, I supposed.

Then I came across a document held down by

something familiar. It was a silver tablet about a foot long and as broad as a palm with a hole at one end. Inscribed on it was the swirling, fanciful design of a dragon's head. I recognized it because it matched in all but colour, the golden tablet I possessed. Lin did have a special remit directly from Kubilai, after all. I picked the silver tablet up idly, and hefted it in my hand, guessing its weight to be around forty ounces. I was calculating its value, when I saw the document it held down. It was written in Turkish – a language I did understand. I began to read it.

Though my command of the tongue was laboured, and largely confined to expletives of use in conversation with a sea captain or to quantities and materials for use with a merchant, I had an inkling of what the paper described. Inscribed with dates from the Muslim calendar, it gave the intended whereabouts of the Great Khan, Kubilai, over the next few weeks. And it seemed to suggest that the Khan and his court would be departing for the site of the new capital at the end of the month. After a ceremony on the Inner City ramparts in only a few days' time.

I was perturbed. If I was going to win my freedom and a return to Venice, I needed to solve the murder in days, rather than weeks. And get to see Kubilai himself, before someone like Lin Chu-Tsai claimed the glory. I wondered if I could arrange to be at the ceremony mentioned in the document. If in the meantime, I had found Sabattine, and put the fix in on him, who knows how grateful the Great Khan would be? So engrossed was I in this prospect, that I was unaware that someone was watching. Until an indrawn breath told me I had been found rifling through secret papers in Lin Chu-Tsai's room.

I turned to see a tall, thin Chinee man standing in the doorway. His eyes burned with surprise and curiosity, though the rest of his face was cold and expressionless. The contrast startled me, and scared me a little, I have to admit. I also had the impression I had seen him before. Without weapons, as we both were, I could easily have overcome him. But I didn't want to make enemies, or have myself incarcerated for no purpose. I needed to remain free to pursue Sabattine in the Mongol palace.

So I feigned stupidity instead. A random thought told me that if Caterina had been there to see it, she would have teased me that such a subterfuge was not hard for me to play out. I slipped the paper I had been reading back under the pile of documents on the desk, and slid the silver tablet back into place. Then I spoke to the man in the doorway both slowly and loudly in Venetian, throwing in the name of Lin Chu-Tsai for good measure.

On the third repetition of the name, the man nodded his austere skull of a head, pulling the tight skin up round his thin lips in a pale and frightening imitation of a grin. He waved me into the only chair in the room, and stood like a statue at the entrance, obviously prepared to wait out this stand-off until Lin Chu-Tsai turned up. He probably didn't believe my invocation of Lin's name, and proposed to uncover my lie. Then have me imprisoned, or even worse.

I dropped my gaze from the man's implacable stare, and passed the time by examining the fanciful embroidery emblazoned on the Chinee's robe. It was of a crouching, dragon-like beast with one horn sticking up from the top of its head. It suddenly came to me that this man had been present at the banquet. He had stared at me with an incisive expression then.

'Master Nick. What brings you here?'

The skull-face smiled at the sound of Lin Chu-Tsai's voice behind him, and turned. Lin continued in his native tongue. Without understanding the greeting, I noted that the apparent joviality of Lin Chu-Tsai's voice didn't quite ring true. I also noticed the sneer that played across my erstwhile captor's features, before he slid on his impassive mask again. The tall man then spoke to Lin Chu-Tsai. Unable to follow the exchange, I sighed and waited a little longer on Lin's arse-numbing seat. I could just imagine what skull-face was saying.

'I found this intruder in your room, rifling through the papers, that you carelessly left uncovered. I think he claims to know you – he invoked your name at least. Or so I gathered from amongst the barbarian and outlandish barking that he uttered. Of course, if he is not known to you, I shall gladly pass him to the Imperial Guard and have him torn limb from limb.'

Or words to that effect.

Lin Chu-Tsai frowned, and peered around the tall man, who still occupied the doorway of his office like some sentinel carved from stone. He had an apologetic look plastered over his face. Then he smiled coolly at the man, composing his reply carefully. He then translated for my benefit.

'I was telling Ko Su-Tsung – ' I filed the name away for future use – 'that you are assisting me in the unpleasant matter of the murder. I said I told you to wait here when I was called away by Minister Kayyal.' He then spoke in the lingua franca of Turkish, giving me a small bow. 'I am sorry I was gone so long – I hope it hasn't inconvenienced you too much.'

I picked up the threads of the sham. 'Not at all, Magistrate Lin. I spent the time admiring your office.'

Ko Su-Tsung narrowed his eyes, uncertain whether he was being subtly mocked or not. He made to leave, but Lin Chu-Tsai stopped him with a gentle brush of his arm on the man's sleeve. The tall man reacted, pulling his arm away as if struck with a red-hot iron. The touch must have been deliberate by Lin Chu-Tsai, knowing the man hated physical contact. He clearly wanted to disconcert the man, and pressed home his advantage.

'May I ask what brought you here in the first place?'

Ko's long glossy queue waggled as he shook his head in a show of modest embarrassment. He replied in Turkish, so that I too knew where he stood.

'Idle curiosity only. I wondered if you had uncovered anything about the killing.'

I was sure that nothing about this man's actions was idle, least of all his curiosity, which was probably utilized to discover everything there was to know about everyone at the palace. I could see that Lin didn't believe him either. They were obviously playing a subtle game of private politics that probably obsessed those whose life was lived out in the palace. I was beginning to grasp the undercurrents. Lin answered Ko's question circumspectly.

'Nothing of note, I fear. Only the identity of the victim, which this man has confirmed for me.'

I took up the story quickly, knowing that Lin did not know the friar's name. I had not supplied it yet. But I could see he wanted to appear to know more than he did in the presence of this cold man, who clearly hated physical contact.

'Yes, as I told Magistrate Lin, Friar Francesco Pisano was a visitor to the palace, and must have met many officials. I am therefore searching for a man called Azzo Sabattine. He may be the one guilty of Pisano's murder. Did you know either man, by any chance?'

I rose as I spoke, approaching the man closely. Ko was disconcerted both by the abrupt and loaded question and my looming proximity. His impassive mask almost slipped, and he reacted without thinking.

'Know a foreigner? Of course not. My duties place me in contact with the Great Khan's administrators only. And none are foreign barbarians.'

He made the idea sound preposterous, and before I could ask him any more questions, he turned on his heels and stormed from the room.

Lin Chu-Tsai grinned triumphantly, and congratulated me on cracking Ko Su-Tsung's facade.

'You have done on first meeting what I have failed to do in several years of sparring with Ko. I hate the man. He is so ... well, so lean.' Lin Chu-Tsai patted his own round, plump body. 'Positively cadaverous. Mind you, it is said he is a good lover ... of women.'

It sounded to me as though Lin Chu-Tsai envied Ko Su-Tsung for that. And I wondered why he kept his own emotions so carefully suppressed. He shook his head, and continued, appearing to divine my thoughts.

'For me, my work is my life. And if I have to labour twenty-four hours a day, at least it keeps me one step ahead of those who had other things entangling the threads of their lives. Those who would have me stumble.'

I heard the unspoken message. Those like Ko Su-Tsung.

'Who is he, exactly?'

Lin gave the faintest of shrugs.

'His ancestry makes him no more than a Khitan invader from Manchuria, and he should not be in the position he is. Lower than a simple *nan-jen* like me. But he claims ancestry from the Han dynasty. And that has been enough to elevate him to the position of power he now occupies in the Ministry of Rites. I must say he is suited to his role, which is strict, formal and devoted to protocol. I doubt the story of his origins, but be warned. Ko Su-Tsung is a devious opponent, whom it is impossible to underestimate.'

The scent of Kubilai's garden wafted across our nostrils, and a bird sang his melancholy morning song. Lin Chu-Tsai leaned on the cushioned back of the comfortable couch, which was the only soft furnishing in the room. Apart from an upright stool, and the table that overflowed with the reports and directives I had snooped through. In the centre of the table sat the massive pile of documents. Lin saw me looking at them, and shuffled them together.

'That is my life's work. It represents Kubilai's personal wish to fuse the Yassak, the harsh and summary laws of the Mongol nation, with the, shall I say, more subtle procedures of Chin legislation. Of course, grafting the one on to the other is an impossibility. Like trying to stitch the head of a howling dog on to the supple body of a cat, then expecting it to run around lapping milk and purring.'

He didn't mention the document I had spotted. I guessed maybe no one below the Justice Minister was supposed to know in advance what Kubilai's plans were. It was dangerous information to know where he would be from day to day. Whoever knew that could plan and execute many things. Including murder. And Lin had deliberately pushed the document out of sight beneath the other papers.

Leaving my curiosity on that matter aside, I explained my problem concerning the maze of rooms in the Inner City, and my search for Sabattine.

'You can have my servant, Yao Lei. He can be our go-across.'

'Go-between.'

Lin looked confused.

'The word is go-between. Yao Lei will be our go-between.'

Lin frowned at having been less than perfect with his English.

'Go-between indeed. A warning, though. Let me tell you a little about Yao Lei. It was when I awoke this morning here at the table. I had had a long night.'

Lin Chu-Tsai told me how he had been

pondering on the matter of the go-between. How he wanted to be sure of the man. What he didn't make clear was that he probably wanted a spy as well. I could understand that. After all, a good gambler always needs to spread his bets. Anyway, Lin had been tired, and he had closed his eyes.

The next thing he'd known was when he had been roused from sleep by the scuffing of bare feet on the tiled floor of his room. He half-opened his eyes, and had seen his servant Yao Lei sneaking round the massive table, and shuffling through the papers piled on it. The skinny little man appeared to be leafing through them as if looking for something. As he did so, a sheaf of documents slid from the heap, and plopped to the floor. Guiltily, Yao Lei cast a glance at his master, who promptly closed his eyes, then stretched as though he had been awakened by the sound of the falling documents.

'Is it morning already?'

Yao Lei hissed subserviently. 'Master, forgive me. I tripped, grasped at the table, and the papers just fell. I was just about to return them to the stack. Forgive me for waking you.'

The man was quaking, and Lin Chu-Tsai guessed not simply because he had awakened his sleeping master. What had he expected to find amongst the documents on the table? And why was he looking? More importantly, for whom?

Lin Chu-Tsai told me he had made an immediate decision.

'Yao Lei. I want you to do something for me.'

'Master?'

'I need someone to pass messages between myself and one of the Westerners who recently arrived in Shang-tu. It concerns the body in the chest. You will be my messenger.'

Yao Lei hadn't suppressed the sly smile that had flickered across his thin lips. He must have imagined his master had been fooled again, and that he was being taken even further into his trust. Lin Chu-Tsai, for his part, had bowed his head over the documents on the table, barely able to conceal his own pleasure at having outflanked the treacherous servant. He would rather have the traitor on the inside, where he could feed him half-truths, than poking around in the shadows undetected.

Now Lin warned me. 'You suggested to me yourself, Nick Zuliani, that duplicity was probably as rife in Shang-tu as in your own city, Venese. How close to the truth you were. You had better take your own warning into account when dealing with Yao Lei.'

11. SHI-YI

*The beginning of wisdom is to call things
by their right names*

I wanted to talk to Alberoni after returning
empty-handed from the Inner City. Lin had
promised Yao Lei's assistance no earlier than
tomorrow, so my search for Azzo Sabattine
was stalled. I still thought Sabattine's behaviour
our put him in line for being the friar's
murderer. After all, he had acted in a typically
Genoan underhand way, and then had resorted
to cowardly flight at the first hint of a fight.
And even if he wasn't guilty of the friar's
murder, I wanted to know why he had ransacked
the man's quarters. I needed to question
Alberoni about the dead Dominican. I needed
to know as much as possible about Pisano in
order to even begin to understand why he had
been killed. Of course, the reason probably lay
within the walls of the Inner City, but it would
do no harm to know everything Alberoni knew
from the friar's time in Rome.

The Franciscan was still closeted in his own
little room, and remained uncommunicative.

He hadn't even come out to eat any of the boiled offal that Khadakh had prepared for us the previous day. Not that I could blame him for that – the meat was now greyish and flyblown, and the water it had been boiled in was greasy, cold and thin. I had deadened my palate with the goat-skinful of kumiss the old Mongol had thoughtfully left behind before tackling the meat myself. It still tasted foul. So it was with a real bad taste in my mouth that I entered Alberoni's cell of a room. He was morosely staring at the wall.

'Alberoni, you must talk to me about Pisano, or I shall never solve his murder. Why was he here, and why were you seeking him?'

'What is the point, when he is dead, and all his treasures are gone?'

'What are you talking about, Alberoni? Treasures – what treasures?'

Had there been gold or jewels? Had I missed such obvious treasure? Alberoni read my mind, and his lower lip curled in a sneer.

'Not something you would have seen as treasure. Merely copies of letters.' He paused. 'But such letters.'

I suddenly recalled the bundle of old papers I had picked up in Pisano's ransacked hovel. They had been meaningless to me at the time. Were they so valuable, after all? I almost decided to keep quiet about them, and examine them for myself later. But I knew Alberoni was right. I would not be able to see the value of them, or know who might give me a fortune for them. I would have to rely on the friar to tell me that. Then maybe I could sell them. I opened the flap of my purse, and pulled out the dusty bundle.

'Are you talking about these?'

With trembling anticipation, Alberoni peered at the topmost letter in the bundle. He gasped.

'Yes. Where did you get these?'

'From Pisano's rooms.'

Alberoni contained his anger at my carelessness. He pointed to the inscription on the top letter.

'Look at that one. See how it is addressed.'

I lifted the bundle up to the light, and read it: *To the Illustrious and Magnificent King of the Indies, and a beloved son of Christ.*

'Do you not see what it is? I fear it may only be a copy, but the paper still seems redolent of the history that envelopes it.'

I rubbed the fragile parchment between my fingers. And Alberoni jumped up to his feet.

'Be careful!' he screeched. 'It's a papal letter to King David of India!'

He took the pile of letters from me, and held them reverently in his hand. It was as though the top letter's vulnerability reminded him of the True Church's perilous situation in an embattled world. He began to explain.

'The original was written by the Pope almost one hundred years earlier, and disappeared in the East with the ambassador sent to deliver it.

No one in Rome knew anything more about it. Had the recipient been found? Had his hands touched the letter? Had he perused its contents, and sighed the great sigh of a monarch burdened with unenviable responsibility? Or had it never been delivered? No one knew. Except that the hoped-for deliverance never came then. Now, with the church in an even more perilous state, Friar Pisano was despatched with a copy of the original letter, and with further entreaties for assistance.'

I looked at the small bundle of documents, begrimed by their passage from hand to hand over the years. And saw them as less of a treasure and more like the mariner's albatross. A curse to anyone who owned them, but not a reason to murder. If this had been Pisano's mission, I couldn't see how trying to deliver a hundred-year-old letter to the court of Kubilai Khan could have resulted in his death. The Mongols would have laughed themselves silly. I was suddenly too tired now to argue with Alberoni. I left him seated in the gloom, hugging the papers to his chest, unmindful that the previous possessor of them lay rotting in the ground.

I slumped down on my cot, my mind befuddled by kumiss. For a while I listened to the drone of Alberoni's prayers, buzzing away like a fly over a rotting corpse. I tried to concentrate on the puzzle of Sabattine and the murder, but the friar's droning pervaded my head, and I swatted at it irritably like the fly it was. After a while there was merciful silence, and I began worrying at the strands of errant facts I had uncovered. Pisano had some ancient letters, or copies at least, and was on a secret mission in Kubilai's domain. He had wheedled his way into the Khan's court, and Sabattine had probably seen an opportunity to make his own way there. Then Pisano had been got rid of, and Sabattine had fled on the discovery of the body. End of story.

But I still couldn't square away one problem. Why would Sabattine have killed the friar somewhere in the Inner City when he saw the man regularly in the foreign quarter? Why, when he had so little chance to gain access to the palace, would he have taken the risk? It didn't add up. I eventually tried to sleep myself, but a multitude of such thoughts hovered round my head. I gave up any idea of slumber, and concentrated on what I would do the following day.

The friar hadn't paid me since arriving in Shang-tu, so I felt free to pursue my own ends in the legendary city. If I could help bring the murderer to justice, I reckoned that Lin Chu-Tsai would owe me a favour. Even in this strange and alien land, I was sure indebtedness counted for something. But first I had to track down the elusive Genoan who, if he wasn't the killer, might hold the key to who was. I had been turning this around in my mind when the next thing I knew Caterina Dolfin was leaning over me, stroking my brow.

'Caterina! How did you get here?'

She didn't reply, and it was a strangely changed Caterina. Her finely chiselled features were coarser than I remembered. More cadaverous. It was the face of Ko Su-Tsung that hung over me, and his claw-like hands wrapped themselves around my throat. I tried to call out but my frozen vocal chords refused to come out with more than a high-pitched squeal. It was a merciful release when death and darkness came.

12. SHI-ER

He who sacrifices his conscience to ambition
burns a picture to obtain the ashes

I am fleeing from Ko Su-Tsung and his sharp knife. The faster I try to run, the slower I go. I am running up the soft, yielding dunes of the Desert of Lop, the sand making each step an inhuman effort. My legs are burning, and I am running as if in a dream. I recall nightmares where I have felt similar sensations, and the knowledge that I am dreaming breaks the spell.

I wake up in the dark, and can't move my limbs – am I dead? I try to call out, but cannot speak as my tongue is cleaved to my palate. I am tangled in something heavy and clinging. I panic, and try to pull free. My thrashing only makes my entanglement worse, and soon I am exhausted, flopping weakly like some fish caught in a net. I realize I'm still dreaming, and gasp with relief.

I struggle to wake up.

Suddenly, I felt a hand over my mouth. It was warm and soft. My heart stopped, but I risked a look at the demon on my shoulder. A beautiful girl knelt over me, a skein of her dark, thick hair draped across his cheek. For a moment, I was sure I had slipped into another more pleasant dream. Then I realized I could smell the freshness of her hair, and the heavy scent of some oil that adorned it. This was no dream.

I was in a distant land, whose customs I couldn't fathom, investigating the murder of a man I didn't know. And there was an unknown woman in my room. The troubled thought of my flight from La Serenissima faded rapidly from my mind, as the reality of the woman's presence impinged on me. I could feel her body pressing down on mine through the thick animal skin covering me, and I was filled with lust. The woman removed her soft palm from my mouth, and placed a single finger across her own lips.

I nodded to acknowledge that I understood I was to keep silent. I wasn't sure we shared any common language anyway, so it was impossible to imagine the point of speaking out loud. Besides, I didn't want to rouse the friar, who I assumed was still asleep in the adjacent room with only thin walls between us. I was surprised to realize I knew who she was, and racked my brain to bring her name to mind. It was the Kungurat girl, and it had not been so long since I had seen her distraught face disappearing into a crowded Xanadu.

Suddenly the name came to me.

'Gurbesu! How did you get here?'

I essayed a little of the Mongol tongue I had picked up bit by bit on our journey to Kubilai's court. I didn't know whether the girl spoke it too, not having had the chance to indulge even in conversation with her at that first, brief and lustful encounter. The girl held a slender hand in front of her mouth, and giggled. Her big, brown eyes stared at me longingly, and I felt a stirring beneath the heavy rug draped over my lower body. I thought maybe she didn't understand me, so tried again, speaking more slowly.

This time she pouted in annoyance.

'You don't have to speak to me as if I am a child. I'm not stupid.'

She flopped down, lying next to me. She was no longer wearing her travel-stained Tartar furs, though I could see a heavy old cloth coat carelessly dropped on the floor by my bed. Now, she was dressed in the simple jacket and long cotton skirt that I had seen many of the women of the Outer City wearing. But the wildness in her eyes, and the loose-limbed way she had dropped to my side, meant she would not have blended in easily with those demure Chinee women. I ran my fingers through her thick hair, noticing for the first time how it was covered in dust, greying it.

'Then tell me how you got here. You were supposed to be ... meeting the Great Khan.'

I left it unsaid that at our last encounter, she had been destined to be a potential concubine to Kubilai. And, as the prettiest of the bunch that had been delivered to the palace, I was sure that Kubilai would have especially selected her. So what was she doing here, on my bed? Moreover, was I in danger because of her actions? I did not know what the punishment might be for being caught with one of the Khan's brood of women, but I could guess. I went limp again at the thought.

Gurbesu clasped her hands behind her head, and lay back. I could see her breasts pressing against the thin silk jacket.

'I don't know how it happened. One minute I was pining for my red-haired lover...' She smiled sweetly at me, and my senses rallied. 'And then the old woman, who was in charge of the Hall of Earthly Tranquillity – that's the place where all the concubines live – said someone had arranged to smuggle me out of the Inner City. I thought she meant you.'

I had to admit it wasn't me, but was glad the unknown person had done so. Most girls in her position would have been resigned to their fate. In fact, I understood from Khadakh that all the concubines apparently lived a most comfortable life, with a healthy pension when they became too old to attract the Khan's attention any longer. But I had also seen, on the smallest acquaintance, how wilful Gurbesu could be. She giggled again, and I could feel the bed rocking.

'I was dressed as an old servant woman, and just walked out through the big gate the other night. I lay low in the Outer City for a while, and now here I am.'

I thought of the old woman whom the thieves and I had nearly bumped into on my first illicit foray into the Inner City. The crone with the sweet scent. Had that been Gurbesu?

'Why come here? And how did you know where to find me?'

'So many questions. Everybody knows everything here. I just thought that even if it hadn't been you who released me –' she pouted at the thought – 'you might at least help me. I just asked about the big, flame-haired man.' She snuggled against me, and I felt aroused again. 'Now you will help me, won't you? I could be your maidservant.'

I sighed, and wondered how I was going to explain this to the friar. A bodyguard with his own maid, who apparently was ready to share his bed. Did I really need this right now? Oh, well, that was a matter for later. For now, I took Gurbesu's shoulders, and pulled her towards me.

I was relieved that from now on we could get on famously with my Mongol, and maybe some of the lingua franca of Turkish too. 'What shall we do with you? I'm afraid there are only two cots in this place, and my very religious companion is in the other one. So unless you want to sleep on the floor...'

'You could share with the priest, of course. So that I could sleep alone here.'

I showed her what I thought of that suggestion.

It was much later that we were disturbed by a scratching sound at the door of the hovel. I slid out from Gurbesu's warm embrace, and pulled on my Tartar jacket to ward off the chill of the room. Sliding the door cautiously back, I was confronted by a skinny Chinee man, dressed in a patched but serviceable shirt and pantaloons. He was of an indeterminable age, like a lot of his compatriots, with a wrinkled face and shaven head. He bowed, and grinned obsequiously, though I could see my bare legs shocked him. Then he thrust a piece of paper at me nervously, hardly seeming to wish to release it.

When I managed to tease it from his grasp, I was at last able to open and read it. It was from Magistrate Lin.

'Have my servant, Yao Lei, bring you as soon as possible. I have found the place.'

I knew instantly what the equivocal statement meant. Though Lin could not openly say it in a document that might be intercepted, I knew what he meant. He had discovered where Pisano had been murdered. I began dressing immediately.

'Where are you going?'

Gurbesu's head emerged from the tangle of furs on my bed, her mane of hair rumpled and her eyes sleepy. Lin's servant ogled her surreptitiously from the door.

'I cannot tell you. It's business.'

I didn't know if the girl knew about the death of Pisano, or that I was involved. What I did know was that I needed to meet Lin Chu-Tsai alone.

'Stay here. Do not go outside, and you will be safe enough.'

'Can't your business wait?'

'No. I'm afraid it can't.'

Looking at her languorous face, and the way the furs were sliding down her chest, I wished it could. But Yao Lei was hopping from one foot to the other in the doorway. Maybe it wasn't all from an anxiety to obey his master. I insisted that the Kungurat girl stay indoors.

'Introduce yourself to the good friar.'

Grinning at the thought of that confrontation, I got the wizened messenger to lead me to his master.

He took me through the Meridian Gate, the great entrance to the Inner City, and on into the palace complex. We soon exited a long hall-way, and I found myself at the entrance to a massive parkland that must have bounded the western edge of the Inner City. Here, the same wall that enclosed the palace encircled miles of groves, lawns and wild scrub, all well-watered with springs and streams. Apparently it was the personal hunting grounds of Kubilai Khan, extremely private and only accessible from the palace itself.

I leaned on the wooden archway that gave on

to the pleasure grounds, staring into the far distance in awe. It was the only part of the Inner City that afforded such a vista. Elsewhere, some views could be long, impressive, and designed to dwarf those who visited the Great Khan. But ultimately the views inside the palace ended in a wall, an archway, a gate – or a throne. Every vista had its limit, every direction was circumscribed. This had all the appearance of open country. But even as I stood there I knew it too was enclosed, sealing the Great Khan off from his subjects. Even here, in the pleasure grounds, the sense of distance was an illusion. Once you knew the apparently endless, rolling parkland was itself bounded by a high wall, albeit unseen until you were close to it, the world closed in again. In fact, the whole country itself – *Tian-xia*, All Under Heaven as the native population endearingly called it – was bordered by the Great Wall, once designed to keep the very barbarians out, who now pretended to be Chinese emperors. Much good it had done.

I followed Yao Lei along a winding pathway to a stand of trees. In the middle of the stand was a small grove. The ground was churned and scarred; the patches of yellow grass looked like they had been caused by the exclusion of light. So the grove now seemed somehow spoiled – damaged beyond repair. Though I supposed that it would not be long before nature recovered. Yet for now, the glade was not as pleasant as it could have been. And I wondered why Lin had had me brought here. And, for that matter, where was Lin Chu-Tsai?

'It is where Kubilai has the cane palace erected.' He stepped silently from a group of trees, the ease of his movement in stark contrast to his size. 'He has the palace erected every summer so that he can enjoy the pleasure grounds and the pursuit of hunting in comfort. It can be built anywhere, though this is his favourite spot. It was taken down some days ago. But it was the place where Pisano was murdered.'

'Which is why the location of the murder was difficult to find. But then how did you manage to uncover it, Lin?'

The magistrate tilted his head slightly.

'I overheard Sun Yun-Suan complaining about the state of one of the rooms after it had been used by our masters. It was smeared with blood, which he assumed was from the carcass of an animal. The coincidence was too much to believe though. Sun, by the way, is the Master of the Pleasure Grounds, and a talkative individual.'

'Where is the cane palace now?'

'Yao Lei will show you. I thought you would want to see the actual location first.'

I paced out the extent of the yellow patch on the grass. It was greater than the interior of the Church of San Zaccaria in Venice. A magnificent size for a temporary structure. My pacing took me to a small rise at the edge of the grove. Further out on the plain, I could see a group of yurts squatting like blackened mushrooms on the lush grass. I pointed them out to Lin.

'What's that?'

'Prince Arik Boke and his barons.'

He explained that the vast jumble of tents and temporary structures housed the senior barons whose clans served the imperial family. They still adhered to the old ways and lived at least a nominally nomadic existence.

'Indeed, there are those who despise the ruling class's aim to strengthen their hold by pretending to have assimilated the culture of their subjugated nation. The old men think all Kubilai does by his actions is lose his own identity, and destroy the very thing that holds them together in the first place. The will of conquest and expansion. Just who they see as the head of the royal family is at present in doubt, and the encampment seethes with dissent and conspiracy.'

'And this Harry Boke...?'

'Prince Arik Boke is Kubilai's younger brother, and his implacable opponent. He made a bid for the role of Great Khan when the other brother, Mongu died. But Kubilai outflanked him. As you can see, he is now his brother's prisoner. The rest of the tents belong to those barons who have thrown in their lot with the treasonous younger brother. Of course, they had to show their face at the banquet the other day, but then left as soon as everyone else was too drunk to notice their absence. Arik Boke, on the other hand, was persona non grata at the sumptuous celebration. You see, it was for the new heir to Kubilai's throne. And how could he be expected to celebrate the birth of another usurper to that which is rightly his?'

I stared with curiosity at the tents. Then, at that moment, the sun slipped behind a great black cloud, the shadow of which fell like a long grey shroud over Arik Boke's encampment in the pleasure grounds of Kubilai's palace. Lin Chu-Tsai shivered at the inauspicious omen, and waved at Yao Lei to escort me to where the cane palace was being unpacked.

'Won't you come with me, Lin?'

'No, Zuliani. I have some ... matters to attend to.'

I left him deep in thought in the quiet grove, and followed Yao Lei back towards the palace. At least the sun's rays were not blocked there. They flooded the pillars and walls of the shimmering Inner City with light. I was grateful for the feeling of warmth on my back as I stepped once more into the sunshine.

I watched as the scurrying servants unwrapped the bundles of canes. They lifted them from the carefully stacked piles next to the red wooden posts and cross-beams that gave the structure strength when it was built. This was the summer palace on whose grassy site Lin Chu-Tsai and I had recently stood. It was constructed of cane around a set of pillars carved to resemble rearing dragons that have their tail planted in the earth and their outstretched limbs supporting a roof of varnished shingles.

The structure was gilded with fanciful beasts and birds that sparkled and shifted with the moving rays of light that penetrated the interior of the structure. When built, it would seem light and airy, yet so solid that it is impossible to believe it was held together temporarily with silken cord alone. I admired the craftsmanship of the dragons that topped the posts, their tails made to curl down around the post itself.

For now, the canes were bundled up with those silken cords, and each vast bundle looked the same to me. But Sun Yun-Suan, the supervisor of the Khan's pleasure grounds, bustled around, and snuffled at the heaps of canes like some overfed boar. It was a resemblance enhanced by the bristly stubble on the lower half of his face. But it was clear he knew exactly what he was looking for. When asked earlier in the day, he had explained to Lin Chu-Tsai the trouble he had had when dismantling the palace. Now he repeated it to me in execrable Turkish.

'Of course, I thought the Mongol barbarians had slaughtered an animal inside the palace. I wouldn't have put anything past Prince Arik Boke. So I thought nothing of it, and ordered the room affected to be washed before packing,

147

but there was not much time, and I will wager that the job was not done well.'

Now he saw that what he had feared was true.

He pointed at a particular bundle of canes, and flapped his hands in impatience, urging the servants to their task. Four of them lifted the tall bundle from the stack and lay it flat on the ground. Then they began to untie the silken cords, fumbling in terror as Sun's impatience grew, and his hands flapped faster and faster. At last, the recalcitrant rope was unfastened and the bundle of canes unrolled.

'It was this wall that was the worst, so you will be best able to see the staining here.' I could see he was berating himself for his lack of supervision at the time. 'What we are going to do with it next year, I don't know.' He sighed deeply at the profanation of the summer palace.

The servants began to unroll the bundle of canes, each of which was more than ten paces long. The canes were linked and intricately carved across their surface. As the bundle rolled out on the floor, I saw revealed lion-headed beasts, their heavily maned upper bodies ending in a scaly serpents' tail, and dragons expelling fiery breath, their fishy extremities writhing in loops and whorls. The curve of flanks, and the dragon's flame, was picked out with gilding, and the shapes enhanced with vibrant colours. The artistry was dazzling, but a whole section in the centre of the panel was dulled – marred by some staining that had been ineptly washed. Someone had scrubbed at the marks and ruined the delicate artwork. It began as a small mark, low on one surface, then grew as the bundle unrolled. I looked at Sun, who stood beside me, frowning at the damage.

'Are we standing at the bottom of the wall?' I hoped I made my question clear.

Sun nodded, and motioned for the servants to reassemble the room section on the edge of the pleasure grounds near where we stood. Soon I could make out the extent and shape of the staining. I looked along from the base of the canes at my feet and up the unrolled portable palace wall. I could see that at its most extensive, the staining was much greater than the height of a man. I now knew where Friar Pisano had stood when his life-blood spurted from the gash at his neck.

This also had implications for the identity of the killer. For Pisano to have been murdered in the cane palace, the murderer must have been freely able to enter the Inner City, and the private expanse of the pleasure grounds. Was such a man Azzo Sabattine? The Genoan had certainly had time to finagle introductions to whomever mattered at the court and the merchant guild – the so-called *Ortogh*. And had been wheedling his way into the circle of Pisano's contacts. But could he have found his way into the Khan's private game reserve? It was now more likely to have been a Mongol or one of the Chinee officials buzzing round the corridors of power. I would have to watch my step.

13. SHI-SAN

A gem cannot be polished without friction,
nor a man perfected without trials

I had thought that I was becoming familiar with the layout of the Inner City by now. But when Yao Lei began to lead me back to the Meridian Gate, and the Outer City, I felt lost all over again. There was definitely an intersection of passageways where I thought we should turn right, but Yao Lei led me straight on. I hesitated, but the skinny servant stopped and waved me on, so I followed. As we passed along a particularly gloomy passage at the heart of the palace, I felt a presence hovering in the archway just ahead of me. I tried to shrug the feeling off. Maybe my worries about the murderer continuing to stalk the palace had struck an unreasonable fear into my heart.

Still I hesitated. Yao Lei was now standing at the end of the passage he had dragged me down. Beside him, a great bronze urn with dragon-like handles on either side dwarfed his scrawny frame, casting him even deeper into shadow. He looked frightened. So it came as no

151

surprise when a demon stepped out of the darkness ahead of me. I almost turned to flee, then saw that the cadaverous figure was dressed in ornate robes. And I recognized the motif on the front. No demon this, merely a unicorn.

As he stepped further out of the shadows, Ko Su-Tsung's skull-like face was revealed, though his stony features betrayed no feelings. Even the dark pools of his eyes hid unfathomable depths. They were matched by the motif on his gown, which was an animal with a scaly body and a single horn in the centre of its forehead. Its eyes, too, stared out at me. I looked past Ko Su-Tsung to the end of the passage. Yao Lei had disappeared.

'Forgive me if I startled you, Master Zuliani.'

His command of Turkish was imprecise, his tones thick. So much so that I could barely understand him. No matter. From my previous meeting with him, in Magistrate Lin's presence, I knew I would have to fence carefully with this man. The excuse of not comprehending what he had to say might be useful.

'Not at all. Do you wish to tell me something about the matter we discussed earlier?'

Ko frowned unconvincingly. I could almost hear his papery skin crackling with the effort of creating any sort of expression. Then he smiled. The rictus was even more unconvincing.

'Ahhh. The matter of the missing murderer – your fellow countryman.'

I refrained from denying that a Genoan was any countryman of mine. Or that I was sure of his guilt.

'Indeed. I am still looking for him. Have you located him?'

A crestfallen look was the next mask he essayed. It was even more unconvincing than the first. Maybe he had covered the full range of facial expressions open to him. I hoped so – so far, the results had not been very pleasant.

'Alas, I have not. But I will continue to look. However, there is a matter I wish to draw to your attention in connection with Lin Chu-Tsai. Please, come into my office.'

With a raised arm, he beckoned me into the room from which he had so startlingly emerged. He was at pains to make sure no physical contact took place in the process, standing back as I passed. The room was more opulent than Lin's austere little room. Dark wall hangings threaded with gold glimmered in the light from several candles. There were no pierced screens here to allow either light in, or the prying eyes of people intent on knowing Ko's private business. Overall the room's atmosphere felt heavy and oppressive. At one end stood a massive chair with elaborate scroll-work arms in a dark wood of some sort. Similarly ornate wings protruded from either side of the padded cushion of the chair back. There was a matching footstool below it. It was a throne to all intents and purposes, and Ko walked over to occupy it himself. I was left standing in the centre of the room like a supplicant.

'I have to warn you about Magistrate Lin. As a newcomer to Shang-tu, you do not know the full facts.'

It was my turn to frown. I hoped I did it better than Ko, because I was getting truly confused. 'Why should I be wary of Lin?'

'Let me explain how things work here. A Turk by the name of Alawi Kayyal is nominally the Justice Minister, because no Chin could occupy a position of authority at Kubilai's court. The fact that Kayyal drinks himself stupid all day, every day, despite being a Muslim, and Lin Chu-Tsai does all the work, does not change things. Lin is a mere clerk as far as Kubilai is concerned. As a *nan-jen* he can be no loftier.'

'A what?' I had heard Lin use this expression before, and been lost as to its meaning. From the curl of his lip, it sounded as though Ko was accusing Lin of being a baby-killer.

'There are certain ... hierarchies in the Great Khan's court. I am *han-jen*. And as a *han-jen* I fear I am a second-class citizen to the Mongols. No, to be more correct, coming from Northern Chin means I am in the third rank of citizenry in the Mongol Empire. First the Mongols themselves, naturally, then the foreign auxiliaries, mainly natives from parts of Central Asia – they are the *se-mu jen*. Then my caste. But at least I am a cut above the *nan-jen* Chins from the South. They are the lowest of the low. Northern Chins and our Mongol overlords are agreed on that one thing. The *nan-jen* Southerners are *man-tzu* – barbarians – and therefore undesirables and untrustworthy into the bargain.'

I did not care for this social claptrap. I'm a republican at heart, and it all reminded me too much of the friction between the old aristocratic families of Venice, and their disdain for the upcoming merchant classes. Like the Zulianis. Besides, Lin had disparaged Ko in exactly the same way.

'If that is all, then I can't see anything to fear from Lin. But thank you for your history lesson, all the same.'

I turned to go. But Ko stopped me with a sharp retort.

'There is more.'

I sighed, knowing I wouldn't like what he had to say. 'Go on.'

'Lin's parents were very backward people, and thought that the only way of ensuring his entry into the service of the new emperor was to do what had been done for centuries in *Tian-xia*. You know the expression, *Tian-xia*?'

I nodded. The words referred to China, and meant 'All Under Heaven'. As though no other country existed for them.

'Long ago, the Chin emperors feared for the honour of their wives and concubines, so they made sure that all male servants were rendered incapable of sullying that honour in any way. It then became a long accepted tradition. Of course, things had moved on by the time it was Lin's turn to seek employment at court, and by then the Mongol overlords had imposed their own practices. But his parents were from the country and things don't change much there. They were living in the past, and assumed that the sacrifice was still necessary. Lin found out too late that it wasn't.'

This time, the grin on Ko's face was convincing. He was enjoying this. I merely felt sick. 'You mean...?'

'Yes. Lin Chu-Tsai was castrated while still a child, and he had no say in the matter. It has warped his mind, and his behaviour. I am convinced that Lin has such a modest room for an office only as show. I am sure that he has some secret boudoir somewhere in the Outer City for his squalid assignations with men. He is so full of rectitude with his public face on, he must be leading a double life. Wallowing in sinful sodomy in his private moments. The trouble is, so far I have been unable to trace this sordid nest of Lin's. But I will eventually.'

He paused, as if needing to recover from this foul invective. Then he continued with a colder, calmer voice.

'That is not important, however. What you must realize is that now, as a grown man – or to many, something less than a man – he knows

156

his parents made the wrong decision. It has affected his ability to make the right decisions – perverted his very life – until he cannot see beyond the outrage. And guess who he sees as the cause of his misfortune? The Great Khan.'

'Why should he blame Kubilai for something his parents did to him?'

'Because the Great Khan is our emperor, and he was castrated to please the emperor's wishes. The fact that it was a long-dead emperor, and Kubilai had already banned the act of castration, only makes it worse in Lin's eyes. His sacrifice was all for nothing. And that is why he is a traitor.'

When we had first arrived, I had seen a consistency in the Mongols' rule, a slick and even stonework where the joins are hardly visible across the whole empire. Beyond the Iron Gates, it had seemed that subject nations happily served the elite, and grew off the security that the empire provided. But once inside the impenetrable walls, I had found nothing but the same sort of internal bickering, power plays and in-fighting that typified Venetian political life. And which betrayed the instability of the Mongol succession.

Suppression was the Great Khan's chief implement of empire, for his subjects and his rivals. How else would a Mongol nation numbered only in hundreds of thousands control the millions in their conquered lands? Even so, the players eternally jostled for position, and created camps and influences that cause dangerous tides and fluctuations in the apparently even flow of the mighty river of an empire. Beneath the surface, cross-currents and rips were liable to drag the unwary under, and drown them. The press of water on the banks were causing landslips and losses.

And I was now in the centre of the maelstrom.

I left Ko's dark and depressing rooms, and found my way back to the pleasure grounds. I needed to breathe fresh air, and think of the implications of Ko's revelations. I passed the cane palace which had been left partially erected by Sun. The rest of it was heaped on the ground still in its silken-tied bundles like so much kindling. Crossing the grove where it had stood when Pisano was murdered, I sat on the little grassy knoll that overlooked Prince Arik Boke's encampment. The sun was dropping down, blood-red behind the yurts, reminding me of death and decay.

Just when I had begun to trust Lin Chu-Tsai, his servant had led me to Ko Su-Tsung, a man whose very appearance screamed distrust. There I had learned things about Lin that confused me. He was certainly a eunuch, though for me that did not detract from his honesty. I was more inclined to pity him than distrust him.

And what about Ko's insistence that he was

also a traitor to his current master, Kubilai Khan? I had seen Kubilai's itinerary in Lin's office. Was it there innocently or as a means for Lin to help arrange an assassination attempt on the Khan? The hint was that Lin had thrown in his lot with the Great Khan's rebellious younger brother, Arik Boke. The younger man had already once attempted to fill the power vacuum left by the death of their mutual father. But he had been in the wrong place at the wrong time, and Kubilai had prevailed. His elder brother had let Arik Boke live, subject to him becoming Kubilai's prisoner. A bird in a gilded cage, like the songbirds the Chinee were so fond of. But even under Kubilai's benign supervision, it seemed the prince was once again fomenting rebellion.

If that were true, and Lin was assisting him, how far could I trust the magistrate? And for that matter, was the proximity of Arik Boke's camp to the murder scene another factor I had to take into account? I had to know more about Friar Pisano and why he had come to Xanadu. I needed to speak to Alberoni about the Dominican's specific mission, and this damned letter Alberoni so coveted. As I sat deep in thought – well, as deep as my addled brains allowed – one of those questions appeared to get answered.

Below me, the princely enclave inside the Inner City's pleasure grounds looked all bustle. Tents and temporary structures were already being dismantled. I guessed it must be in preparation for the massive transfer of the court that I had read about in the document from Lin's desk. Some tents sat on the ground, some on the back of squat wagons set with heavy wooden wheels on each corner. The state of the prince's encampment gave the opposite impression of Arik Boke to that of Kubilai. The Great Khan wanted to absorb or be absorbed into Chin culture. But Arik Boke stood for an occupation force that, unlike any other that had fought over the lands of northern China, was reluctant to settle and be absorbed. If the younger brother had his way, that attitude would ever be the case – the Mongol overlords would always be alien.

Then amidst all the hustle in the camp, I saw an event that confirmed my worst fears. Two men had stopped at the edge of the clearing where stood a large, imposing black felt yurt that was slightly apart from all the others on a patch of lush green grass. The well-flattened path to the entrance conveyed to me a sense of its importance, of the frequency of supplicants visiting its owner. It had to be Arik Boke's yurt.

One of the two men I saw was a Mongol. The other was Lin Chu-Tsai. So this was the business he had to attend to, and which prevented him from watching the cane palace being rebuilt. Ko had been right after all.

Lin Chu-Tsai stopped in the shadow of a massive wagon, and the Mongol was about to take his arm and usher him forward, when the flap of the tent opened. A portly figure stooped under the low arch, and when it straightened, I saw it was the old woman – the witch Bolgana. I watched as Lin Chu-Tsai squeezed even further back behind the wagon's wheel, dropping his face to the ground. He obviously didn't want to be seen in the prince's company by someone so close to Kubilai as the old aunt and nursemaid. From where I sat even I could hear Bolgana's shrill voice calling sharply back into the darkness of the yurt.

'And be sure you never do anything so foolish again.'

The imprecation, spoken in the Mongol tongue, was clear, even to me. She was actually reprimanding the prince for some perceived misdemeanour. Lin stayed under cover until he could see the old woman waddling off back to the palace, her head held imperiously in the air.

The Mongol escort spoke again in Lin's ear. Acceding finally to the command, Lin Chu-Tsai reluctantly approached the tent. He must have been hoping that Arik Boke's pent-up anger from Bolgana's visit wouldn't be vented on him. In the circumstances, his reception could not have been friendlier.

A large, imposing Mongol man stepped into the tent opening. His finery meant it had to be Arik Boke, and I could see the Khan's brother was livid. His face was flushed crimson with anger. Bolgana must have truly treated him like a child, and you might have now expected him to behave like one. But he forced a smile, slapped Lin Chu-Tsai on the back, and ushered him into the tent like he was his closest ally. The flap dropped, and I was left to imagine what conspiracy was brewing inside the prince's yurt with the man who knew Kubilai's movements over the next few days in full detail.

14. SHI-SI

Crows everywhere are equally black

I hurried back to the foreigners' quarters in the Outer City, deep in thought about what I had been told. And had seen. I had jokingly referred to the problem of trusting people in Xanadu when I had spoken to Lin Chu-Tsai. Now it looked as though he was one of the people I needed to be most wary of. It was a mortal blow, because I needed someone on the inside, and intimate with the workings of the Inner City, if I was ever to find out who had killed Friar Pisano, and why.

Ko Su-Tsung had apparently been frank with me. But I would rather be heading out into the Adriatic in a storm aboard a rotten Pisan hulk than trust myself to his mercies. Only the little silversmith Tadeusz Pyka could help me. He had been here long enough to understand how the place worked, surely. But first I needed to speak to the friar about these crazy letters of Pisano's. I remembered something about the top letter now. It was an old story of a letter purportedly written by Pope Alexander the

163

Third nearly one hundred years ago. And was itself in response to letters said to have been brought by Philip the Physician from a place that no lesser person than Alexander the Great had seen. The far-off Indies. These letters concerned the existence of an Eastern Christian monarch called Prester John, who it was said, would at some critical juncture invade and liberate the Holy Land. Most Venetians, being of a pragmatic nature, saw that as pipe dreams for optimists. But if it was real, what had the letter to do with Kubilai?

Though outside our quarters the evening was warm and balmy, inside I soon discovered that the atmosphere was frosty. I had forgotten about Gurbesu's presence, and the subsequent ménage à trois it created. As I slid back the door, and stooped to cross the threshold built for a shorter race than us Venetians, I was hit by the friar's invective.

'What do you think you were doing? Are you insane or have your brains descended to your Tartar breeches?'

'What have I done now, Alberoni?'

'Her,' he hissed, pointing at a sullen Gurbesu, who sat on the edge of my cot teasing the ends of her glossy tresses with her fingers. 'Do you know who she is?'

Before I could concoct a suitably bland response, he provided the answer to his own question.

'I recognize her, if you don't. She was on

board that cart of Kungurat girls the old woman was escorting. The virgin tribute for Kubilai.'

I grinned knowingly. 'You singled her out yourself, then, from all the beauties on display?'

Alberoni's face turned purple. 'What are you suggesting, Zuliani? It is more likely you singled her out. And defiled her.'

There was no joking with Alberoni. And I could see that if I wished to get Alberoni's continued cooperation, I had better be more contrite. Striving to pull on a solemn face, I assured him that I had done no such thing. Po-faced lying was, after all, an asset useful for both trading and gambling. And I had been suckled on both skills.

'Listen, she has come to us ... to you ... as a priest. For sanctuary. She does not wish to become a virgin sacrifice at this heathen court of Kubilai's.'

The friar eyed me with suspicion still in his gaze. But he couldn't help but take my statement seriously. I beckoned Gurbesu forward, and taking the cue well, she threw herself at Alberoni's feet, crying out. Though she misinterpreted my intentions for her somewhat.

'What is she saying?'

Not wishing to spoil everything by translating the girl's licentious suggestions precisely, I told him she was repentant of her life of sin. Alberoni's face glowed with religious pleasure,

165

and he made the sign of the cross. All was well, apparently. It was with some difficulty that I extricated his limbs from Gurbesu's grasp though. Maybe I had misled her as to what was expected of her in convincing the friar to allow her to stay. I told her to sit on the cot in the corner of the room and keep quiet.

'And be demure,' I hissed for good measure. I was not sure Gurbesu knew what the word meant. She sat down cross-legged on the cot, showing her pretty ankles and bare feet. I flapped a hand anxiously, and sulkily, she pulled her skirts over her feet. Then, when Alberoni turned his back, she risked sticking her tongue out at me. With the friar duly placated, I broached the matter of Pisano's hoard of letters.

'Those letters. May I see them again?'

He pulled the bundle of crumpled and torn old documents from his purse, and reverently passed them to me.

'Read them,' croaked Alberoni, a tear in his eye. He sat on a low stool, and encircled his knees with his arms. It was as though he was trying to contain some force, some holy energy within himself.

I unfolded first the letter I had looked at before. It had the intended recipient's name in faded ink on the outer fold.

To the Illustrious and Magnificent King of the Indies, and a beloved son of Christ.

166

It confirmed what I now had recalled. I was a letter supposed to have been written by Pope Alexander III about 1177, and despatched along with a papal ambassador, who disappeared without trace. I shuffled the pile of papers and selected another one. It was also a letter but, having been folded a thousand times, it had lost the top portion.

Seventy-two Kings are under my rule, and my Empire extends to three Indias including Farther India where lies the body of St Thomas. In my dominion are the unclean nations of Gog and Magog whom Alexander the Great walled up amongst the mountains of the North with Iron Gates.

The reference reminded me of our position behind those Iron Gates, so far from Venice and my family. I almost forgot my resolve to sweep the sweet memories from my mind, but I read on nevertheless.

By the power and virtue of God and the Lord Jesus Christ, King of Kings, I will come forth soon with three hundred and sixty-five dukes, ten thousand knights, and a hundred thousand foot soldiers to destroy Islam.

It was signed as being from a 'King David'. I looked quizzically at Alberoni, whose face still

167

bore a fanatical glow.

'Where did this one come from? Do you know?'

'The letter to Pope Honorius? Written by King David in the year twelve twenty.' He almost chanted the words as if they were holy writ. 'This copy came from an Englishman called Bernard de Genova – a Black Friar. He was a close confidant of Sir Geoffrey Leyghton, who perished at the hands of the Mongol war machine at Liegnitz. It was said they used some fiendish sort of gas to win the battle.' He fixed a manic gaze on me. 'Just think, not more than twenty-five years ago, Leyghton fought and died a glorious death along with Henry of Silesia and the cream of Templar knights. And now, here your sort are ... trading with their murderers.'

I ignored the implied condemnation of Venice, who had long ago thrown their hand in with the godless Tartars in return for lucrative trade deals. But then, as traders on the rim of the two worlds, a Venetian always knew where his best interests lay. I scoffed also at Alberoni perpetuating the myth that Henry of Silesia had lost because of some hellish noxious fumes. The Mongols had employed a simple smoke-screen at Liegnitz to hide their advance. Sometimes such a ruse worked for Venetian sailors at sea too. I ruffled through the papers in my hand again.

Alberoni jabbed a finger at a dusty, dry fragment of vellum.

'The others are remarkable. But this is the best of the lot.'

I opened the crackly parchment, and read the only part of the letter that was still legible.

My desire is to visit the Holy Sepulchre, and rededicate my fight against the enemies of the Holy Cross...

'Is this all there is?'

Alberoni squirmed impatiently on his seat.

'Read the signature.'

I didn't really need to, but there it was at the bottom of the fragmentary document.

Prester John.

'How did Pisano lay his hands on this one?'

Alberoni's eyes lit up like a ship's lanterns in a darkening sea.

'That's why I am here. Let me explain.'

'I think you had better.'

'It all began for me when I started to read about distant lands...'

It gradually emerged that Alberoni considered himself as well travelled as any Venetian. A greater traveller, if the truth be known. It mattered not that prior to this great journey to Xanadu, he had hardly set foot outside Rome. His travels had all been in the mind, but none the less real for all that to him. Giovanni Alberoni knew of lands where I had never trod. He had read all about them. But he had been simply set on a life of piety.

However, during his youthful studies in the libraries of Rome, the quiet friar had come across a single letter that had fired his imagination. It had been a copy of a letter from Alexander the Great to Aristotle describing the wonders of India. In it Alberoni read stories of the Indian desert, and of white lions, tigers, and bats as large as pigeons. It was the beginning of his study of far-distant places, and his interest in natural history.

His insatiable curiosity and voracious reading had one day led him to another letter that had had an even more profound effect on him, bringing him to where he was today.

That letter, uncovered in the dusty archives of the Papal library, was itself a hundred years old, and came from the far East – from a Christian leader who was prepared to march against Islam. It told of marvels such as giant ants, fishes that bled purple, and pebbles that gave light. More inspirationally to the young friar it, and the other letters I now held in my hand, represented the correspondence of one great defender of Christianity to another. Prester John. And now I learned that this was the very reason why Francesco Pisano had travelled so far. To find this Christian leader in the East at the behest of the Pope.

'But in Rome,' continued Alberoni, 'we did not

hear from him for five years or more. So I was sent to find out what had happened to him. Whether he had been successful, and if necessary, to continue his mission myself.' He looked back up at me then. 'You will help me find Prester John, won't you?'

Untouched by the friar's plea, I passed the letters back to him. What he sought was a chimera, and I tried to convince him what the letters really were. Oh, they were all compelling documents but, with the possible exception of the one from Alexander the Third, they were complete fakes. Not copies of an original, mind you – just utter fabrications. I saw that only too well. Being a dealer in men's dreams myself, I had once met one of the clever forgers who crafted such letters to sell to the gullible. In a grubby, damp workshop overlooking the deep, winding channel of the Grand Canal, I had seen the forger at work. The artist had been most adept at copying old-style handwriting, and ageing parchment by dipping it in the very canal that bisected Venice. After having a grubby-fingered boy fold the document countless times, the forger maintained no one could tell the difference between his forgery and an original old letter.

Especially if the dupe who was going to buy the letter yearned for the contents of the letter to be true. And there were countless priests, from the humblest to the highest, from prelate to Pope, who had longed for the arrival of a

171

Christian saviour monarch from the East. The original saviour had been named Prester John, and it was said he visited the Pope in Rome in 1122. Whether this was true or not mattered little. While Christianity fought a losing battle with Islam over the Holy Land, desperate hopes of a saviour from the East had revived the myth of Prester John.

Letters began to appear supposedly from Prester John himself. The desire for these letters raged unabated, but by about 1220, the forgers must have realized that the man would have been over one hundred years old by then. If the myth was to be maintained, new letters would have to appear from his descendants. It was then that letters started appearing supposedly from his grandson, King David of India. One of these was the second letter I had read.

Amusingly, one of the letters that reached England at the time had been miscopied by a poor forger as 'King David of Israel', which had induced the Jewish population to send a chest full of gold to the invading army. It only got as far as the Caucasus, and there fell into the hands of local bandits. If it had got any further, it would have no doubt ended up in the coffers of Chinghis – Kubilai's grandfather.

'The letters are ridiculous, unbelievable. I have seen this one ... the very same words –' I waved the King David letter – 'signed as being from Prester John himself and addressed to the

Greek Emperor. But it was written in Latin, not any eastern tongue.'

My scorn stirred the torpid Alberoni into action. He leapt from the stool, and snatched at the letters, tearing them in the process.

'Then explain to me one thing.' He smoothed the crumpled letters lovingly. 'Tell me how the letter from Prester John came to be in Pisano's possession.'

'What do you mean? I thought you said he got them all from the Pope.'

'The letters to Prester John and his grandson King David, yes. But he was never given any correspondence *from* Prester John. So this...' He waved the scrap of parchment that I had read in the air. 'This was never forged in the West. And if Pisano laid hands on it here, don't you understand the implications? It proves the man exists.'

'By now he would be at least one hundred and fifty years old.'

Alberoni brushed aside my cynical comment. He was now in full flow, and as excited as a virgin boy with his first harlot.

'Whatever you think, it makes it more likely that he or his descendant is to be found here. Right here in Xanadu. Isn't that truly a treasure worth discovering?'

I refrained from commenting that I would prefer to take home to Venice something more negotiable than an ancient prelate, or a sacred bag of bones. I could see the friar trembling at

173

the thought. That he should be the one to uncover the man who would save Christendom from the threats that encircled it. And find salvation from deep inside the evil Mongol Empire. All other plans he had were clearly subsumed to his search for the writer of that original letter. Prester John.

'Why do you think he is to be found here? Pisano could have picked up the letter anywhere. Venice, Sudak or Caffa – they all have skilled forgers in abundance.'

'You still don't believe it's real, do you? Then look at this.'

He held out the Alexander letter and pointed at the bottom of the document. I peered closely at an illegible scrawl in a Latin hand. I had to admit that knowledge of the ancient tongue was not one of my better accomplishments.

'It does look more recent than the letter's main text. What does it say?'

'It is recent, and has to be Pisano's hand. The word is – *evestigatus*.'

'What does that mean?'

'Discovered. He is found.'

15. SHI-WU

*Of all the thirty-six alternatives,
running away is best*

Due to Alberoni's history lesson, I had some difficulty concentrating on a little local murder. Though equally it might also have been the drink that I consumed later that evening. That all kicked off because I reckoned I needed to know more about Xanadu, and I hoped that the little silversmith, Tadeusz Pyka, could enlighten me about the ruling elite. So I left Alberoni drooling over his letters, and made for the silversmith's shop. I decided also to take Gurbesu with me to avoid any other misunderstandings. I wouldn't have given much of a chance for the priest retaining his virginal state alone with the Kungurat girl. I think she still assumed that seducing him was a requirement of her staying. So I was glad that she seemed eager to accompany me.

When we reached Tadeusz Pyka's tiny workshop, the diminutive silversmith said he would help all he could. But in return, I first had to tell him all about the Inner City. So few

175

foreigners were allowed within its walls, that anyone who was, was obliged to slake the thirst of their fellows' curiosity. In return, he produced some wine, and a skinful of the Mongol's favourite drink – kumiss. My resolve to learn all about Kubilai and his clan weakened. Soon, I was regaling Tadeusz and the girl with details of the bloodied bamboo palace, the discovery of which seems to have been solely down to me now, excluding Lin Chu-Tsai all of a sudden. Gurbesu squealed with unconcealed delight at all the horrific detail, clutching my arm in horror. Then, as the levels in the kumiss skin and wine bottles dropped, my description of the secret palace behind the great walls grew more and more grandiose. Gilded panels became walls of solid gold, ceilings soared to inconceivable heights, and I found I could not stop myself. Even as I exaggerated, I could not stop myself from trying to impress Pyka and the girl. We continued to drink and tell tales well into the night.

Waking, my left leg felt numb and as cold as ice. I tried to move it, to slide it back under the covers on the low bed, but there was something resisting my efforts, pinning my thigh down. I moved my left hand down underneath the layer of animal skins thrown haphazardly across the couch, and felt the warmth of a soft, downy thigh across my own. Then I remembered the progress of the previous night's events – even

176

after the kumiss had numbed my brain. I vaguely recalled Tadeusz Pyka offering the girl and me a bed for the night, which I graciously accepted. We stumbled together down the alley leading to his sleeping quarters, which rocked and rolled like the deck of a storm-hit ship.

I couldn't recall pitching into bed. But now, when I looked down into the crook of my right arm, there nestled a moon-shaped female face. Her fair skin and dark tresses wound around my shoulder, and I smelled the sweet exhalations of her skin. I was glad it was Gurbesu. I knew that when I was drunk, I was sometimes capable of getting amorous with whoever was to hand.

I reached lower, and eased the girl's thigh off my own. I drew my leg back under the heavy animal skins. The warmth of the girl's body pressed against me, and soon restored the circulation to my leg. Then I felt the blood coursing into another part of my anatomy. Dammit, it had been a long time. What did I expect? As if in response, the girl stirred against my side and began to roll over. I started to accommodate her movements, but then she supported herself on her elbows, and looked at me with curiosity.

'Do you have a wife in your own country?'

'No,' I replied, only half lying. I reached out for her, but she resisted my advances, sitting up at the end of the bed with the fur pulled round her, covering her nakedness.

'But you have a woman who you love.'

It wasn't a question.

'Why should you think that?'

Gurbesu screwed her face up in puzzlement at my response. There was still a barrier of language between us.

I tried again. 'Why do you think I have a woman?'

'Because you called her name in your sleep – Kata ... something.'

'Caterina.'

I felt sick at the sound of the name on the lusty girl's lips, and my ardour for Gurbesu drained away at my mention of Caterina's name. It was true a Venetian wife expected her husband to be faithful to her. But when a merchant was away on business for years at a time, the conundrum was that she didn't expect him to be celibate either. For me to be taking sexual pleasures in this way, did not mean I would have been thought unfaithful. I had done with the Kungurat girl no more than I had with other girls since my exile from Venice. The trouble was, I wasn't sure I felt no more for Gurbesu than for a whore. But then, what did it matter? Caterina Dolfin was not even my wife. So I could not be considered unfaithful as I had no one to be unfaithful to. Damn it all, I had lost Caterina, and the sooner I got her out of my mind the better.

So why did I still feel guilty?

I decided the only way to proceed was to put

all thoughts of both Caterina and Gurbesu out of my mind, and concentrate on the murder again. I sat on the edge of the pallet, and shuffled the jumble of characters I had so far met around in my head. Azzo Sabattine, Lin Chu-Tsai, Ko Su-Tsung, even Prince Arik Boke and the little thief Zhou – and still nothing made sense. The biggest question had to be why Pisano was killed. Who would kill a Dominican friar who had travelled to the ends of the earth in search of a myth? Something prickled at the back of my brain. But it was no good – the clouds of stale wine obscured it.

'Tell me why you lost her.'

'What? Who?' I was not entirely lost in thoughts of murder, and knew to whom Gurbesu referred. But even though I still felt like I was betraying Caterina, I pretended I had forgotten what we had been talking about.

'This Cata...' Gurbesu had difficulty with the rolling sound of the name again.

I sighed in resignation.

'Caterina. Caterina Dolfin.'

'Cata-Ina.' This time she produced a good approximation of the Venetian inflection in my voice.

I told her of my fall from grace. And though I knew she wouldn't understand half of what I was saying about so foreign a country to her, I was glad to be telling her. It was a starry tale of high politics and low conniving. I had tried to subvert the election of the new Doge. Not for political reasons, you understand, but for the best reasons of all. Money and pride. I had been wagered I could not rig the election, and that had been like a red rag to a bull. I had almost pulled it off too, except some rats had set me up from the start. I had been a patsy, a fall guy in a convoluted Venetian political manoeuvre, and had had to flee both Venice and Caterina Dolfin.

Gurbesu rolled over, rested her chin on her upturned palms, and put on her most sympathetic look.

'You have told me all about yourself. What I wanted was for you to tell me about Cata-Ina.'

How did she know so well what was bothering me? I couldn't deny that thinking of Caterina Dolfin was hindering me from finding the murderer. So, like husbands down the centuries, I told my latest lover all about my nearly-wife. I told her of our romps on down-filled mattresses in gilded beds, of romantic evenings spent sharing the exquisite cuisine of sea-girt Venice. I also spoke of that final moment of intimacy with Caterina. And how, one morning long ago, she had seemed so pale and wan, so edgy and remote.

'I suppose it must have been the wine we had drunk the evening before, though she could hold her own with any man.'

Gurbesu hooted with laughter, rocking backwards and forwards on the bed. The fur slipped from her breasts, and I was confronted with the alarming vision of their heavy undulations as the girl continued to laugh. I grinned, a little embarrassed at whatever inadvertent joke I had made, and its effect on Gurbesu. But I still could not take my eyes off her heavy breasts. They were so unlike Caterina's, which were small and firm.

'What have I said?'

'You do not know? Why she was sick?'

I was still at a loss, and getting a little annoyed at Gurbesu's amusement over my lack of understanding. 'Tell me.'

'She had a child with her.'

Well, that was what I thought she said, and did not at first understand. A child? There had been no child in the room with us. I thought she had used the wrong words in a tongue that was not familiar to her. But she sat on the end of my bed, miming a protuberant belly under her own fine breasts, and giggling. Suddenly it all made sense. What a fool I had been. That was why Caterina had wanted me to propose marriage. And when I didn't, why she had latched on to Pasquale Valier. I myself had made her pregnant, and she needed a husband. When the preferred choice – Niccolò Zuliani – had shied away from the proposition, she had taken what she could. The unprepossessing, but ardent Pasquale Valier. And who could blame her? I certainly couldn't.

I groaned. I was the father of ... of what? A three-year-old child – and I didn't even know if it was a boy or a girl. Somehow, out of the blue, I felt a responsibility to this child of mine. A father's duty to a child whose name I didn't even know. The thought hounded me.

'Caterina!' I leapt out of bed, and began to pull on my new Mongol breeches, hopping on one leg, and getting the material in a tangle.

'What are you doing? It's the middle of the night.' Gurbesu could hardly restrain her laughter at the sight of me struggling, and clutched her heaving bosom.

'I'm going back – I must get back to Venice.'

'Right now? How are you proposing to do that? Anyway, you are three years too late already – a few months more won't go amiss.' Her giggles had subsided, and she spoke more seriously, almost pleadingly. 'And there is the matter of the murder. The Khan won't let you leave until it is solved.'

I didn't see why it mattered to the girl if I solved the murder or not, but I knew she was right. Pulling on a jacket over my silk shirt, I mumbled a curse, and began to see reason. Caterina might have forgotten me by now. After all, I had failed her. I would have to sort out this stupid mess of the killing of Friar Francesco Pisano first, and then petition for my release. Hell's teeth, I wanted to see fair Caterina again.

Gurbesu too was now dressing in her Chinee finery, hiding those magnificent breasts under a high-collared blue jacket with buttons down

182

the front. She looked at me with a frown.

'You know, if your life was in peril in Ven...'

'Venice.'

'In Ven-eez ... because you became involved in affairs of state, do you think the priest might have been killed for a similar reason?'

'How do you mean?'

I rammed my feet into my Mongol riding boots, and began to pace the room. Gurbesu leaned forward eagerly on the pallet bed.

'Did he find something out that would harm either the Great Khan or his brother, and was he killed because of that?'

What the girl said had a ring of truth. I was lit by a fever to solve the riddle of the murder, burning with desire to finish with it, and leave. But I was being frustrated at every turn. Magistrate Lin seemed intent on dragging out the investigation while he accumulated facts like a ... I racked my brain for a suitably detrimental word – like a dock-side clerk. Yes, a dock-side clerk tallying bales of goods. While my own nature was to cut to the core of the matter like a soldier, or a trader bargaining for the best deal. My inclinations were so Venetian, whereas Lin's were so ... well, so foreign. And a dirty political reason struck a chord with me.

I had to take into account Pisano's finding of someone he thought was Prester John. The inscription on the letter indicated 'He is found'. Who could Pisano have thought it was? Kubilai was the obvious candidate. Or was the discovery of Pisano's body near to the camp of the younger brother Arik Boke significant? Was he Pisano's saviour of Christendom? And if so, why should Pisano have been killed because of this knowledge? It struck me I needed to find who it was Pisano had picked out as Prester John. And so I still needed to get my hands on the Genoan, Sabattine. He must have had some idea what Pisano had found out in his final days. Suddenly, it looked as though my search for the killer and Alberoni's hunt for Prester John were converging.

16. SHI-LIU

Heaven lends you a soul,
Earth will lend a grave

Once again I made my way into the Inner City to find Lin Chu-Tsai. Double-dealer and traitor or not, I needed him to tell me if he had discovered anything. Only he could verify once and for all whether Azzo Sabattine was inside the palace grounds. I could not imagine being allowed to conduct a sweep of the whole maze of palace rooms myself. I had left Gurbesu in the care of Tadeusz despite her protests that she wanted to come with me. I had told her she would be mad to enter the palace she had so recently escaped. She had no answer for that. To be truthful, I was glad to be without her for a while. She reminded me too much of what I had lost in Venice.

As I approached the main southern gateway – the Meridian Gate – I could see the guards leaning on their spears. It was still early morning and there were precious few people about. Waving my gold *paizah* imperiously, I entered the Inner City through the red-pillared portal on the left of the main gate. The great gate was for the Khan alone, and I, as a mere mortal, passed through one of the two lesser openings. Inside, I crossed the great ceremonial courtyard behind the Meridian Gate, which the Chin officials called Wai Chao – Outer Court. Here were the thirty-two doors of Kubilai's treasure house. Their main security was from being in full view of everyone who passed by. All well and good, except after dark. I wondered if the Khan knew it was being systematically plundered by two small-time thieves and one of his officials. Maybe one day I could use that knowledge to my advantage. For now, I left Da and Zhou to their depredations.

Before I bearded Lin in his den, where I had no doubt he would be toiling away, even at this early hour, I decided to have another look at the section of the cane palace that had been re-erected for me. I fancied that, if I stood inside its walls, I might gain some feeling for what happened there. I cut through the palace towards the edge of the Khan's pleasure grounds, where it had been set up. As I approached the archway that gave out on to the open parkland, I thought I could smell burning. At first I imagined it must be someone burning incense, then I realized the odour was acrid. It stung my nostrils. I rushed out into the open air.

Part of the cane palace was ablaze, flames already leaping above head height. The bulk of the palace that had remained unrolled was

186

where it had been left, piled next to the rebuilt murder room. I was reminded of my image of kindling from earlier. I called out for assistance, and looked for the nearest source of water.

Then I saw him. Inside the room, trying to force a way through the flames that were already shooting up round the entrance, was Lin Chu-Tsai. He raised the long sleeve of his gown over his face, and tried to press forward, but the heat was too much for him. I watched as he fell back, beating flames from his smouldering clothes. I called out again. Though I knew no one would understand me, surely they would hear my cries and investigate. Where was everybody anyway?

I tried to pull away the big bundles of canes from the base of the fire, but it was no good. With a terrifying roar, the whole edifice was suddenly ablaze, fire shooting upwards and sending sparks and ash flying up to the heavens. I saw Lin fighting for breath, and collapsing, his hair shrivelling in the heat. And then all I could see was a huddled figure on the ground as his gown caught fire. The flames seemed to be sucking the breath out of me too, and I sank to my knees. I felt dizzy, and a dark shape like a cloud was looming over me. There was a sharp pain at my throat, and I felt it closing. Was it the fumes? All I knew was that I was suddenly gasping for breath myself. I heard cries, and then I blacked out.

'Even as Kubilai is invoking the gods to protect his possessions – slaves, beasts, birds, crops and everything besides – we will deprive him of them. We will show him what the gods think of his false existence in that palace of the dead.'

The voice was harsh and guttural, speaking the Mongol language in low tones. It was far away in the darkness that I swam in. Was I in the Venice Lagoon drowning? I was not sure. Maybe the whole journey to Xanadu had been a drowning man's dream. The waves bore over me, rocking my body as if in a cradle. I was floating face down in the water, and at death's door. The voice echoed distantly in my brain once more.

'This year I have ascertained that he will perform the ceremony on the plains of Camp Field in the east, rather than the ramparts as other years. I have got this information directly from one of his minions – a Chin who it seems did not live long enough to tell anyone of his treachery.'

This statement was followed by sycophantic laughter. The barking laughter of the Tartars. Was the man talking of Lin Chu-Tsai and his immolation? Was this man the person who had set fire to the cane palace, killing the magistrate? It hardly seemed to matter, if it was all the fantasy of a dying man, drowning in the Venice Lagoon. I began to sink below the waters, falling longingly into the arms of oblivion. Then the voice dragged me back.

'It is time. Are you ready?'

There were ripples of assent to the man's query. I wanted to call out, to beg to be allowed to drown. To stop this voice calling me back somehow. Then I began to be aware of hard ground pressing on my chest and knees, and the discomfort of my neck being twisted to one side. A stinking carpet half-filled my mouth, suffocating me. I wasn't drowning – I was lying face down on solid ground. I squeezed open my eyes and saw a forest of legs across an expanse of rugs scattered on the earth. I was inside a yurt, and what I had heard was real not fantasy. Lin Chu-Tsai had really died in a fire in the cane palace, and I had been taken for dead. Maybe I really was. They had dumped me in the corner of the yurt belonging to whoever was speaking. It had to be Arik Boke.

I cautiously opened my eyes again, and took in what I could see with my limited range of vision. The princeling, seated on an ornately carved chair set opposite the yurt's entrance on the northern side of the interior, was sweating inside his heavy body armour. His face glowed red, and I could smell the heavy odour of kumiss exuding from the pores of sweating bodies. The yurt was full to bursting with Arik Boke's sworn allies and cronies. Every man wore his full body armour in emulation of their leader. And the tent bristled with swords and

189

spears, though the princeling, as Kubilai's prisoner, was not supposed to hold any arms. Arik Boke, as if he wasn't dripping sweat from his brow already, could be said to be warming to his task as he fancied he was rousing the spirit of battle in his men. He explained how they would fall upon Kubilai and his cowardly guards at the very point he made the annual sacrifice of mares' milk in the ceremony in a few days' time.

If these men were all on Arik Boke's side, then the auguries were bad for Kubilai. I set my mind to listening to Arik Boke as he outlined his plan. There was a murmur of assent from his followers, who clearly were dreaming of the riches that might follow from their bold action. The princeling was emboldened by the men's reaction, and pressed on recklessly.

'I am minded of my brother Hulegu's actions against the Caliph of Baghdad, who had the greatest treasure house stuffed with gold, silver and jewels that ever belonged to man. Before my brother Kubilai came along, that is.'

There was some nervous laughter at this sup-posed joke. Ignoring it, Arik Boke pressed on, even though everyone present knew the story of old.

'The Caliph refused to spend his riches to bolster up his army, and lost in battle against Hulegu. When my brother saw what the trea-sure house held, he was amazed, and asked the captive Caliph why he hadn't spent his riches.

190

The Caliph had no answer to this, so Hulegu said that as he loved treasure so much, then he could have it to eat. He locked the Caliph in his treasure house, and ordered he be given nothing to eat or drink, telling him to eat his fill of treasure because that was all he was getting. He took four days to die surrounded by his useless wealth. That is where the accumulation of riches gets you.'

Arik Boke grunted in satisfaction at his homily, and sat back in the chair, his arms folded across his ample breasts. I suppose he took the silence that followed for the awe he had inspired in his *noyans*. I knew what the silence meant, though. They were thinking of backing out, if plundering the treasure houses was not to be part of the pact.

As the motley assembly shuffled out of his presence, murmuring to each other in tones they hoped would not carry, Arik Boke waved for a Mongol warrior to approach him from his lowly position by the door where servants and the poor stood in any assembly. The *bahadur* was a squat man, and almost as wide as he was tall. His head sat directly on his shoulders with no intervention of neck between the two, and resembled the large ball which Mongols employed to play a sort of horseback war game. His pockmarked face, evidence of childhood disease that had simply run its course, added to the resemblance to a battered ball that had been bashed about. The princeling leaned over to

191

whisper in his ear.

I thought the round-faced prince's eyes were too close together. And his brow was one hairy caterpillar that straddled his forehead – a sure sign that he was not to be trusted. The warrior smiled agreeably as the round-faced man with the narrow eyes stamped around the room, raising dust with every step, and haranguing him. The warrior nodded uneasily, and fingered the short curved blade hanging at his side. Arik Boke's sumptuous silk tunic had sweat stains under the arms, for despite the hot weather he had insisted on wearing a heavy cavalryman's fur-lined tunic and layered leather armour. Foolish to affect the demeanour of a warrior, seeing as how he was the Great Khan's prisoner. I allowed a smirk to twist my lips, but only as the man turned his back and paced away from me. After all, I was dead. Or I would be soon, if Arik Boke discovered I wasn't. I closed my eyes as Arik Boke turned back and strode towards me.

I waited for the kick in the gut that would come to establish my state. But it never came. There was a familiar voice outside the tent and the next thing I knew a cool hand felt my neck for a pulse. I risked a shifty glance up into the doctor's eyes, and hoped he understood my plight. He winked impassively.

'Yes, he is dead,' said Masudi al-Din. 'Shall I remove the body?'

'Do what you like with it,' grumbled Arik

Boke. 'Only get the stinking thing out of my yurt. It was only brought here to make sure no one else found it beside the fire.'

The Arab doctor must have come prepared for a body with some pall-bearers, because I felt myself being lifted by two men. I tried to relax, slumping in their grasp until I assessed we were well clear of the Mongol encampment. Then I cracked an eyelid.

'I knew your diagnoses were suspect, Masudi.'

The terrified pall-bearers dropped their supposed corpse on the ground, and fled. The doctor grinned.

'Think yourself lucky I was there to pronounce you dead, or I would be trying to stitch together the pieces of you left after the horses had pulled you apart.'

I shuddered at the thought and sat up. I had been dropped back by the blackened ruins of the cane palace. The pyre was still smoking. And I could feel the heat even though we were yards away. Masudi stared into the glowing embers.

'I was told Master Lin was in there when the fire started. We will have to sift the ashes when they have cooled.' He turned back to me and gave me some advice. 'And you had better lay low, until the court and Arik Boke has departed in a few days' time. The prince will not take kindly to your resurrection. Good job that I guessed you were laying doggo. Whatever did you overhear in that tent of his?'

'You don't want to know.'

I got shakily to my feet and wiped my brow. I winced. The heat from the flames must have singed my face, because it stung.

'Let me see,' offered Masudi. He gently probed the sore flesh. 'Nothing a little ointment won't cure. But look here.'

'What is it?'

He was peering closely at my neck.

'It looks as though you have escaped death twice today. There is a bite mark on your neck, just like that on Pisano's body. It would seem that you had a very close encounter with a murderer. Unless you have a lady friend who is a little too excitable.'

I couldn't recall Gurbesu biting my neck, but I did remember the dark shape and a choking sensation just before I blacked out. Could that have been the murderer? If it had been, then the people uttering the cries I had heard must have inadvertently interrupted him, and saved me.

My legs gave way, and I sank to my knees again. I surveyed the watery, charred heap that was all that was left of the cane palace. Somewhere in the midst of it lay Lin Chu-Tsai.

'Masudi, will you remove Lin's body and examine it?'

'Of course. Though I cannot be sure what I can gather from the corpse. It will have been badly burned.'

17. SHI-QI

When your horse is on the brink of a
precipice, it is too late to pull the reins

Murder and mayhem were still rattling round my head as I fitfully slept that night. I was back in Venice, being pursued endlessly by the Signori di Notte. I was not even safe in my uncle's house. The sound of the pursuit was echoing down the narrow alleys.

I grabbed my uncle Matteo's arm.

'Tell Caterina that I love her, and that I will contact her somehow, Uncle Matteo.'

'You better forget Caterina Dolfin, and think about saving your own hide.'

'Uncle!' My pleading look softened Matteo's heart, as it always did. After my parents had died, he had taken me under his wing. I suppose I had always been a trial and tribulation to him. I knew my uncle – a steady if unspectacular merchant – had always predicted I would come to a bad end. He had felt both frustration and envy when all my risky trading ventures had prospered, and the *colleganzas* paid off handsomely. Now my charmed life of thirty-three years had apparently come to an end. The thunderous knocking at Matteo's door energized us both. Matteo Zuliani pulled a fur-trimmed robe over his sleeping gown.

'Very well, I will speak to her – put in a word for you. Though God knows you don't deserve it.'

He watched while I pulled on his boots, and grabbed a meagre sack of possessions. I had taken the precaution of not undressing the night before.

'Make for Sudak, and stay there. I will be in touch.' Matteo obviously hoped the distant Black Sea port on the edge of the Tartar Empire would be far enough away. 'And keep out of trouble.'

'Thank you, Uncle Matteo. I will be the dullest of honest citizens while I wait to hear from you. I promise.'

Matteo snorted. 'You could no more stay out of trouble, than Prester John will come to save us from the Saracens.'

As if to put the lie to his words, the door flew open, and there stood an imposing figure with a full, long beard, clad in heavy brocade robes and bearing a cross in his right hand. He raised his left hand towards me...

I awoke shivering and alone. There was no sign of Gurbesu and that troubled me. She was too vulnerable to being revealed as a runaway, if she was found. I sat up, and shook the nightmare from my brain. It seemed that wherever I pursued the murderer of Friar Pisano, and now of Lin Chu-Tsai, if it be the same man, I was confronted with the image of Prester John. The trouble was I still considered the ghost who had haunted my dream to be a myth. Even if everyone else, including Alberoni, thought otherwise.

I was now fearful of a greater crime concerning both victims. That of treason and conspiracy. If Pisano's search for Prester John had led him to the tent of Prince Arik Boke, then he could have been embroiled in his plotting. In the same conspiracy that Lin seemed to have been involved with. Indeed, I was now sure that Lin had been part of the Mongol's scheme to topple Kubilai. That much I had heard in the tent. So Arik Boke had all to gain from the deaths of Pisano and Lin. I had not tied up all the loose skeins, but I decided it was time to pass on my evidence. I threw on my threadbare clothes, and dusted them down. It was time to share what I knew with Ko Su-Tsung. And through him hope to gain an audience with Kubilai.

It was the twenty-eighth day of the month that I knew as August, which in the Muslim fashion adopted by the Mongols was Shawwal. Therefore, it was the time for the Great Khan to take his leave of Shang-tu and the palace of the Inner City. He was already building an even grander palace on a site north of the old Chin

197

city of Yenking. This would be his central capital – Chung-tu – and the one he was about to leave would become nothing more than a summer retreat and hunting reserve.

As I was led into Ko Su-Tsung's presence by Yao Lei, Ko was preparing himself for the ceremonial leave-taking. He was pulling on his black, knee-high leather boots. He nodded to acknowledge my presence, and stood up, stroking out the creases in his *bei zi* under-robe of silk, embroidered with chrysanthemums. Behind him a servant held up the red damask robe denoting his high rank. It was a formal robe with its *bai*, or panels, in each side that added bulk to the skirt. This was not practical in everyday use, but the ceremony obviously demanded the most formal of court wear. Ko Su-Tsung was clearly looking forward to it with the deepest satisfaction.

Encouraged by his master's unusual cheerfulness, Yao Lei stepped up behind Ko Su-Tsung. He helped ease the robe on to his new master's shoulders. Immediately, Ko Su-Tsung could feel the weight of it. He shrugged his shoulders to settle the robe more comfortably on his spare frame. The deep sleeves reached down to the end of his fingers, hiding his hands from view, and showing he had no need to indulge in manual labour. He patted the one-horned beast emblazoned on his breast, and then screwed his face up with exasperation when he saw the servant approaching with his everyday *fu tou* cap. He swiped the offending object from the hands of Yao Lei, and swung a series of blows at him. The man cowered in fear at his master's anger.

Ko screamed something in Chinee at his servant. Yao Lei scuttled out, scooping up the black felt cap which had caused his new master's outburst. One of the stiff wings had been bent and torn, and he would have to repair it. He had brought the wrong item, and returned with an extravagant coronet with seven ridges that showing that Ko was an official of the highest rank. He went to place it on his master's head, but Ko Su-Tsung snatched it from the incompetent's clutches and settled it in place himself. Yao Lei hurried out of the room, relieved to have only received a buffeting around the shoulders for his grave error. With a swish of silk against damask, Ko Su-Tsung swung imperiously towards me, having kept me waiting for a suitably humiliating time. He spoke in his halting Turkish tongue.

'What is it you wish?'

'To see the Great Khan.'

For a moment, I don't know why, his eyes narrowed. No mean feat for such a beady-eyed man.

'Impossible.'

'I regret it is imperative. I believe his life is in danger.'

He favoured me with that rictus of his face that was meant to be a smile. On this occasion, it was to illuminate my stupidity.

'The Great Khan lives a life in peril. But he is well guarded. Now, if you will excuse me, I have a tedious Mongol ceremony to attend.'

I stood firm in the entrance to his quarters. I knew I needed something to hold his attention. To convince him to give me access to Kubilai.

'I believe that both Pisano and Lin were killed because they were involved in a treasonous plot.'

'Lin Chu-Tsai?' The man was immediately hooked by the idea he could blacken his old rival's name further. I had his attention now, and I could see he was curious.

'Why do you say that Lin Chu-Tsai was a traitor?' I asked.

Ko sneered – an expression that came more easily to his skull-like features than a smile.

'I told you. His family had him castrated as a child, so that he could become a clerk in the emperor's court. It was unnecessary, and Lin blames his parents and Kubilai for him being less than a man.'

'How do you know that he still blamed his parents?'

'I once made the mistake of asking about his childhood – his ancestry. He told me he had long ago lost contact with his family. Once they had done to him what they did, and sent him to the Mongol court ruling China, he had not had the opportunity to maintain any contact with them besides sending them some money from his meagre earnings as a clerk. But as his skills were recognized, and his rise through the ranks took him to positions of influence, he had little time for the family he had left behind. When he had the power to find out anything about his brother or his parents at little cost to himself in terms of time, merely by willing it done, he did not do so. He still sent them money. That had been the purpose of their sacrifice after all. But it was clear he felt like only he had sacrificed anything at all. He could not bring himself to want to know what had become of them. Of course, he rationalized to me his lack of action by saying that, the break having been made, it was better for his parents not to be confronted by their son again. But I knew that the truth was he resented their using him in the way they had, resented his older brother in particular living comfortably off his labours, and his sacrifice. It was after all his brother who had a future, the ability to produce offspring.'

'And your proof of his hatred of Kubilai?'

Ko looked sharply at me, his eyes pools of mystery.

'If I'd had proof, I would have denounced him when he was still alive.'

'Maybe we can be of help to each other then.'

In return for my information about what I had overheard in Arik Boke's tent as I lay 'dead', Ko promised to take me to Kubilai. My plan

201

had worked. Once in Kubilai's presence, I could warn him of the plot, and explain my other suspicions about the murders. I was going to say that I needed more time to be sure of the latter. But Ko insisted he would take me to the Khan only if he could be the one breaking the news initially. I was sure he would cheat me in some way, but I had no choice. I may have held the Khan's *paizah*, but it would not have got me into Kubilai's presence with the speed that was now required. The ceremony at which Arik Boke, using information supplied by Lin Chu-Tsai, was to make his move would shortly take place. Alone, it would have taken me days to cut through the red tape of the Khan's court. Reluctantly, I acceded to his stipulation.

Using Ko's standing, we were swiftly led towards Kubilai's private apartments. Down a vista of open double doors, each artfully pierced, I could see into a softly lit room. Servants scurried back and forth through the final set of doors with arms full of cloth and robes. I noticed there was nothing that struck me as typically Mongol about the rooms through which we were ushered. Latticework screens were carved in Chinee designs featuring fanciful dragons, and a heavy aroma of incense hung in the air. Maybe it was designed to mask the aroma of Kubilai's body, I don't know. I was made to stand outside the final set of doors as Ko went in. It was a golden room, and basking in its glow stood Kubilai, centre of all attention.

The servants fussed around him, dressing him in a sort of hybrid costume that reflected his attempt to bridge the two worlds he ruled. Despite being originally brought up to act first rather than think, he had come to admire the Chinese culture with its interest in the contemplative sciences of astronomy and mathematics. He was supposedly impressed, and a little intimidated, by scholars. But that was a weakness he couldn't show, and his militaristic upbringing no doubt trampled over his finer feelings. So it was rather symbolic, if unconsciously so, that the fine red brocade dragon robe he affected as a nod towards the Chinese emperors whose throne he had usurped was topped by a rich Mongol coat. The coat was of the finest white fur with black monkey tails sewn in it, a matching black fur collar, and cuffs that hung warmly over his hands, hiding the calluses raised by regular holding of horse reins.

Having had the coat arranged to the satisfaction of his fussy servants, Kubilai moved towards the ornate throne that was set seven steps up from the floor. He sat down for the servants to pull on the gleaming red leather boots that completed his ceremonial outfit. As they struggled to force his swollen legs into the boots, he gazed fondly at his wife Chabi. She sat in the light of the morning sun as it

203

cascaded through the high-arched window on to her lap, where she was occupied turning old bow-strings into thread for use in mending clothes. The story was that Kubilai had once been exasperated by Chabi's outward show of frugality – a trait she had inherited from her mother. But he had long since given up any hope of curing her of it. In fact, amidst the excessive splendour of his court, her little weakness now almost endeared her to him all the more. Especially since she had provided him with a little male heir, who now lay gurgling in the crib that sat at Chabi's feet. The baby's round red face was a perfect replica of Kubilai's own, though of course the baby did not yet have the straggly beard and moustache of his father. Kubilai probably dreamed of the time when he would take his son on his first hunt – perhaps in the grounds of the very palace where they now resided – and blood him with his first kill.

Ko Su-Tsung bowed low before the Great Mongol Khan and Emperor of China, and waited for Kubilai to usher him forward. Having been given the signal, Ko knelt on the lower steps of the throne's dais, and leaned forward to whisper in Kubilai's ear. I was furious. He clearly did not intend for me to hear what he was saying to Kubilai. Ko was taking all the credit. And there was nothing I could do.

Suddenly Kubilai cackled, his rotund face splitting in pleasure. He asked a question of

Ko, and he turned and pointed me out. His dark eyes pierced me like Mongol arrows, and then he looked back at Ko. The Chinee shuffled on his knees down the steps. Then, when he was no longer likely to tower over Kubilai, he stood up and backed out towards me.

Kubilai must have immediately forgotten about me, and begun thinking about what was ahead of him this day. For he squared his shoulders, kicked the stupid servants away who grovelled at his feet, and stomped the ground in his red boots to force them finally on to his swollen legs. He groaned a little at the pain they caused, and I could see Chabi cast an anxious glance at him, and yet say nothing. It was obvious that Kubilai did not like anyone – even his favourite wife – reminding him that he was less than a god, and suffered pain and illness like any mortal. I had also heard rumours that he yearned to change the date from the Muslim year 661 to year one of the era of Kubilai, Emperor of China.

Under protest Ko dragged me with him. As we retreated from Kubilai's presence, I hissed at him.

'What did you tell him about me? Did you claim all the credit for uncovering the plot? What did you tell him about my ideas of who the murderer is?'

'I told him what he wanted to hear. That you had solved the matter of the priest's death, and it did not concern the palace.'

'You told him that? I have discovered no such thing. I believe it to be Arik Boke who killed both Pisano and Lin Chu-Tsai to prevent them telling the truth about the plot to kill Kubilai. But I cannot be sure. You did tell him about the plot, I assume.'

Ko nodded curtly as we backed out of Kubilai's presence.

'Of course I did. I told him of Lin Chu-Tsai's treachery, and Arik Boke's plan to kill him today at the ceremony.'

'And?'

'That was when he laughed. He said his brother has been trying to kill him for years, and hasn't succeeded yet. Though he did thank you for alerting him to the possibility of Arik Boke trying again.' Ko stopped in the first outer chamber, as though reluctant to leave the aura of the Khan behind. He clasped his hands, half hidden in the long sleeves of his gown, in front of him as if in prayer. 'And he invited you to the ceremony to see how tight his security is.'

From where we stood, I could still see Kubilai and Chabi. It was a temptation to stride in, and present my case personally to the Khan. But I didn't think he would take kindly to my bold approach. Nor might his bodyguards, who hovered on the periphery of the domestic scene. Still I was as reluctant as Ko to leave. Just to be around such power was a heady intoxicant.

Then I heard Kubilai bark a question at his wife.

'Where's Aunty?'

'She will be here soon. Don't fret.' Chabi, already dressed in her finest gown of deep blue silk, and wearing a neck band dripping with jade, rose to her feet, her round, chubby face showing concern. 'Aunty knows we have to go soon – she will come.'

Even as she spoke, the familiar clomp of Aunty Bolgana's stumpy legs could be heard in the long passageway. We stood humbly to one side, as her bulky figure, wrapped in its familiar, stained jacket, with a talisman bouncing on her chest, rolled through the doors leading to Kubilai's private chamber. Compared to Chabi, Bolgana was positively dowdy, her only adornment the thin leather pouch that always seemed to be hung round her neck. I noted the stench of old and slaughtered animals that seemed to emanate from the old lady's every pore as she passed. As I was standing in the shadows, she didn't see me, or she might have wondered about my remarkable resurrection. The last time she had seen me was in Arik Boke's tent as a corpse.

'Here she is.'

Chabi hurried over to the old woman, and guided her to the seat she had just vacated next to the precious baby's crib. She tried not to flinch at Bolgana's odour. Puffing out her cheeks, Bolgana waved them away, and gazed lovingly down at Kubilai's offspring. Satisfied all was now well, Kubilai bowled, bandy-legged, out of the room to his appointment on the Camp Fields, followed by the ever obedient and equally rotund Chabi.

The earthen rampart, the height of several men and stretching across the whole horizon, formed a magnificent backdrop to the long procession that wound its way along the base of the wall from the south. The phalanx of horses, headed by an imposing figure in red and white, wound away into the distance further than the spectators could see, as though it went on for ever. At one side of Kubilai Khan rode Chabi, uneasy on horseback, but determined to play her role to the full. And on Kubilai's other hand rode a standard-bearer proudly holding aloft the spear from which hung the nine shaggy yaks' tails, a symbol of the first Great Khan, Chinghis. The hammering, jarring trot of the small horses stirred the earth, creating a cloud on which the procession rode, giving the appearance that the Khan and his entourage were floating on the mist of a choppy sea.

The snaking line of horses turned at one of the buttresses to the great wall, and slowing to a walk, wheeled out on to the broad expanse of open plain between the great, permanent city, and the bustling temporary encampment of yurts that housed the Mongol families of lesser station, who did not live inside the palace enclave. Several tents had already been cleared to create sufficiently grand an arena for Kubilai to perform the libation ceremony.

I was standing below the wooden rostrum that had been hastily erected to provide a platform for the stocky Khan to rise above the heads of his subjects, and could still see the marks on the earth where the yurts had stood.

The workmen who had constructed the platform that very morning were now lounging below it, pulling on the mouths of several skins of kumiss. The edges of the arena, east and west of the plain, were crowded with people. They were lined up, to my mind, in some symbolic, undeclared battle formation. Below the walls of the city, silently stood the Chinee and Middle-Eastern officials of Kubilai's administration, resplendent in their silken dragon robes and conical black hats. I could make out individuals I knew in the throng, especially Ko Su-Tsung. He was actually standing a little apart from the rest of the Chinee clerks and scholars. Opposite them, flowing in and out of their encampment, the horde of Mongols roiled and intermingled, like some horncts' nest stirred by a child's unwary stick. The crowd only broke ranks briefly, as a man on horseback dressed in heavy cavalry armour emerged from the throng.

It was Arik Boke, and I discerned some scattered cries of support for him. I could see no sign of the *bahadur* knight, whom Arik Boke had instructed in his tent about killing the Khan. All I could remember was the man was squat, and had an ugly pockmarked face. Most of the time, my face had been pressed to the ground. God knows how I would identify him in the milling crowd where there were plenty of squat men with pockmarked faces.

Ko had thought it had been madness when it was announced at the last minute that Kubilai would hold the ceremony on the Camp Fields. Standing on the high walls – his normal position – he would have been relatively safe. Down here, at the edge of the Mongol encampment, it was chaos, and anything could happen. I had known from the document in Lin's office that the location would be here. It seemed that Ko had not, and it obviously irked him. I turned away from the princeling's rowdy entourage, and slipped discreetly into a group of Westerner onlookers to hide. I had to remind myself that I didn't want Arik Boke to see me.

The sun was high by the time Kubilai reached the rostrum, and the haze of rising dust behind him sparkled in the light, almost painful to the eye. Far to the south, black, louring clouds hung in the sky with the threads of distant rain dropping from them. They hung back from the plain, as if they were afraid to overshadow the military pageant created by the Great Khan for his subjects. And it was true that, though storms raged all around, the sun

210

shone down on Kubilai. A fortunate shaft of light actually fell on him as he dismounted, causing the blood red of his Chin robe to stand out against the whiteness of his Mongol fur jacket. He strode over to where Chabi waited patiently on her horse, and assisted her down. Together, they walked towards the high rostrum, bedecked with banners and flanked by the fortunate workmen who had built it, and who were now to be afforded a good view of the ceremony.

It was then that Arik Boke chose to spur his horse forward, crossing Kubilai's path. For a while, he loomed over his older brother from the back of his mount. But then Kubilai spread his arms in a show of brotherly friendship, and Arik Boke was forced to dismount or seem unmannerly. He was then manoeuvred to a place on the opposite side of his brother to Chabi, embarrassingly like some minor concubine. I was perfectly placed to see the flush of anger on Arik Boke's cheeks at being outflanked so easily. But then I knew that was not the end of the game. What was Kubilai playing at, allowing his conspirator brother so close to him? Hadn't he heeded my warning? I stayed close to hand at the foot of the steps, which Kubilai now approached ahead of both his wife and younger brother. If something went wrong, I thought I might be able to reach the Khan in time to save him. But from the bottom of the steps, I could see nothing. Everyone, Chin and

Mongol, had pressed forward, and I was enveloped in a jostling throng. If the *bahadur* was making his way through the crowd right now, I would not see him. I needed to get higher up.

I looked up from the foot of the wooden rostrum, raised high so that Kubilai could be seen by all as he performed the August ceremony. Its blocky shape and wooden structure reminded me of a funeral pyre, or perhaps a mausoleum. I hoped that was not prophetic. I had a clear sight of where Kubilai would be standing, and if I could get up on the lower steps of the rostrum, I reckoned I could see over the crowd too. That way, I stood more chance of spotting the likely assassin. By stepping on a few toes, and applying some judicious jabs with my elbow, I at last got myself on to the bottom step. Now I could look across the sea of faces, and search for Arik Boke's man. It wasn't long before I spotted him.

The squat figure was nervously stroking his trusty blade stuck through his leather belt, flattening it against his thigh. But he was not yet close enough to Kubilai to act. He was several yards away from me, being pressed up against the sides of the rostrum by the mob. Everyone was fighting for the best view. One of the rostrum builders standing next to the man pushed his elbow in the assassin's ribs, trying to improve his own position. The man backed away, and I could see the naked blade of his knife, now held low in his fist. There was a great cheer, and the man was jostled again as everyone threw their hands in the air. For a moment, I lost sight of my quarry, and then saw Kubilai's round head bobbing about in the throng. He was much closer already, forcing his way into the handful of Mongol *noyans* who were trying to push up the steps and on to the rostrum before the tide was held back.

I couldn't see the pockmarked face of the assassin anywhere.

The cheer that greeted Kubilai as he mounted the rostrum echoed across the plain, and he raised his arms in acknowledgement. This occasioned a great cheer, and a flock of black crows rose from somewhere in the Mongol encampment where they had been taking advantage of the absence of people to scavenge for food. They rose like a cloud, and flew off south merging with the real storm clouds in the distant sky. Indeed, there were those who claimed later that what they had seen was the dispelling of all the rain clouds by Kubilai's astrologers, using enchantments and diabolic Tibetan arts. The crowd's eyes were carried away by this miraculous sight, and when they returned to look on Kubilai, he held a bulging animal-skin container aloft. Everyone could hear the slopping sound, and knew it contained the milk of the mares in Kubilai's fabulous herd of white horses.

Then Kubilai spoke.

'When he was dying, my grandfather Chinghis said, "My descendants will wear gold, they will eat the choicest meats, they will ride the finest horses, they will hold in their arms the most beautiful women... "' He paused, and looked fondly at Chabi. She blushed, and he went on. '"And they will forget to whom they owe it all." '

I heard the words, and knew that only those closest to the rostrum would have heard them too. But hearing the words or not, the look on Kubilai's face as he stared at his younger brother must have pierced the hearts of everyone present. Arik Boke heard the words, knowing they were a rebuke to him, and he cast a glance around for his man. The *bahadur* was nowhere to be seen, and the impetuous Arik Boke suddenly drew a blade he had secreted under his ox-hide cuirass. I knew this was the moment I had feared, and tried to push my way up the steps past the horrified and static onlookers. But an elbow struck me in the side, and I stumbled, slipping back down the steps. I fell amongst a sea of legs. Now I would be too late to save the Great Khan, and all was lost.

Then I heard a great sigh – a combined release of breath from the whole crowd. When I hoisted myself back up and peered over the shoulders of those around me, I saw that Kubilai had anticipated everything. As soon as Arik Boke had committed himself, the workmen who had been standing, apparently drunkenly, at the base of the rostrum surged up. It was one of them who had knocked me over. They had surrounded Arik Boke before he could even get the knife clear of his jacket. The men were from Kubilai's loyal *Keshikten* guard, and Arik Boke knew immediately he had been out-flanked, and out-thought. I watched as he drop-ped the knife, and grinned in embarrassment at his older brother, shrugging his shoulders in a gesture that said, 'If it had been you, you would have done the same, brother.'

Kubilai's face was inscrutable.

I watched the drama play out before my eyes in wonderment. So I hardly felt someone brushing past me in the crowd. I had a fleeting glimpse of a pockmarked face. But when I did turn round, the squat figure had been swallow-ed by the amorphous mass of the crowd, still transfixed by the scene being enacted on the rostrum. Perhaps it had been the assassin, relieved at having failed to reach Kubilai, and saved from becoming a regicide. He had seen who was the winner in the contest of brothers, and drifted quietly back into the throng, his knife firmly back in his belt. He had no com-punction in switching support to the stronger, more cunning man.

Kubilai was unperturbed by his brother's treachery. Warned of the plot, he probably de-liberately provoked his brother's intemperate action by holding the libation ceremony in

215

such an apparently dangerous place. Arik Boke had ensured no Mongol in any way favouring his brother had been included in his coterie, but had been lax with his tongue. He had failed to keep his secret. And I was sure he would pay for his indiscretion with his life. Maybe not immediately, that was not always the Mongol way. But eventually he would die of a convenient fever, or an excess of drink. Something degrading and unmanly. For now, he was hustled away from the crowd's curious gaze under close guard.

Unperturbed, the Great Khan Kubilai stepped forward, untied the leather string at the neck of the skin container, and flung it high into the air. Everyone watched in hushed silence as it arched up into the wide, blue sky, then lazily descended like some bloated sheep, crashing to the ground on a wide patch of lush, green grass. The skin's mouth gaped, the stitching burst asunder, and the bluish-white milk inside sprayed in all directions, providing a copious libation to the gods. The roar of approval devoured the empty air like white-hot flames rushing from the mouth of a furnace.

18. SHI-BA

He who asks is a fool for five minutes, but he who does not ask remains a fool for ever

There was a great deal of good cheer in our little hovel that night. The murderer had been caught, and I could look forward to being rewarded by a grateful Khan. Tadeusz Pyka and Gurbesu helped me celebrate my imminent access to the court. Even Friar Alberoni was sufficiently impressed with my elevated status to take a small quantity of wine. It appeared to suffuse his face with a rosy glow. The heat I was experiencing was caused by the proximity of the voluptuous curves of Gurbesu. I stroked her oiled, black hair with one hand, as I quaffed a goblet of wine with the other. There was nothing more a man could desire.

So why was I not entirely happy?

Alberoni clapped my shoulder in an unusual expression of bonhomie.

'See, I told you it was a Tartar who had killed Pisano. They are all barbarians and heathens. You can even forget about accusing that Genoan, Sabattine, now.'

I shrugged, trying to make a jest of it.

'Yes, I suppose so. Though that's a shame in itself.'

I gazed fondly at Gurbesu, the wine beginning to mellow my concerns. Not for the first time since trapping Arik Boke, I caught a frown on her rounded face. Noticing my look, she banished it with a broad smile. Rats of doubt began to gnaw at my brain. And I challenged her.

'You are not convinced about Arik Boke being the killer we sought, are you?' I looked straight into Gurbesu's dark eyes. She lowered her gaze, the fringe of her thick hair masking her face from me.

Alberoni was incredulous. 'Why ever not? Wasn't he prepared to murder his own brother?'

Gurbesu shrugged. 'Yes. For the highest of stakes. He stood to gain the world – almost literally – for that deed. But why kill a mere priest, and then...?' There was only a momentary hesitation, but I noticed it, and finished her sentence for her.

'Then a Chinee magistrate?'

My gloomy look stopped both Pyka and Alberoni from their carousing. They were quite prepared to object to Gurbesu's assertion that all was not set to rights. The silversmith chipped in first.

'We know that Pisano, in his search for Prester John, had encountered Arik Boke.

Maybe he overheard as much as Master Zuliani did concerning the prince's plot against his brother.'

'And Magistrate Lin?'

Pyka was now more hesitant.

'Well, perhaps he was threatening to tell Kubilai, so Arik Boke had to finish him off too.'

I snorted. Gurbesu's doubts were infecting my mind too.

'What? Tell Kubilai that he, Lin, had sided with Kubilai's brother, and provided Arik Boke with secret details of Kubilai's movements in order to assist in his murder? But that he had changed his mind now, and wanted to return to the fold? That is not the cautious, clever Lin Chu-Tsai I knew. If he had thrown in his lot with Arik Boke, then he would have done it knowing there was no going back. It would have been certain death to throw himself on Kubilai's mercy. He well knew Mongol law. He was trying to formalize it himself. And I saw the document on his desk that told him about Kubilai's itinerary, then his meeting with the prince. After which, Arik Boke was well informed to take action during yesterday's ceremony.'

'Perhaps Lin's usefulness had come to an end, then.' This was from Alberoni.

'You could be right. But that still does not explain Pisano's murder. I only overheard the details of the plot because I was thought to be dead. The prince would not have spoken a word of it in the presence of a babbling, old fool of a priest.'

'Friar Pisano was no fool!' Alberoni sprang to the Dominican's defence. 'It was he who came to the edge of the world alone, followed the trail, and found Prester John, after all.'

'Exactly,' I sneered. 'There are no greater fools in Christendom than those who believe in Prester John.'

I suppose it was the wine that had gone to his head. I mean, Alberoni would not have normally done what he then did. So I was caught entirely on the hop, when he leapt across the room, toppling me off the bed end, and on to the rush-strewn floor. I lay there stupefied, while the friar windmilled his arms, battering me round the head. It was Tadeusz Pyka who had to pull him off me. Gurbesu simply sat back laughing, obviously quite amused at my downfall. Sitting on the floor with my ears ringing, I had to laugh too. Maybe that was the wine's effect also. And what Alberoni had said set me to thinking.

'I take it all back. You are right – Pisano was no fool. Misguided perhaps.' Alberoni growled, but I pressed on. 'But no fool. He thought he was close to what he was searching for. So indulge my doubt for a moment. Maybe we should search for the same thing.'

This immediately interested Alberoni, who forgot his anger with me.

'You mean we should search for Prester John?'

Reluctantly, I nodded. And was surprised when Gurbesu tossed a suggestion into the ring.

'Perhaps the magistrate was on the same trail too.'

'Then, if I follow in their wake, I may uncover the identity of the real murderer of Friar Pisano and Lin Chu-Tsai.'

I felt helpless and isolated. I felt small and lost – a headless chicken flapping around in a yard so big I could not tell where the edges were. A brainless fool pretending I could solve two murders in a land which until a few weeks ago I had no knowledge of, except in travellers' yarns. In the Inner City on my own, and with the only man I could easily communicate with dead, everything seemed suddenly so vast and complex. I had meddled in the plot by Arik Boke to kill the Great Khan, when my instinct told me to keep out of that quagmire. I had tried to mess with politics in Venice, and it had led to my exile. Now, I had to leave it to others to play that game. I would stick to the simple detection of a murderer. Did I say simple? The trouble was I no longer knew where to start looking. Whatever Lin had discovered had been lost with his death.

At least Ko Su-Tsung had listened to me when I suggested that there were some loose ends to tie up concerning the murders. In fact, I was a little surprised that he was so accommodating. I was sure the matter had been concluded to his satisfaction. Still, he allowed me to install myself in Lin Chu-Tsai's office for the time being. In the aftermath of the murderous conflagration, and Arik Boke's arrest, it was Ko who had turned up to take over Lin's duties. When I asked for somewhere to work in the Inner City, an enigmatic smile played on his thin lips, and he had led me through the Palace to Lin's old rooms. I imagined he was triumphant now that Lin was dead.

The ostentation of the other gilded rooms that gave off the passageways leading back to Lin Chu-Tsai's office, and the half-glimpsed images of sumptuously clad officials beyond the lattice screens that hid them, seemed all the more extreme to my eyes now. I thought of La Serenissima. It too was a place of beauty – especially the interiors of the churches dotted around the marshy land on their wooden pilings. But it was a quiet beauty, a beauty visible through a veil of miasmas, and yet at the same time grounded in the practical common sense of the bankers and traders who had caused it to grow.

This already legendary Xanadu had about it a harsh beauty of ostentation and showiness. It was Kubilai Khan's proclamation to the world that he had most of its riches at his fingertips, and what he didn't have he could reach out and take. Each room I passed was a cell of activity in this beehive at the heart of an empire. Until recently, I would have revelled in being here, where I could gain most profit and advantage. I was a Venetian, after all. But another voice now spoke inside my head. The cry of home. I was glad finally to be ushered into the refuge of Lin Chu-Tsai's office.

Not for the first time I noticed how simple and austere it looked in contrast to the rooms I had observed in passing. It was a working man's room, with the only furniture in it a couch, a chair and a table, which was piled high with paperwork. The walls were bare and lime-washed, as though Lin could not bear any distraction. The tidiness seemed at odds with his apparently treacherous act, and I felt that I had not really known the man. But he was dead, killed either by Arik Boke or another person. I didn't even really know whether his death was related to Pisano's or not. Or because he might have turned over the stone that hid Sabattine. So there I sat wondering what I should do next, and not knowing how I could begin to question those who might know something of Lin's movements prior to his murder. Then Tadeusz Pyka arrived, and I should have been relieved. But I wasn't very happy when I saw who accompanied the little silversmith. Despite the layers of clothing over her body, the smelly Mongol jacket, and the hat covering her tresses, I recognized her instantly.

'Gurbesu,' I hissed. 'It is not safe for you here. Why have you come?'

The girl made an apologetic grimace. 'When they came to fetch Tadeusz, I thought I could help too. Last time we left you on your own in the Inner City, Magistrate Lin was killed, and you almost died too.'

'Yes, and that's all the more reason for you not to be here. Especially if the murderer is still loose.' I was picturing some monster lurking in the passageways, ready to spring out at a moment's notice. Gurbesu's face fell. And Pyka quickly apologized for bringing the girl with him, though in truth I could see that there had been no way he could have made her stay. She looked quite determined.

'What do you want me to do? Shall I take her back?'

I sighed, and shrugged my shoulders. This was all going wrong.

'The deed is done now, and I need you here now to translate for me. My Turkish is fine but my Chinee is non-existent.'

Pyka proudly puffed out his chest at the thought of how useful he could be to me. It was also his chance to see more of the inside of the Inner City.

'I can help you with that. Who do you wish to interrogate first?'

I needed to know what Lin had been up to. Bearing in mind that I couldn't imagine the snooty official Ko happily offering himself for interrogation, I was reduced to the duplicitous Yao Lei.

'Let's start with Lin's own servant.'

Yao Lei sidled into the room, casting fearful looks around at those present. His gaze lingered longest on the strangely bundled-up figure in the corner of the room. Gurbesu turned her face away deliberately as he looked at her. We didn't know what he knew of her, and I didn't want to chance him recognizing her for who she was. He knew who I was, and looked as though he had seen the little man with the scarred face before somewhere. He frowned in half-recognition at the sight of Pyka.

Tadeusz was perturbed. 'If this is Lin's servant, Niccolò, then I would not trust him. I was dealing with Master Ko some months ago. The pieces I showed him were beautiful, even though I say so myself. But Ko threw the best piece – an engraved dish – aside like some piece of trash, and pushed me out of his chamber. I was forced to leave the engraved dish behind. It was only later I heard that Master Ko had picked it up, and stowed it away in his cupboard. And that he had used the same ploy with other craftsmen so that he did not end up paying for goods. But what I want to tell you is that this man...' He pointed at Yao Lei, who stood wringing his hands and grinning obsequiously. 'This man was the servant who threw me out. He serves two masters.'

I patted Pyka's shoulder. 'I know. Lin himself warned me about his duplicity. Please ask him if he will assist us.'

The cheated silversmith spoke to Yao Lei in his own tongue. He answered deferentially, but noncommittally. I could see he was waiting on what best to say when he saw how the land lay.

'He says he will assist you in any way he can.'

'Ask him what Lin did on the day of his death, from first light.'

Pyka turned to the Chinee, and he began to tell us what Lin Chu-Tsai had been doing prior to his death. He spoke to the silversmith, but he knew his words were for me. I listened to the silversmith's translation, but pinned Yao Lei down with a hard gaze as he spoke even though I didn't understand the language. Yao Lei began to sweat. To Pyka's next question, he put on a look of surprise. Pyka translated for me.

'He says his master was not pursuing the matter of the Westerner's death. He thought that is what you – ' Yao pointed slyly at me, whispering – 'were doing. Master Lin trusted you to find out the truth of that matter.'

'Then what was Master Lin doing?' I waited impatiently while Tadeusz Pyka translated first my question, then Yao Lei's response. I didn't like the shifty look in the servant's eyes. Nor his constant sidelong glances at Gurbesu. I trusted the man about as far as a Genoan fish-seller. And in fact, he smelled as rank as one.

The man's answer made Tadeusz go pale, and he gabbled the translation.

'Niccolò, he says that Lin Chu-Tsai was pursuing the most important matter of theft from the Great Khan's treasury. The night of his death he had set a trap for the thieves, and their co-conspirator.'

The thieves plundering Kubilai's treasure house? I was now confused. I had assumed that Lin Chu-Tsai's priority had been the same as mine. The death of Pisano. Now it seemed he had merely been preoccupied by Da and Zhou's little scam. Was Yao Lei suggesting it was thieves who had killed him? Or did Lin know something that connected the two affairs? I asked Tadeusz if he could contact the thieves.

He looked very nervous, wary of even mentioning his fencing activities for Zhou. 'I can't. Zhou comes to me when he has something to sell. I could ask around other silver workers.'

'How long will that all take?'

He pursed his lips as if in calculation. The whole idea was making him fidgety. 'Weeks, probably.'

'Weeks!'

I was thinking of Kubilai's impending departure. Once the court was on the move, it would be impossible to stop the murderer slipping away unseen. Besides, I had my own reasons for a speedy conclusion to the investigation. I wanted to depart as soon as I could.

'I do not have that amount of time. The thefts may be related to the deaths of Pisano and Lin. And by then the murderer could be clean away.'

I was thinking about where I went next – which included the option of forgetting about everything and getting stupendously drunk – when a figure appeared in the doorway. Pyka pulled my sleeve, and I looked up at the face of Ko Su-Tsung for the second time that day. The man was constantly peering over my shoulder, it seemed. Still, I had to be polite, knowing how useful he could be. I was also still hung up on the idea of finding Azzo Sabattine. Not that I had him down as the killer. How likely was it that a Westerner could strike twice in such a closely controlled citadel as the Inner City? The niggling thought in the back of my mind had surfaced at last. I remembered Pyka saying he had rarely had a chance to get a look inside the Inner City. So, if few Westerners were allowed access, how could it be that Sabattine had so easily killed two men in the very heart of Mongol power? And where could he hide himself without sticking out like a sore thumb? But then I was assuming he hadn't fled Shang-tu altogether and was still alive. The longer he failed to surface, the more ominous it looked.

I knew I needed to uncover some connection between the two murdered men. But my uncertainty that the connection would prove to be Sabattine, meant it was all the more urgent

228

to flush the man out, and quickly. Then at least he could be eliminated from the investigation. I told Ko Su-Tsung what I wanted, and urged him to help find the Genoan. Through Pyka, I gave Ko the impression that I still thought Sabattine was the killer, because I wanted some urgent action. Fortunately, my own doubts seemed not to communicate themselves to him.

'Then I will order an urgent search begun for this Sabattine. If he is in the Inner City at all, he will be found.' Something seemed to amuse Ko at this, and the flicker of a chilly grin ran across his lips. 'Now, forgive me, I am called away on another matter. Unfortunately, I now have to do my own work and Magistrate Lin's, or I would assuredly assist you more.'

'I do have one more request, Master Ko.'

Ko Su-Tsung tilted his head in a gesture that suggested I was pushing my luck. But I pressed on anyway.

'Ensure Masudi al-Din has examined the body of Lin Chu-Tsai, and see if he can find any similarities with Pisano's death.'

Ko continued staring narrow-eyed at Zuliani while Pyka translated.

'Similarities?'

'He will know what I mean.'

Pyka looked very relieved when Ko left, slumping down on the only seat in the room.

'When you started talking about Zhou, I nearly died.' Pyka clutched his chest as though his heart was bursting. 'All I could think of was that chalice in my workshop. I felt sure Ko was lurking nearby, and then he appeared. That man gives the impression he can almost see into your soul.' He was babbling and knew it, but he could not stop himself. The sense of relief at not being found a party to theft from the treasure house was immense. It was then I realized what a fool I was. I began to ask Pyka about the stolen chalice, and the thieves who had supplied it.

19. SHI-JIU

*Vicious as a tigress can be,
she never eats her own cubs*

The plan was simple, but like many simple plans it did not work at first. If Lin had been seeking the thieves, Da and Zhou, then he had been doing it for a reason. I would pursue the same goal and hope it led where I wanted to go. Pyka asked around his usual contacts, but it seemed the avaricious Chinee pair had gone to ground. We would have to find another way of flushing them out. The first step had been for Tadeusz the silversmith to let it be known on the quiet that he had a gilded chalice that had once belonged to a Chin Emperor, and that it was worth a Khan's ransom. I arranged to spread the news around the Inner City in the swiftest possible way.

I passed the story to Sun Yun-Suan, the guardian of the royal park. Lin had told me that gossip came as second nature to Sun – it was the currency that ensured the fat man's popularity with his peers. On the back of the rumour went the story that the chalice was stained with

Magistrate Lin's blood, and that Tadeusz Pyka knew who had spilled the blood. The final link in the chain was that the silversmith was open to offers to sell both the chalice, and the information relating to the identity of the thieves who had murdered Lin. Either way, I hoped the thieves would be drawn into ensuring the chalice or the information went no further than Pyka's workshop.

Nothing happened on the first night, except that Pyka and I lost a lot of sleep. And I had plenty of time to think about my own predicament. I asked Tadeusz again, if he had not dreamed of going home.

'Sometimes. Soon after I was brought here. But they were just that – dreams.' He told me that in the past he dreamed of his wife Irena, and his two boys. Though long dead, he said he'd often imagined them still alive, and overjoyed to see him again. It had taken a long time for those dreams to fade. When they were gone, he ended up wishing he still had them. They were the only remnant of his former life that he had.

'But my life is here now.' These were his final words on the matter during our cold, fruitless vigil.

I grunted, and stretched my stiffening limbs. I wasn't sure if that was the message I had wanted to hear.

'Maybe you're right. I have to forget the past, and live for now. It's gone and can't be recovered.' I wasn't sure if I meant the past, my former life in Venice, or simply Caterina. I did know I had begun to get scared about returning. Not for my life, which could still be forfeit if I was caught, but for the gulf that might exist between Caterina and me. What if she didn't want to know or acknowledge me? I wasn't sure I could bear that.

'Maybe you're right.'

Pyka snored, ignoring me. And no one took our bait.

Come morning, I wended my way back to my home through the now familiar streets of the foreigners' quarter. I no longer cared that I had not spoken to my former employer, Friar Alberoni, for days now. Even when he had been in evidence, he had kept to his room, mumbling prayers, or slipping into the night on unexplained errands. Our lives no longer intersected with any purpose, and so I put him out of my mind. Tired and disheartened, I slumped down on the still-warm bed, only just vacated by Gurbesu.

'Nothing?'

She still wore the rumpled under-robe that had served as a nightgown for her, and I could smell the earthy warmth of her body, as she leaned solicitously over me. She had begged me on the previous evening to let her sit in the back of the workshop with us, but I had insisted that it was too dangerous. If a fight had ensued, she would have been in the way, and in danger herself if the thieves prevailed. Gurbesu had snorted, and asserted that she would have been of more use to me than that ancient midget of a man, Pyka. I forbore from setting her right about Tadeusz's fortitude in a fight, and simply refused to take her with me.

'I do not doubt that you would fight like a tigress. But I might be distracted from the fray in order to defend you myself. No – you may not come.'

Gurbesu had snarled at me in her best imitation of the striped beast of the Indies, and had launched herself at me. I forced any thoughts of Caterina out of my mind, and the struggle had turned inevitably into the most lubricious of entanglements. But when both our lusts had been sated, and Gurbesu lay on top of me licking my chest like a contented cat, I still refused to take her with me.

Now, with a fruitless night of waiting behind me, she still wished to know everything that had happened.

'Nothing at all, I tell you, save that Pyka nearly suffocated me with his farts. He blamed the capsicums he had eaten for his dinner. I said he should stick to boiled mutton today, then we might survive the vigil tonight. And no, you may not accompany me this time either.' I had already seen the pleading look in Gurbesu's eyes. Prepared for the inevitable lasciviousness that would accompany her appeal, I closed my eyes, pretending to sleep. Gurbesu sighed, and I fell asleep watching her dressing in her best silk *bei-zi* robe. When I woke up in the afternoon, and begun preparing myself for the second night's vigil, Gurbesu was nowhere to be found. I briefly wondered where she was, but was glad that at least I didn't need to argue about her coming with me.

The second night, we revised our plans. I ended up crouching beneath the bench in Pyka's workshop. We had decided that to have both of us in the back room would give any intruder the opportunity to escape through the front door unimpeded. There were only two ways into the workshop anyway – either the front door itself, barred and bolted from the inside, or the tiny window set high in the passageway that ran alongside the rear room where now Pyka waited. The window gave out on to a back alley, and was too small for anyone to wriggle through except the slimmest of youths. Like the thief Zhou.

To hide myself from any prying eyes, I was buried in a pile of greasy rags that Pyka used to burnish his wares, and store them away from the corrosive effects of the air. The golden chalice, now sitting temptingly on the bench, was half-wrapped in a similar cloth. They stank of rancid mutton, and I wondered if I would ever be free of the stench after this long night.

And a long night it was proving to be. I was

even beginning to think that my plan had failed yet again, when I heard a scraping sound followed by a thump and a groan. It sounded like the bait had been taken, but I remained patient. It could be that Da had sent his child in through the rear window to then open the front door for him. No point in pouncing now on the urchin, and losing the prize catch. I held my breath, and hoped that Pyka had not dozed off like I had nearly done.

I heard a hiss of voices as whoever it was exchanged angry comments with each other through the rear window. Then there was the soft pad of bare feet on the floor under my very nose. I risked a look out of the bundle of rags wrapped round my face. It was too dark to see much, but I fancied I saw a shadowy form feeling its way across the workshop towards the front door. The scrape of the bolts being drawn tore the silence apart, and another sharp hiss of warning was given – this time from out-side the front door. Then the door itself was drawn back, and I could at last see something by the faint glow of a candle lantern shrouded in a cloth to hide the light. A hulking figure in a long, ragged robe slipped into the workshop, sliding the door closed behind it. The candle-light fell on the smaller figure, revealing a slim, hard-faced boy of about twelve years. The boy screwed his eyes shut as the yellow light took away his vision temporarily, and grunted in annoyance. I decided the moment

236

had come to act, while at least one of the intruders was blinded.

'Get them.'

Calling out to Pyka, I surged up from under the bench, knocking the larger man over. The lantern tumbled from his grasp, and everything was plunged into darkness. While I struggled with the man, I heard Pyka stumbling out of the back room, groping his way forward in the dark.

'Get the boy,' I called out, momentarily relaxing my grip on the hard, muscled arms of my opponent. The man managed to pull free, scrabbling across the floor towards the door. I stretched out, and grabbed the long robes that enveloped the man. Meanwhile I could hear the squeal of the youth as someone took hold of him.

'Lord, he has a knife.'

That was Pyka's voice, followed by a gasp as though the air was being driven from his lungs. I hoped it was only air, and not his life's blood too. I had already seen one slashed corpse in the past few days. I clasped the man's legs tightly to stop his kicking, and reached out for his balls. I could tell the man was no eunuch, and squeezed hard, twisting at the same time. This was no time for fair play. I could feel the fight going out of the man, as he yelled in pain. Then the scene was lit up, and all the scuffling ceased.

Pyka, who had recovered from what was only

a blow in the stomach, had relit the tumbled lantern. The light fell first on the boy who Pyka held firmly in his grasp, and then on the man who still sat on the floor nursing his groin.

'Well, well. It's Zhou and Da.'

Pyka was triumphant at our successful springing of the trap.

I shoved past the squirming boy in Pyka's grasp, and bent to pick up the blade Zhou had wielded in the dark. It was a large and murderous knife with a crude horn hilt, well worn and stained by many sweaty hands. There were even dark stains still on the blade itself.

'Did he cut you, Pyka?'

The little silversmith locked one muscled arm round Zhou's throat, and grinned.

'This little tadpole? No, he just caught me a lucky blow with his fist.'

The boy's face turned purple as Pyka's grip tightened, his eyes bugging out of his head.

I held the knife up to the feeble light of the swaying lantern, and saw the cause of the dark staining.

'It's not blood, it's rust. The blade is rusted through, and the edge is like a carpenter's saw, it's so jagged. Not really a murder weapon, unless you wanted your victim to die of an infected wound.'

Not that I was going to tell them I knew that.

'Well, it is to our advantage that we haven't been speaking in their native tongue. They won't know what we have been saying. Let them think we have proof of their part in Lin's murder – we have this knife after all. Let's scare them a little.'

Pyka grinned wolfishly, and turned to the father-and-son team of thieves. He spoke in such authoritative tones I had no need to know what he was saying – it scared even me. The boy at first seemed defiant, but I could see Da's face pale, until he looked almost green. Whatever Pyka had said had seemed to have diverted his attention from his aching balls. He scrambled from his sitting position on to his knees, and clutched at the hem of my jacket, begging for mercy. Pyka spoke again, and the father waved his arms at his son as though pushing him away.

It was the boy's turn to go pale, which was no mean feat as Pyka's arm still encircled his neck. The two thieves then fell to bickering until Da rose from his knees, strode across to Zhou, and silenced his son with one crashing blow to his mouth. The boy was stunned at the unexpected reprimand, and lifting his fingers to his mouth in shock, was horrified to see his father had drawn blood. I saw surprise on the father's face too, and guessed he was totally unused to dishing out such punishment to his unruly son. He was probably wondering why he had not tried it sooner.

Pyka took my arm, and pulled me to one side.

'The father claims he didn't know the boy had stolen the chalice, or had tried to fence it with me. He regrets the boy getting them both into so much trouble, when they were doing so well as ... well, as honest thieves is the way he put it. It appears they did have an arrangement with the keeper of the rolls for the treasury – a man called Yu Wan-Chu – to remove selected items that Yu then erased from his rolls.'

Of course, I already knew that. But now I had a name for the greedy Chinee official. Pyka continued.

'The boy just got greedy. Of course, they deny killing anyone. They say they have not been inside the Inner City for days.'

'And you believe them? They could be lying.'

'I regret to say, I do believe them. I told them you worked for the Khan and could deliver them to a nasty Mongol death – being crushed under heavy stones – but it did no good. The father even begged me to tell him who I wanted to implicate, then he would have a name for me. I was tempted – for a moment only – but I regret I am too honest, so could not help him with even that.'

'I had hoped this would lead somewhere more positive. Unless this Yu has information, we are no further forward.'

Pyka turned on the shaking thieves, and delivered another tirade. It brought forth a little gem.

'Da did tell me that Yu boasted of a secret treasure worth more than all the Khan's gold put together. Something that only he knew of.'

'A secret treasure? Does Da know what it was?'

'I didn't ask.'

'Then ask now.'

Pyka did as I requested. The answer was disappointing.

'They do not know what the treasure is – Yu would never show it to them. Nor do they know where it is. All they can say is that it is locked in a hidden room off the Wai Chao.'

'This sounds more like wishful thinking than the truth. A thief's dream of the pot of gold at the end of the rainbow. Still, if it was what Lin was seeking, then we need somehow to get access to this room.'

Pyka shrugged his shoulders, knowing that even if it were possible, it would take some time to arrange the opening of one of Kubilai's treasure rooms. Even if we knew which one it was. I pulled the golden tablet out of my purse.

'This may help. It's a *paizah* – a direct symbol of the Khan's authority. Most of his fellows are illiterate, you see. But when they see this, they know to obey whoever holds it. Especially one with the imperial dragon on it. It's the highest civil authority you can get.'

'How did you get it?'

'Let's say I appropriated it. It's very difficult for a Venetian to let gold slip through his fingers. But don't get worried, I hold it legitimately now.'

'Then let's make use of it.'

We were so busy warning the thieves never to show their faces in Xanadu again, that neither of us heard the rustle of silk from the darkness outside the door.

20. ER-SHI

The man who removes a mountain begins by carrying away small stones

A stony-faced Mongol guard, whose eyes were barely visible under the thick, fur-lined hat that sat deep on his brow, looked ferocious when Pyka and I arrived at the Meridian Gate. But I showed him the golden tablet, and it acted like a magic key to open the doors of the Inner City to me once again. The guard bowed his head, his hat flopping lower over his eyes, and stood aside. Pyka and I entered through the gate, and into the vastness of the Wai Chao. The problem was knowing just where to start. We needed to find Yu, the elusive little Chinee who had sold his soul to the family of thieves, without scaring him off completely.

As I stood in the open courtyard, I heard a call behind us, and was surprised to find Ko Su-Tsung hurrying down the palace steps. He was attempting a smile again, but it came out no better than last time. His face looked like that of a long-desiccated relic of a holy saint. His accent had not improved either, though I could just follow his Turkish.

'Good. I am glad to have found you here. I have something to show you. Follow me.'

The man then led us not back up the steps and into the palace, but round the side and down into quite another world. A short flight of stone steps led into a dark nether region of rough stone walls and packed earth floors. A little light filtered in through a row of narrow horizontal slits above eye level. I figured the apertures were hidden in the base of the palace itself which stood on a raised platform above the level of the courtyard. We were under the very feet of Kubilai, his entourage and his myriad servants. In fact, I fancied I could hear the muffled thud of their footsteps above my head.

As our eyes gradually adjusted to the gloom, I became aware that the half-cellar stretched away into darkness before us, and that the earthen floor was piled with boxes. They were heavy wooden chests, each padlocked and bound in iron, each about five feet long and a couple of feet deep. I wondered why Ko had brought me to a storehouse, and what he had to show me in such a place. Then I fancied I could hear low moaning sounds coming from somewhere.

I stood still, listening, and realized that the sounds must have been floating in the air all the time. I had only become aware of them because I had now fallen silent, leaving a stillness that was forced on us by something in the air around us. Something more horrifying than just the uncanny noise. It was more a deadening sense of human despair.

I could not figure it out, until I saw a human hand push out of the side of one of the nearest boxes. It was filthy, claw-like and wrapped in a rag, but it was palpably human. Silently, it begged for help. Shocked beyond belief, I saw other arms appear from the sides of other boxes, all of which I now saw had small apertures in them. At one hole I saw framed a grey, gaunt face with reddened eyes that bored into my soul. The moaning sounds increased like a wave rolling towards the shore, only to break on my shocked senses. I heard Pyka utter his own moan of horror at my side. This was some godforsaken prison. The cells were coffins, and the prisoners the living dead.

'How long are they kept like this?' My whisper hardly disturbed the heavy air, but Pyka understood my question whether he heard or not.

'I have heard of this place. The old Mongols believe that you might as well be dead if you live in houses and cities. They call them cities of the dead. But this is truly a city of the dead within the city of the dead. Some are doubtless kept here until they die. The few who are released might as well be dead.'

Apparently unconcerned, Ko led us past piles of chests, and I felt the brush of fingertips against my legs. It felt like seaweed clinging to the legs of a dying sailor. Pyka gave a little whimper, and scuttled after me. He was in silent shock.

Eventually we were joined by another man, who simply stepped out of the gloom as though he had been formed from the very fabric of the darkness. He motioned our little band forward, bowing before Ko Su-Tsung. This jailer of Hell stood before a row of chests lying on their own in the light of a torch that burned fitfully over them. The stocky man, whey-faced as if he never emerged into the light, had a bunch of keys in his beefy fist.

'This is inhuman,' I spluttered, more to myself than to Tadeusz Pyka.

Ko was talking in a low whisper to the jailer, who led him further into the gloom.

'Zuliani?'

At first, I thought that Pyka had whispered to me, but when I turned and spoke to the silversmith, Pyka too looked puzzled. The hoarse croak came again, and Pyka pointed into the darkness. The sound had come from the corner of the prison. From where Ko and the jailer had gone.

'Zuliani. Is that you? For God's sake, help me.'

I didn't know what to think, and I peered into the gloom. Was this Alberoni, locked away like a criminal? Who else here knew my name? A hand waved maniacally from one of the boxes.

At Ko's curt command, the jailer stooped, and fumbled with the padlock to the chest. He lifted the lid, which rose with a squeal of its little-used hinges, and stepped back. I moved forwards hesitantly.

I was suddenly reminded of the time as a child I had been lifted up to look into the coffin where my father lay. I hadn't recognized the face under my gaze – it was more like a poor wax copy than the true features of my father. I was afraid of what I might be confronted with here. I forced myself to look in the prison box, and like before, almost didn't recognize the figure inside. My father had looked waxen, his normally animated face so fixed as if death had sneaked up unnoticed and surprised him. The face that looked out of the prison chest was equally horrified and fixed, and it took me a few moments to recognize it.

It was Azzo Sabattine.

Ko stood at my shoulder. He was gloating. 'Is this the man you were looking for?'

Sabattine's body was crammed into the inadequate space inside the coffin-box. It was less than five feet long overall, and perhaps adequate for a Chinee or Mongol. But far too small for a Westerner like Sabattine. The Genoan lay partly on his side, his legs bent at the knee and his feet pressed against the end of the box, the ankles forced into one corner. His upper body was twisted so that from the waist up he lay on his back, his arms crossed over his stomach. But it was his face that shocked me. His beard was long and untrimmed, pierced by a pink tongue that flickered round his cracked, white-rimmed lips. The beard was as matted as the thatch of black hair on his head. From below the bird's nest of hair squinted two red-rimmed eyes – twin pools of terror unused to the light.

Sabattine's hands scrabbled at the sides of the box, but he seemed unable to lift himself from his tomb. I leaned over him, and scooped the Genoan up with a hand under each shoulder. He groaned as he tried to force some life back into his contorted, dead legs. Once sitting up, Sabattine gasped for breath, his eyes squeezed tight against even the feeble light of the flaming torch. I pushed the Mongol guard back, and helped Sabattine lift his trembling legs over the side of the chest. For a moment I thought the man would collapse as his limbs wobbled underneath him. It was all Sabattine could do to kneel. A shuddering gasp racked his whole body.

'May God protect me from experiencing that again. I have been there since the banquet, and I thought I was dead, and in my coffin.'

He crossed himself, and cast a horrified glance at the narrow confines of his former prison. Then he looked up at me. For the first time, he became aware of my companions. His gaze lingered in curiosity on the stooping little man with the particoloured face. Then moved

are all the voices of innocent men. If you did not kill Friar Pisano, why is it then that you were constantly in his company, and seen arguing with him before he was found stuffed in a chest with his throat cut?'

The last statement was a lie, but Sabattine was not to know that, and paled. He would have collapsed if he had not clutched at the lid of his former prison, and supported himself on it.

'I had nothing to do with his murder. You have got to believe me.' He seemed hardly able to look at the box that he clutched on to for support. Whatever happened, I was sure he felt he would not – could not – be locked in it again. 'It's true we had a falling out – the old fool kept promising me that he would get me an audience with the Great Khan. But all he did was take my money, and repay me with empty promises. He took to hanging around those camped in the Khan's pleasure grounds. They returned his fawning by treating him like a favourite dog – a slavering, faithful hound, which performed tricks at their dinner table. I was angry when I realized he was useless to me. I pushed the old fool around, smashed a few of his pots. But I did not kill him. I could see even his enthusiasm was faltering. Then he told me he was near his goal, and...' He was about to say something else, but stopped himself. He glanced upwards uncertainly, not daring to look directly at Ko Su-Tsung. 'He

251

had seen some Chinee official called Yu, who he said would help him. Could arrange an audience.'

Sabattine stopped, and clutched at my knees, deathly pale at the dilemma he found himself in. He was behaving like some supplicant on his knees before an awesome majesty. I looked away in embarrassment, staring instead at the Mongol guard, who stood in the shadows holding the sputtering torch.

'And the friar said Yu would take him to the Great Khan?'

'Yes.'

The reply was almost a whisper now – the scratchy rustle of a broken reed. And about as convincing to me. I looked questioningly at the silversmith. Pyka too shook his head sadly. He knew there was no way that Friar Pisano had direct access to Kubilai Khan, especially if he had been sniffing around Prince Arik Boke and his followers. If Sabattine was to be believed, Pisano had promised what he could not deliver.

I decided to demonstrate to the Genoan I did not believe him. My ears had been stuffed with fables built on greed – first a secret room housing treasure, and now access to the Great Khan himself. I pushed him away, and the enfeebled Sabattine collapsed on the ground. The man railed in the dust at his fate. 'Oh, why did I believe the priest? I swear that is what he told me. Pisano said he knew of a place where he could meet the Khan alone. He said he would soon speak to him.'

Tadeusz Pyka understood the last words. He snorted in contempt, doubting Sabattine entirely now. A secret meeting room where the friar could commune with Kubilai alone?

It was ridiculous. I was just as bewildered by all this nonsense, and wished only to be out of this living graveyard. The Genoan's body stank of fear, and his clothes were sweat-stained and soiled with his own bodily fluids. Still something made me hesitate. Even though Sabattine was guilty of only one crime in my eyes – that of being a Genoan – I could not in all conscience consign him to this living death for that. And I had a sense that he was hiding something from me at the last. I turned to go. Suddenly, Sabattine, grovelling on the bare, pounded earth, grabbed my ankles. His eyes bulged with fear, and I could see an inner struggle going on within the Genoan.

'Save me, Zuliani.'

'Only if you tell me the truth.'

'Damn you, you Venetian filth. Then take my treasure, and do with it what you will. Only have them release me.'

I spoke briefly in Turkish to Ko, who nodded. Sabattine sighed, and gave up what he thought was his most valuable secret.

'Pisano was not going to see Kubilai, but another, greater man by far. You see, he had seen Prester John.'

21. ER-SHI-YI

*The man who strikes first admits his
ideas have given out*

So began our crazy hunt for Prester John – a
man who I was convinced we wouldn't find
because he did not exist – in order to find a
man who did exist but who had so far eluded
me. The killer. I began by once again trying to
find Yu Wan-Chu. He was the Chinee official
who stole for Da and Zhou and, according to
Azzo Sabattine, had led Pisano to the Presbyter. Pyka and I spent most of the day trying to
track him down, only to discover finally that he
had apparently travelled to Sindachu on
business. The town was fifty miles or more
away, and it appeared Yu had left days earlier,
though no one had actually seen him leave.

Alberoni was distraught that our hunt had got
off to such a bad start.

'Sindachu? Can't you get him to return?'
'How?'
'What about that Chinee who got you into
Kubilai's presence? Ko Su-Tsung. He could
recall Yu, surely.'

Pyka squawked in horror.

'Ko Su-Tsung? Don't you know who you are dealing with? He is the most senior member of the Censorate.'

'The Censorate?'

'It's the organization that spies on government officials throughout Kubilai's vast empire, and is used to keep bureaucrats on the straight and narrow. Ko keeps records on everyone. Records that are far more searching and broad in their scope than are required by the censorate office's need, merely to stifle corruption. In reality, Ko uses his office for other purposes – mainly to compile information that can be used to further his own ends. Ko's entire experience of those he spies on is that without exception, everyone has something to hide, a guilty secret that would bring them down if revealed.'

Pyka shuddered, thinking of his fencing of stolen property from Kubilai's treasure house. 'You have seen the badge on his robes. It is both an emblem, and a reality. It is the *xie zhai* – a mythical animal with a scaly body and a single horn in the centre of its forehead. The horn is to gore any wrongdoers, and its eyes are constantly on you. Believe me, the beast is the very symbol of Ko Su-Tsung.'

'Then we can use him well.'

Pyka could not believe what I was saying.

'Use him? How?'

'We need to see his file on Yu Wan-Chu. If

255

what you say is true, then the records should be as good as talking to the man himself.'

Pyka and Alberoni looked at me hard with doubt written on their faces. The friar wanted to know how we were going to lay our hands on secret records.

'I have the very man for the job.'

Yao Lei, former servant to Lin Chu-Tsai and spy for Ko Su-Tsung, was petrified when I got Tadeusz Pyka to explain to him what I wanted him to do. He refused at first. And I knew threats were hopeless – Yao was more afraid of Ko than he was of anything I could do to him. So I had to resort to good old-fashioned Venetian bribery, and I soon won him over with gold from Alberoni's purse. You have to speculate to accumulate, after all. Within the hour, the scrawny Chinee was back with a bundle of scrolls. There were plenty, and we settled down to work.

Pyka scanned through them, and translated as much as he could of the Chinee writing, while Alberoni and I hung on his every word. Gurbesu had seemed interested in the process too at the beginning. But she soon appeared to get bored, and said she would get some fresh air. I warned her to disguise her looks, and let her go. It was going to be a long, tedious afternoon.

As Pyka stumbled through the first scrolls, it became clear from Yu's records that the silversmith had been right. As chief of the Censorate,

Ko Su-Tsung had unparalleled access to secret information about everyone in the Inner City and beyond – indeed on almost anyone of account in *Tian-xia*, or All Under Heaven. Yao Lei had pulled down a surprisingly heavy set of scrolls on Yu Wan-Chu, and the man would have been horrified to learn what Ko knew about his activities through his many Censorate spies.

'He knew Yu was pilfering from the Khan's treasure house. In his post as ... what does he call his official post? Here it is. As Recorder of the Treasury in the Directorate for Imperial Accessories, Yu had unprecedented access to the treasury.' Tadeusz stole a sidelong look at me, glad his name didn't appear there too.

Alberoni peered at the symbols under Pyka's finger. The friar obviously thought he could decipher them merely by staring hard. 'What does this say?'

Pyka blushed. 'Apparently, he was working with two unnamed Chinee thieves.'

'Read on,' I said. 'That does not interest me.'

Pyka gulped and read on. 'Ah, look. Here Ko states he confronted Yu with this, and the man admitted to his deeds.'

'Then why wasn't he arrested?'

'Don't be so naive, Alberoni,' I retorted. 'He was much more use to Ko with the knowledge held over him. He was probably an excellent spy for Ko after that little disclosure.'

What I had guessed appeared to be true, for

what followed was a series of titbits of information about other officials' peccadilloes, fed to Ko over a period of months. Then Pyka found the mother lode.

'Look at this.' He held up a long scroll covered in a minute scrawl. 'It's a statement from Yu about someone he calls "the black priest". It refers to the discovery of his body at the banquet.'

Alberoni sat up sharply.

'It's about Pisano. What does it say?'

As Pyka slowly translated the document, an amazing story emerged.

Yu Wan-Chu had asked to see Ko after the murder of Pisano, because the Head of the Censorate was aware he knew the black priest. He had feared Ko might think him implicated in the death. It was enough to convince him to impart to Ko his one big secret that he felt would be of value to his master.

Yu had long known there was a secret door leading off the Wai-Chao. He had not noticed it at first, looking as it did all of a part with the others. But one morning its existence sprang out at him, and he couldn't believe he had missed it for so long. It had been under his nose all the time. The door wasn't obviously different. But once aware of it, it seemed to Yu to stand out clearly. He could not imagine why he had never seen it before.

The problem was that he didn't have a key

for it. In fact, it appeared he was not to be allowed the key to this door, even though he was entrusted with the keys to everything else that Kubilai held in his treasury. For months that other door had irked him, rankled and got under his skin. At first, he had tried not to bother with the contents behind that door, and be grateful that he had been given the honourable position of Recorder of the Treasury in the Directorate for Imperial Accessories. Week after week, he walked past the locked door, and did not give it a second thought. But as the weeks turned into months, and Kubilai's storehouse of riches increased, Yu fell to imagining what might be behind the door.

He soon discarded the idea it might contain yet more saddles, bridles and stirrups, or weaponry such as bows, quivers, arrows, or even the very best of armour made of metal or boiled leather. There were three storehouses full of such equipment, and Yu could not imagine that yet another storehouse of the accoutrements of war should be so jealously guarded from his and others' gazes. For weeks he toyed with the idea it might be yet greater stockpiles of gold and silver, lapis lazuli and sapphires from Badakhshan, or balas rubies and pearls. He even conceived of exquisite furniture wrought from these precious elements by expert craftsmen. For a week this conclusion satisfied him, and his curiosity felt assuaged.

But then he fell to thinking again.

All these things he could picture, because he could see them in the other storehouses to which he did have the keys. He was a man of little imagination, only believing in what he could feel and see for himself. His father had died when he was a little child, and his mother had struggled to bring him up, drumming into him the lessons of their poverty. He had been taught to believe they would only eat at the end of the day if there was already millet in the jar earned by yesterday's labours. His diminutive mother convinced Yu that the only truth worth knowing, was one you could roll between your fingers, and taste with your tongue. No, Yu had not been brought up to be a dreamer. He could only imagine what was in the locked room by reference to what he saw every day in the other rooms. But whenever he thought he had worked it out, a little worm fell to gnawing at his brain, telling him that it must be something other than what he had guessed it to be so far.

So he struggled again to imagine what lay behind the locked door he was not allowed to access, convinced only that it must be more precious even than anything he currently recorded in his scrolls. He eventually realized that the only way he would learn what was stored there, was by seeing it for himself, like the millet in the kitchen jar. Being a cautious and law-abiding man, he thought about asking permission to enter the room. It had taken him three months to pluck up the courage to enquire, albeit indirectly, of his Mahometan overseer, if there was not something missing from the inventories. 'Nothing at all,' had been the terse response. It had been that retort, stinging to his pride and sense of face, which had set Yu on the dangerous course of his conspiracy with Da and Zhou. Theft was a sweet, if solitary, revenge on his untrusting masters.

Then, the change in his routine occasioned by his thievery, suddenly gave him an opportunity to find out what was hidden behind the secret door. One night he slipped out into the courtyard to oil a particularly stiff lock before plundering the treasures behind its door with Da and Zhou. He was afraid and didn't want anything to go wrong. So the hour was unusual for him, and to his surprise he saw a kitchen girl, carrying something, hurry across the courtyard. He snuffed out the candle he was carrying and hid in one of the deeply recessed doorways. From there, he watched as the girl moved into shadows along one side of the square. He pulled back in case she saw him. When he looked again, she had disappeared into the darkness. Half relieved at not being seen, he waited until she reappeared, which she did very shortly.

When she had gone back to the kitchens, his curiosity got the better of him, and he approached the place where the girl had vanished. Walking past the irritatingly secret door as he had done a thousand times before, he hardly registered that there was something different this time. He had gone a dozen paces past before his brain had worked out what that difference had been. He had to turn back though and was standing in front of the door before he really believed it. But it was true – the door was slightly ajar and there was a key in the lock. He still couldn't believe his eyes, but when he reached out to touch the door, it creaked alarmingly, and moved on its hinges. It truly was open, and this was his chance – perhaps his only chance – to find out what it protected. But first he drew the key from the lock and pressed it into the base of his still warm candle. Then, having taken an impression of the key, he slid it back in the lock. Did he now have time to see what was behind the door? Still he hesitated, for he was not a man who was capable of swift decisions, and he was scared of what might be inside. His mother had also drummed into him the litany of thinking, and thinking again before doing anything. Sometimes he hovered in a perpetual stew of indecision, sweating over the tiniest choice – should he wear the blue robe or the green today? Was it cold enough for leggings with his trousers? But the door beckoned enticingly, and he glanced nervously about him, making sure the expanse of the Wai Chao was empty, before sliding through the narrow opening. He

262

didn't want it to creak again and give him away. He was in and out before the girl returned, scared by leaving her key behind.

What he had discovered inside was deeply puzzling. But as he began to think about it, he could see ways he could profit from what he had found. His father had impressed on him that there was a buyer for everything – the trick was to find him. Then, one day the black priest spoke to him, and he realized the buyer had been under his nose all the time.

I saw immediately where this was leading. This was the fantastical secret room of Pisano's imagination, reported by both the thieves and Sabattine.

'What does he say was in the room? Why would Pisano have been interested in the information?' Alberoni could hardly wait for Pyka's laboured translation.

The silversmith looked at us both, puzzlement in his eyes.

'Some of the last line has been scratched out. Ko merely records it was a treasure without price.'

Alberoni's eyes, however, sparkled with excitement. He was convinced he knew what lay behind the door in the secret room.

'The only treasure Friar Pisano sought was Prester John himself. We must find this room immediately.'

It took some persuading to get the friar to

wait until the morrow. No good sneaking around the Inner City in the dark. Tomorrow was soon enough to begin the hunt for the room.

22. ER-SHI-ER

Better to light a candle than to
curse the darkness

I don't know what it was that woke me. Maybe it was my dream of Caterina disappearing in the thick mist of the Venice Lagoon. Or maybe it was a rustle of silk that bore no resemblance to the swish of the simple gowns she wore. I reached out. There was a warm hollow where Gurbesu had lain. I turned my head to see the exterior door slide gently shut. The sound reverberated in my brain, and set me thinking of other occasions when I had ignored such a silken rustle. How often had Gurbesu been close by, when vital information had been revealed to me? And how many times had my intentions been anticipated? It had also been Gurbesu who had been the cause of my own nagging doubts after Arik Boke's entrapment.

I slipped off the cot, and pulled on my boots. Crossing the room, and sliding back the door, I was just in time to see Gurbesu's shiny silken robe disappear round the corner at the end of the street. I followed in the same direction, a

265

thousand thoughts coruscating round my brain. Had I been spied on all along, and led by the nose to point the finger at Arik Boke? Who had pointed me at the unfortunate prince, leading me away from the real investigation? And who was Gurbesu about to report my current misgivings to? I didn't know where she was going, or to whom. But she was leading me out of the foreign enclave, and deep into the Chinee sector.

This was the old city on to which Kubilai had grafted his Mongol palace. It was far older than the invaders' imposing monolith. The buildings had steep roofs tiled in wood, with curved ridges and ornate eaves that spoke of wealth and age. If this was the home of the wealthy Chinee who acted as officials to the Court of the Great Khan, then Gurbesu's master had to be either the weaselly Ko Su-Tsung, or the elusive Yu Wan-Chu. I hoped I would soon find out.

The quiet of the night was broken only by the trill of a caged bird that hung in the window of a house whose interior was lit by a dim, yellow light. Someone was up late, waiting impatiently no doubt for Gurbesu's report. She stopped outside the house, and looked round. Fortunately, I was able to merge with the deep shadows cast by the low roof ridges of the adjacent buildings. She scratched at the door, and entered when a shadowy figure slid the door open.

The house looked modest in comparison to its neighbours, bare of ornament and yet neat and clean. It did not smack of Ko's desire for aggrandizement. Yu Wan-Chu, perhaps, was not in Sindachu after all. The light cast through the window moved, as though someone had shifted the candle to a more secretive position. And a tall shadow played on the far wall. The shadow of a tall man. It was time to find out who Gurbesu was spying for.

I crossed the thoroughfare, and slid the door open with a jarring crash. Gurbesu's face was a picture of shock and embarrassment. The two men, one a Chinee reclined on a couch, the other an Arabian standing over him, were not quite so surprised. The Chinee's face in particular creased in a grin. I was astonished, not having anticipated what I was seeing.

'Lin Chu-Tsai! But you are dead. I saw you burn to death myself.'

It was Masudi the physician's turn to smile.

'I told you I was a great physician. Look, I have brought Magistrate Lin back from the dead.'

Perhaps not back from the dead, but close enough. I could see that Masudi had to assist Lin to rise from his couch. The skin on his face was scorched red still, though not as severely as Tadeusz's scarred features. And his hair was unusually short for a Chinee. Lin saw my look, and rubbed his head ruefully.

'I am afraid I have lost a lot of hair, and the

267

luck that goes with it, my mother would have said. Would that she had had such concern about my precious jewels.'

I winced at the thought of Lin's childhood castration. He stared off into the corner of the room, where motes of dust hung in the air, no doubt imagining that childish, carefree time. A time when he was whole.

'Yes, I can recall a time still, when my only burden was such fleeting troubles as making my cloth-bound bundle of cooked millet, provided by my doting mother, last until evening. She had loved her little Chu-Chu, and wailed in despair when my father had mapped out my future for me. She hadn't wanted her little man ... spoiled in such a cruel way. But father had pointed out that the family line was assured by Hujia, my elder brother. Gawky, hairy-armed Hujia would provide the Lins with children, while I, little Chu-Chu, would bring them ever-lasting fame. And no issue. Not that I under-stood any of that at the time. I only knew that my older brother kept smirking at me, and clutching his groin for weeks after the decision had been made. And my mother had done nothing but cry, and shake her head when I asked her what was the matter.' He sighed. 'However, that is in the past. I think I owe you an explanation, Nick Zuliani.'

Still puzzled at the turn of events, and sore at Gurbesu's treachery, I nodded grimly. I needed to step carefully. I still did not know of the depth of Lin's involvement with Arik Boke. If he was hiding from Kubilai's retribution, then my knowing that he was alive, and being in his company, endangered my life too.

'If you escaped the fire, then whose body was it that Masudi here examined?'

'Why, Yu Wan-Chu's, of course.' Lin settled gently back down on the couch, his skin still clearly tight and painful from the fire. 'You see, I had already pinned him down as the inside man involved in the thefts from the Khan's treasury. And suspected him of trading information to Friar Pisano. If I was to do anything though, I needed to extract a confession from him. So I arranged for him to meet me at the cane palace.'

'What? How did you know about his involvement with Pisano?'

'Ah. It all started when I helped Gurbesu escape the Khan's harem.'

I looked questioningly at Gurbesu, who hung her head, obscuring her beautiful brown eyes with her dark and glossy hair. Lin Chu-Tsai explained.

It was as Lin Chu-Tsai was returning to his office, and the mountain of paperwork that awaited him, that the only beneficial moment of a wearisome day occurred. And even that had an inauspicious beginning. He was hurrying, head bowed, along the corridor that led to his sweet-smelling sanctuary, when a familiar voice stopped him in his tracks.

'Master Lin. A moment of your time.'

He gave an inward sigh, and turned to face the old woman, his most obsequious smile on his lips. Her beady eyes fixed him to the spot as firmly as if he had been transfixed by a cavalryman's lance. He hoped that whatever she wanted would not be as painful to endure. As it turned out, the favour she required suited his own purposes entirely.

'I am at your service, Mistress Bolgana.'

The old woman harrumphed in apparent embarrassment, and fingered the talisman round her neck.

'It is a ... delicate matter. Concerning the Kungurat tribute.' Her lips pursed in distaste, sending further striations shooting out from her mouth across the permanent ridge and furrow of her visage. Lin Chu-Tsai inclined his head questioningly, wondering what the problem was with the gaggle of pretty girls who were soon to titillate the jaded palate of the Khan. Bolgana frowned, deepening the furrows.

'It appears one of the items is ... faulty. I need to dispose of it.'

Lin agreed to assist her in sneaking the girl out of the harem. It remained unsaid between them that Bolgana herself was in danger, and could be accused of failing in her duty to protect Kubilai's property. It had been embarrassing, and not a little frightening to smuggle the girl out of the Hall of Earthly Pleasures. She was in effect the Khan's property, after all, and his action could be deemed to be theft – a capital offence. But Bolgana had bluntly told him the girl was not a virgin – apparently she had slept with a red-haired stranger on her journey to Shang-tu, and made no secret of it. She was better lost in the *demi-monde* of courtesans that thronged the Outer City. There, her temperament would suit some of the men who frequented such girls. She had wondered if Master Lin knew of the man, and if he could get rid of her on him. Lin Chu-Tsai said he would help. The ensuing subterfuge – dressing the girl in layers of clothes to bulk out her slender figure, coarsening her face and fine dark hair with grey dust, and allowing her to walk through the Meridian Gate like an old maidservant – had passed unusually easily.

It was then Lin Chu-Tsai had his only lucky break of the day. After getting rid of the 'faulty goods', he was returning late across what the Chin officials called Wai Chao – the Outer Court. The sun had virtually set, and the beaten earth of the courtyard glowed red in its dying rays. A marble avenue ran through the centre, continuing the line of the corridors of the Inner City. Around the courtyard were arrayed the galleries in which were housed the libraries and storehouses of the riches of Kubilai Khan. Weapons, silks, precious stones and rare objects lay hidden behind the thirty-two doors that debouched on to the courtyard.

The area itself was vast and empty – some two hundred yards north to south and a similar distance east to west. Lin Chu-Tsai seemed to be alone in this great vacuum. Then, along one side aisle, in the shadows cast by the distant, towering Meridian Gate, he saw some movement. Two men were making their way towards Lin Chu-Tsai and out to the teeming Outer City.

From the start, he saw there was something about the demeanour of the men that smelled of conspiracy. So he slipped into the shadows on the western side of the square, not wishing to be seen. Their movements were guarded, their glances stealthy. He had seen it so often before, indeed knew the feeling as he himself became more and more involved with Arik Boke and his supporters. He knew the tension and the fear that induced a drumming heart, and shallow breathing. It was as though every breath might expel a whiff of betrayal into the air, creating a rancid aroma that would be sniffed out by your enemies. He even fancied he could smell it now himself.

Sidling nearer to them, he could see their clothes, though they had their backs to him now. They were both of his caste and no doubt held some position of authority within the palace just like him. Their voices were pitched low, but Lin knew that it would be foolish to go any further and expose himself. He hung back in the shadows of the great gate, straining to hear what they were saying. One voice dominated – that of the taller man. He caught a phrase that drifted to him on the light evening breeze.

'A single death may not be the end of it...'

The comment brought a gulp of indrawn breath from the shorter man, and a tensing of shoulders. Lin Chu-Tsai wondered whose death they were discussing – was it that of the Westerner? The shorter official looked uneasy at the idea, but the speaker was obviously made of sterner stuff. He patted the other man on the shoulder, and whispered into his ear something that Lin Chu-Tsai couldn't catch. Then the nervous man turned, and though his face was partly in shadow, the rays of the sinking sun caught his profile such that Lin Chu-Tsai felt sure he would remember it.

Then they moved further into the shadow of the deep, wooden colonnade around the courtyard. Lin Chu-Tsai just had to get closer to the conspirators, and prayed the colonnade would allow him to do so unseen. The deep shadow of each red-painted, gilt-edged arch afforded him good cover, and his tread was light despite his bulk, his felt boots soft and quiet on the hard earth. He was glad that they still had their backs to him however. Something about the big man's air – the way he held his shoulders – told him the man was preternaturally sensitive to being observed. But soon, Lin Chu-Tsai was only a few yards away, and could now hear

273

more of the exchanges.

The nervous official was extremely scared of some proposal, his edginess betrayed by his quivering lips. 'They must never know, or we are finished. You know how they would deal with us if they found out. The Mongols prescribe the death penalty for stepping on a threshold, let alone what you propose.'

The big man's laughter was chilling, and he poked the other man. 'Then we must say nothing about the black priest Pisano, nor what you led him to. Eh, Yu.'

Yu Wan-Chu bared his teeth in a forced grin that ended up more like a grimace. Now Lin Chu-Tsai knew him. He was the bookkeeper of the treasure house. Lin wondered what he had shown to Pisano that had proven so deadly. Then the big man was speaking again, and Lin finally recognized his voice.

'We must take heart. Now give me the key and let us go our separate ways before we are seen.'

Yu Wan-Chu handed over something – obviously the key – and turned tail, keeping to the shadows. The big man sighed, and then called after him. 'And behave naturally – no one will ever know what has been done if you just behave naturally.'

The tall, cadaverous man shook his head at the sight of the departing Yu Wan-Chu, watching him march with fake nonchalance across the square. He looked absurd – as though his arms and legs were being manipulated by a puppet master in a shadow theatre.

'I would be best rid of him,' muttered Ko Su-Tsung to himself. He was standing half in the rays of the sinking sun, and half in the shade of the colonnade that still hid the shivering Lin Chu-Tsai. Then he turned in Lin's direction, and took a few paces along the edge of the colonnade. Lin held his breath, and prayed. If Ko approached any further, Lin knew he couldn't help but be seen.

Then Ko grunted, turned towards the gate, and walked through it into the maze of the Outer City. Lin Chu-Tsai let his breath out in a long, relieved sigh, and dropped his shoulders to ease the tension that had come with his near discovery. He wondered what the key was for that Yu had given to Ko. As the shadows lengthened, he marvelled at the towering size of the Inner City walls that managed to exclude even the sun in the sky from its confines. At this time of the day, the place felt like a mausoleum. He shivered at the thought.

'I was going to tell you all this, Nick. But I wanted to catch Yu out while he was still frightened, and before he made a bolt for it like a scared rabbit. Through Yao Lei, I arranged to meet him by the cane palace, which had been partially rebuilt for you. Although I was chiefly concerned with his involvement in the thefts, I had at the back of my mind that Yu and Ko had

275

been involved in the black priest's murder too. I wondered if the sight of Pisano's blood might shock the truth out of him.'

'You thought Yu had been the murderer?'

Lin shrugged noncommittally.

'I could not say.'

'But what did he say to you when you confronted him at the cane palace?'

'He was not in a position to speak. He was already dead; someone had murdered him. And then before I could check his body, the fire engulfed us both, and I was fighting for my own life. Now Arik Boke is arrested for both treason, and the priest's murder.'

He sounded as unconvinced of the prince's involvement as I was. Maybe he had good reason to, if he was a confidant and co-conspirator of the treasonable prince. I suddenly wondered if this might explain his having hidden away after his apparent death. He obviously read my mind, and smiled painfully.

'You saw me entering Arik Boke's tent, and think I was somehow involved in the plot to kill Kubilai.'

It was a statement not a question. I stared again at Gurbesu, who had the good grace to blush. I'm afraid that all I could think of was that she looked beautiful that way. Lin saw my stare.

'You need not fear the girl being on the wrong side of the fence. She did what she did to protect you, and help you. She acted as my agent at your side, and it was I who asked her to suggest a few avenues of investigation to you. I was too ill, and too scared to stand by you myself. It suited me to be dead for a time. And whilst she is not what she seemed to you, neither am I. I am no enemy of Kubilai's.'

'You were acting for the Khan?'

'Am I not his magistrate? I owe that good fortune all to the preferment of Kubilai. In return I acted as his spy in Arik Boke's camp, and if I stirred things up a little – prompted the prince's treasonous actions – then I don't regret it. I only speeded up the inevitable.'

I was confused.

'But Ko said you hated Kubilai because of...'

'Because of my status as a eunuch? How can I blame the Khan for the actions of my parents thirty years ago, when I no longer blame even them?'

I could see he was telling the simple truth. He went on.

'I will tell you something about Ko Su-Tsung. He doesn't like being made a fool of, especially by some *nan-jen* southerner like me. Especially when his own origins are even lower. He long ago buried those origins in a miasma of obfuscation and half-truths so compelling that he himself has come to believe his own lies. He hated his Khitan parents for having brought him into the world as they had. It was humiliating that his ancestors came from the far north, beyond the Great Wall, and had been mere barbarian invaders before even the Mongols arrived. Khitans are reviled by the native Chins, and had little chance of preferment under the old Chin emperors. So the first lie was the story of the Ko parents coming from the heart of the Han Empire.

'The second lie was the story of their unfortunate demise in an earthquake. Orphaned, if only in his mind, Ko Su-Tsung emerged from obscurity posing as a young Chin in the regional town of Kaifeng. There he set about constructing a noble history for himself. This he conveniently achieved by discarding his family name, and hinting at an ancestry including the famed engineer Su Sung. Next, he concocted an education that included passing the *shengyuan* – the old civil service degree. This allowed him access to important positions at court, and he relied on his native wit and ability to cover up his lack of real knowledge. He has lived with these lies so long, that now he himself believes in his descent from the great inventor whose name he has stolen, and that he passed with flying colours the civil examinations that all Chin officials were required to sit. So now, little or nothing remains of the boy, Ko, who had been the dirty rice-eating Khitan who had left home twenty years earlier.'

I saw I had to reassess Ko Su-Tsung in the light of what Lin was telling me. He was clearly a very devious and ambitious man, capable of anything to achieve his ends.

'No wonder he was glad to see you dead, Lin. Now he is revelling in having taken over your position.'

Lin shook his head sadly.

'It won't stop there for Ko Su-Tsung. If Arik Boke's plot had led to the death of Kubilai, then he would have aligned himself with the survivor. For the time being. If it resulted in the fall of the royal House of Tolui entirely, then that would have suited him just as well. You see, his naked ambition is no less than to fill the void as emperor of China.'

23. ER-SHI-SAN

Experience is a comb which nature gives
to men when they are bald

It took the rest of the day to discover who, in Yu Wan-Chu's stead, was holding the keys to the treasure house, and another frustrating delay while we woke the man. Chen Yun had retired early, and at first refused to be disturbed. He felt under no obligation to open the Khan's treasure up to foreigners. It took my golden *paizah* to persuade him. Even then, Alberoni, Pyka and I had to pace around impatiently outside his door while he dressed. Chen Yun insisted that he could not be seen out in his nightgown, and made us wait while he put on his clothes.

His promotion to the middle-ranking post apparently vacated by Yu Wan-Chu, had come unexpectedly, and I could see that he was going to make the most of his chance. Everything he did would be carried out with such grace and skill, that he would soon be climbing further up the ladder of preferment. Chen Yun was not going to let this opportunity slip by being seen scurrying through the palace in his night attire like some flustered low-grade servant. Finally he emerged from his rooms. He had donned his silk underwear, over which he had pulled on a narrow plain robe, his felt boots, and finally his ornate green *pao* – the outer robe denoting his rank. He was probably already planning to order a blue one from his tailor in anticipation of further elevation.

Finally he was ready.

As the fat man waddled ahead of us down the passageways back to the Outer Court, I did not have the heart to tell him that his coiled-up coif of black hair had come loose from its pins. It was straying from underneath its net cap like a weasel trying to escape a sack. We descended the steps into the square, Chen Yun jangling his bunch of keys, and asking which door it was we wanted opening. Tadeusz translated.

'Which door?' I was beginning to tire of this officious, fat man already. 'How do I know which door? Don't you know what's inside them? It has to be Kubilai's most priceless treasure.'

Chun Yen smirked. He obviously thought we foreigners knew nothing, and were losing face in our ignorance.

'Well, take a look.' The man waved a podgy-fingered hand around the vast square, acting like some pedagogue with backward children. 'There are thirty-two doors – each one a trea-sure house. What is it you wish to see? Cloth of gold, silks, precious stones, pearls, elephants' tusks, spices? They are all here. And for the doors I have thirty-two keys.'

He jangled the bunch of keys again on their huge iron loop to emphasize his point. 'There is a different key for every door, you know,' he said importantly.

I reckoned that he was so new in the post that he had not yet figured out which keys opened which doors.

It looked like we would have to open every one. And I was reminded of Ko Su-Tsung's avowal that it would take weeks to complete an inventory of Khan's treasure. Now I understood why. Would it take us as long to find which one was the so-called secret room housing Yu's hidden treasure, and where Pisano met Prester John, if indeed they were one and the same place? I didn't even know if it truly existed. In this fabled city of Xanadu, wasn't everything just an elusive chimera?

Chen Yun stood impatiently twirling the keys in his fat fist, a superior sneer on his face. I was about to tell him to open each door in turn, when I realized what a fool I was.

'Tell me, Tadeusz, what do you see before you?'

Pyka frowned. 'What do you mean?'

I spread both arms wide, encompassing the whole vast expanse of the darkening Wai Chao. 'Thirty-two doors – all facing into the square – all open to view.'

Pyka shrugged. 'Naturally. It's good security to have what you want to keep safe in open view.'

'Exactly.' I turned round and round, peering into the furthest corners of the square. 'And what did the two thieves call the room that held the treasure, and where Pisano met the Presbyter according to Sabattine?'

'A secret room. Why?'

'Surely none of these doors can be called secret. So they cannot be the one we seek. We have to find what is hidden, not what is visible.'

Alberoni stood irresolute in the middle of the square, while Pyka and I separated, each taking one end of the long sides of the Wai Chao. We walked slowly down the shady colonnades, peering into each nook and cranny, even feeling the earthen walls for cracks in its smooth surface. Anything that might reveal a door. Chen Yun stayed in the middle of the square with the friar, puffing out his cheeks in exasperation at our foolishness. He watched as we reached opposite corners at the bottom of the square, fruitlessly checked for doors either side of the great Meridian Gate, and met under its overhang. We both then walked towards him down the long, central avenue. As we got closer, his pompous face was a mixture of puzzlement and annoyance. But neither of us would give up until we had examined the area round the steps to the palace at the head of the square. We did so with the same care we had lavished on the lower end of the Wai Chao.

Nothing.

'We must do it again.' I was determined, so with a sigh Pyka walked down one side of the square, scurrying to keep pace with me on the opposite. He was not really paying attention to his task, when I suddenly saw it. I called across the square to him.

'Wait!'

With a start, Pyka stopped, and was about to apologize for his lack of attention, when I called out again.

'Stand directly opposite me.'

Pyka thought I had gone mad trying to puzzle out the mystery, but complied, humouring me. We lined ourselves up as best we could using the squares marked out on the floor of the Wai Chao. When I was satisfied with our position, I called across.

'What do you see behind me?'

Pyka frowned, unsure what I was aiming at.

'Why a door, of course.'

'And what do you see behind yourself?'

Pyka turned on his heels, and found himself staring at a blank wall. A gap between two doors. Alberoni grinned and immediately began counting the doors on Pyka's side.

'Sixteen.'

Then he counted my side of the square. There were seventeen doors, not sixteen. The secret door had been in full view, after all. He and

Pyka hurried across the square to join me.

The portly keeper of the keys squinted into the gloom and frowned. For the first time, he noticed the extra door, the central one on the side I had stood.

'I have not noticed this layout before – are you sure this is part of the treasure house?'

I saw the disagreeable look on Chen Yun's face, and although I was not following the conversation spoken in Chinee, knew something was amiss.

'What is he saying?'

Pyka again performed his duty as interpreter.

'What do you mean? It may not be part of the treasury?'

'The door is not matched by one on the opposite side of the square.' He pulled a face at the lack of symmetry, and assumed his argument won in the face of such incontrovertible logic. He turned to go. I grasped Chen Yun's arm in a vice-like grip, preventing his imminent departure.

'Try them.'

'What?'

Pyka translated.

'Try all the keys in this door?' Chen Yun's face contorted in the superior sneer he no doubt cultivated long and hard at night before the mirror in his room. Intended to frighten a common servant, it of course had no effect on Pyka, Alberoni, or myself. My grip on Chen Yun's arm tightened, and the man paled at the pain he felt.

'Yes – try every last one, if necessary.'

Chen Yun suddenly understood me without needing any translation. He pulled the first key round the ring from the bunch, and approached the mysterious door. He poked the key into the hole, and the door gave way under his fumblings, swinging open. Pyka gave him an accusing look.

'I thought you said you didn't have the key.'

'I don't. I didn't even turn the key – the door must already have been open.'

I pushed Chen Yun to one side, and peered into the oblong of darkness beyond the doorway. Alberoni was next, right at my shoulder, followed by Pyka. Beyond the door, we could see a flight of stone steps cut into the thickness of the great protective walls of the Inner City. The steps curled upwards and out of sight, so it was impossible to tell what might be at the top.

But what was more disconcerting was the faint keening sound that drifted down from above our heads. I am not a man given to fanciful thoughts about exotic beasts, but I have listened to travellers' tales. And as I climbed the steps, I was reminded of stories of the islands beyond Mogdaxo, that some called Madagascar, where lived the gryphon bird, big enough to pounce on and carry away an elephant. I had once seen an elephant being trans-shipped to the King of France, and knew how large the beast was. For some reason, the keening sound put me in mind of the gryphon. So it was with great caution that I poked my head above the level of the final steps in the spiral staircase to take a look.

There was a second, inner door at the top of the stairs, and it too lay open. Beyond was revealed a small room with little natural light to see by. Two windows set high in opposite walls, one facing west the other east, were no more than slits. In the evening light that drifted through the westerly slit, all I could make out was an empty room with a small couch in it. There was a shape, a bundle of furs on the couch. Cautiously followed by Tadeusz Pyka and Friar Alberoni, I climbed the final steps, and tiptoed across the dusty floor of the room towards the shape on the couch. I lifted the furs. And found nothing. The keening sound emanated, not from a gryphon, but the wind blowing through the chamber. Whatever bird had been here had already flown.

'He's gone!' Friar Giovanni Alberoni fell to his knees, and slumped in prayer.

I looked around for signs of our mythical man. And a cursory examination of the room was all that was required to confirm that no great treasure had been housed in it. It was a cell – admittedly a cell of luxurious proportions compared to Sabattine's coffin-box – but a cell nevertheless. From the top of the stairs to the outside wall with its slit window was no more than five paces. It was clear that the cell was indeed built within the thickness of the ramparts. A secret room. It was hardly bigger in the other direction, seven paces taking me from one side of the room to the other. I paced back and forth several times, tapping the walls to see if there was a secret door, which would make this space merely the ante-room to a bigger space. I even slid aside the low couch covered in rags that was the only furniture in the cell.

Nothing. Then I remembered something. I pulled a grubby slip of paper out of my purse where I had stuffed it when I searched Pisano's hovel. It had a date on it.

'When was the Eve of the Assumption?'

Alberoni looked puzzled, but responded.

'It was more than two weeks ago.'

The date fitted. Shortly before we had arrived in Xanadu, Pisano had a meeting with someone important enough for him to make a written record of the date on a piece of Chinee paper. I had found it, and held it in my hand now. Soon after, Pisano had been murdered. The only conclusion I could reach was that the former occupant of the room was indeed the 'treasure' that Yu Wan-Chu had stumbled on. But where he was now, was another matter.

The friar had slumped on the couch after I had yanked it away from the wall in my fruit-less search for another door. Alberoni found he still could not speak, but fumbled in the folds of his habit instead. He pulled out the bundle of crumpled and torn old documents, and waved them at me.

'Don't you see? You were wrong about these letters concerning Prester John. There is such a man in the East, and he was here, in this very room. His name is unknown to his guards, because he has not uttered it in over sixty years. But he is Prester John.'

I tilted my head back and laughed.

'Then where is he? He must have died a long time ago. Even a son of Prester John would have to be almost a hundred years old himself.'

Still Alberoni was in earnest, gripping my arm like a vice.

'Suppose he was. A very old man, I mean. It matters not about his age. What does matter is that he has gone, and you must help me find him. He is the one who can rally Christianity and drive the Saracens out of the Holy Land.'

I shook the madman off, and tried to convince him of the foolishness of his statement. But Tadeusz Pyka took my arm, and guided me across the room, whispering in my ear in our common language.

'This may not be as mad as you imagine. There was a warlord called Togrul who was a Nestorian Christian. The Chinee called him Wang. Is that not like your name John?'

I frowned – it was true that the way a Chinee might pronounce the two names – Wang without the hard Northern guttural 'g', and John as the Orthodox Iohann – there was some similarity in their sounds. But it was foolish to leap from this to the idea, firstly that Prester John had once truly existed, or secondly that he was still alive. I said so. Still Pyka defended the friar.

'Alberoni is not saying that Wang, or John, still lives. Indeed Togrul was certainly killed by Kubilai's own grandfather, Chinghis, for betraying him more than sixty years ago. But nothing was ever heard of Togrul's eldest son after the battle. It became as though he had been expunged from history. Even his name is now lost to us.'

I paused, not yet ready to admit the crazy tales might have a nugget of truth. Then Pyka said something else that gave me a clue to Pisano's murder.

'Also, Wang simply means great in the Chinee tongue. So whoever was in this room was the inheritor of his father's mantle. Wang Khan – the Great Khan.'

I knew what he was hinting at. Sabattine had first thought Pisano was referring to Kubilai when he talked of meeting the Great Khan in secret. My compass bearings had been way off track from the start. Pisano had not met Kubilai, nor was his story an idle boast. He had truly met the Great Khan – Wang Khan, son of an old enemy of Kubilai's family – and given him the mantle of Prester John.

And in the middle of it all was Yu Wan-Chu. It was he who had found ... I still can't call him

Prester John. Let's call him the Old Man. He found the Old Man, and sold his knowledge to Pisano, who thirsted to find Prester John. After that, he had done exactly the same thing with Ko. The scroll from the Censorate files told us so. So was Yu Wan-Chu a killer? He struck me as a weak individual, more inclined to wheedle his way out of trouble, than to use force. Or was the Old Man in some way responsible for the deaths? Did he himself want to keep his existence a secret?

I voiced my suspicions out loud.

'No!' Alberoni was adamant. 'You are talking about a man of the lineage of Prester John. Probably David, King of India himself. It is not possible for him to have killed Pisano, the emissary of the Pope.'

I recognized the dangerous glint of madness in the friar's eyes. God's blood, what an unholy mess. Families and secrets – they were always and ever the cause of mayhem. Why could people not be truthful with each other? I could not help but think that, if I had given in to Caterina's wish to be wed, I might not have got mixed up in the fraud that went wrong. And if I had not been involved, I would not have had to flee from Venice. And then found myself in this arse-end of the world. If the Old Man's existence had not been a secret, then it would not have been there to be found out. If the whole Christian world did not openly yearn for an earthly saviour...

My head was spinning. Yu might have killed to keep his valuable secret to himself. Or at Ko's instigation. Or the Old Man himself might have done so for his own reasons. If the door to his cell was so poorly secured, then he could have sallied forth, killing anyone who found out about his presence, and his identity. I reckoned Alberoni had been lucky that the Old Man had disappeared before we found out about him, or we too might have been dead by now.

24. ER-SHI-SI

There are always ears on the other side of the wall

My hunt for the murderer seemed finally to have merged with Alberoni's quest for the mythical Prester John. I could only guess at the motive for Kubilai's clan keeping an old enemy under lock and key for so long. Although the lock wasn't as secure as it perhaps had been. His long incarceration must have driven him mad, and despite Alberoni's protestations to the contrary, turned him into a killer. Whatever was the truth, he was on the loose.

We left Chen Yun to decide how to tell his masters that the Old Man had slipped his bonds. That was his problem. I wanted to figure out a way of finding him myself. I still needed to impress Kubilai sufficiently that he would believe in the truth of Pisano's death, and allow me to return to Venice. Preferably with a purse full of jewels.

When I returned alone to Lin Chu-Tsai's hideaway, he was sitting up, drinking from a

293

shallow bowl proffered by Masudi. I took it to be some medicine, though it was as clear a liquid as water. But whatever it was, it seemed to revive him. And he listened with care to my telling him about the discovery of the secret room. He considered my cast of characters for the role of murderer.

'I myself had suspicions about Yu Wan-Chu. He confessed to me that he had met Pisano, but didn't say why. Then he too was killed. Who is this old man who meant so much to the friar?'

I groaned.

'Prester John. A Western legend, a product of wishful thinking. Take it from me, the Old Man from the treasure house can't be him.'

I explained about our discovery, and the fact that the Old Man was who Tadeusz and Alberoni suspected to be the son of Togrul, or Wang Khan.

'But why do you no longer think Yu was Pisano's killer?' I needed a final confirmation of what I already suspected. 'Could he not have murdered Pisano in some dispute over payment? The friar was well known to be short of funds.'

Lin turned a stiff gaze on Masudi.

'Tell him.'

The Arab doctor twisted round on the edge of Lin's bed.

'You see, Master Nick, when I examined the burned body of Yu, it was still possible to see the true cause of death. His throat had been

294

neatly cut with such a sharp knife that there were nicks in the bones at the back of the neck. I have no doubt that, had the skin not been roasted so effectively, I would also have found teeth marks on the shoulder or neck. The same as on Pisano. And you.'

'On the neck – as if the killer wanted to hold his victim like a tiger does. So, if the two deaths were linked by the same method of killing, then it was not Yu who killed Pisano.'

'Exactly. Unless Yu did it, then slit his own throat in remorse.'

I knew he meant the comment only in jest, and fingered the scarcely healed bite mark on my own neck. I mean, picture the scene. Yu slits his own throat, tries to kill me, then crawls back into the fire to die. Unlikely. No, I only had one suspect left. It had to be the Old Man who killed both Pisano and Yu Wan-Chu to preserve the secret of his identity. I shivered, and Masudi al-Din offered me a dish of the clear liquid. I intimated I had no need of medicine. He laughed.

'This is rice wine. It's very warming. Try it – but not too much. It can cloud the senses very rapidly.'

Oblivion in wine – that's what I wanted right now. I tipped the whole dishful down my throat, gasping as the fiery liquid hit my stomach. I refilled the dish myself from the small glazed bottle Masudi had left on the table. Let the Old Man try to find and kill Kubilai, if that's what he wanted. There were plenty of *Keshikten* guards to prevent him achieving his goal. They would stop and kill Prester John, or King David, or whoever he was. The trouble with that line of thinking was that I would lose the prize of solving the riddle for Kubilai. The second dish warmed as much as the first. It also released any inhibitions I had about asking Lin what should have remained unspoken.

'Tell me, Lin. Have you no regrets?'

The magistrate knew what I was asking, and eased himself into a more comfortable position on his couch. Masudi and Gurbesu were now sitting well back, beyond the small circle of yellow light cast by the spluttering candle.

'For my jewels? Oh, I used to long for someone with whom to share my thoughts – a compliant wife waiting at home to whom I could unburden myself, knowing no word I spoke would be repeated. But of course, she would be a gossip and scatter her secrets like seeds to impress the other wives of the scholar classes. You can imagine the conversation. "Do you know what my dearest Chu-Chu said today?" I just know my wife would have wheedled my mother's baby-name from me, and used it not only to my face, but to her cronies at the tea house. "What Chu-Chu told me last night as we snuggled each other under the quilt?" She would then proceed to expose my innermost soul for the examination and amusement of her friends. She would even drop a hint as to the extent of dearest Chu-Chu's knowledge in the case of the murder. How he knew the identity of the man, even if I didn't. Just to impress – caring nothing for the danger that put her husband in. "He said that..." She would pause for effect, then spill out the story when all hung upon her words. "That the killer lived in the Inner City." This is the deadly secret my wife would impart with not a care for her husband's safety, only excited by the frissons of horror that she would cause in the gathered throng of wives. Who would all go home to their husbands, and cause their own ripples of horror. "Do you know what Madam Lin told me today?" Only, one of the husbands would know the truth already, because he would be the killer. And so his wife would set in train the events that would lead to me becoming the murderer's next victim.

'No, I am far better off not having a wife. Nor even children, come to that. Being alone has its compensations at times – it means I don't have to worry about shooting my mouth off in unguarded moments to those I would expect to trust, and who could, unwittingly or not, betray me. Or be compromised by having to protect my offspring.'

Lin Chu-Tsai smiled rather sadly, and started to settle back on the couch in a doze. I was galvanized, because I had suddenly been vouchsafed the truth.

'The Old Man!' I cried. And leaving my companions open-mouthed, I rushed through the door into the quiet streets of the Outer City, praying I would be in time.

25. ER-SHI-WU

*You can't capture a cub without
going into the tiger's den*

Thanks to my pass, I had a means of free passage through the Inner City without being challenged. The golden *paizah* opened every door. I began quartering the rooms and corridors of the palace in my search. I knew I had little time.

Empty chamber after empty chamber proclaimed my failure to even get a scent of what I sought. Then, passing rooms once occupied by the departing Mongol lords, I could detect a strangely familiar odour. A smell I suddenly associated with maternal breasts, and milky, suckling infants. I was reminded again of Caterina, and could see, in my mind's eye, a chubby boy-child sucking greedily at those ivory bosoms with their tracery of blue veins that I had once so lasciviously nibbled. Rationally, I knew that any child of mine was now more than a suckling. But my soul would not allow a child that I had not yet seen to be more than the baby that would have been imminent when I left Venice. It was as though I could only come to terms with this disaster in my life – and that was the sole way I could describe it – a disaster – by forcing time to stand still in the place I had fled. Venice was still La Serenissima of three years ago in my eyes. Caterina was still aged twenty-two and full of sweet charm. I knew it was foolish, even as I envisioned the suckling infant and mother. After all, Caterina would have got on with her life during my self-imposed, self-inflicted, drunken exile. The milky smell in my nostrils turned sour.

And I recognized it for the stink of empty bags of kumiss – the fermented mares' milk loved by all Mongols. The Inner City should have been throbbing with life, its passages flowing with the blood of activity as a myriad servants, officials and scholars pulsed through its courtly body. The susurration of instruction, intrigue and gossip should have filled the air with a sound not unlike the inhalation and expulsion of breath of some great being sprawled on the landscape. Instead the palace confines felt cold, clammy and dead. Like the oily exhalations of a newly expired corpse, the very air smelled foetid and stagnant. There was no living being in the palace corridors, and it was terribly easy for me to imagine the place abandoned, deserted, left to rot. And the murderer fled.

The change from what I had experienced

before was uncanny, and as I rushed down the maze of passageways, I was hard pressed to hold on to my sense of reality. The race down ornate corridors and through gilded rooms became like one of my nightmares of escaping the Signori di Notte police in Venice. I looked back, and for a moment I saw Caterina running after me. She fell, and in falling, called out. I faltered, then realized it was only a young Chinee female hurrying on some errand. Perhaps she was a courtesan, delayed by a demanding client, or a servant made to clean the pots before she was free to leave. Whatever she was, she regained her feet, and glancing nervously down the corridor at me, sped off.

I realized why there was no one here. The court had already begun its journey to Kubilai's new capital further east. Everyone was on the move. I hoped I still had time, because in the confusion of the preparations, what I feared most could more easily happen. I pressed on eventually, realizing I was in a part of the palace I had not seen before. The wall decorations were subtly grander, the light more all-pervading, unlike the gloomier parts of the Inner City at the core of the buildings.

I slowed to a walk, and felt nervous and edgy about being where I was. My sense of awe almost overwhelmed me, and I stared at the carved door that faced me at the end of the corridor. The intricate work was designed to confront anyone approaching with a rampant dragon that stared straight out with bulging eyes, daring the intruder to have good reason for crossing the threshold. It held my gaze for an age. I was alone outside what must be Kubilai's private chambers.

I tiptoed to the dragon door, and pressed my ear to its gaping, fiery mouth, but I could discern no sound from beyond. I swallowed hard against the fear that lurched up in my throat, and slid the door gently open an inch or two. Still no sound, so I peered into the gap. Inside, the room was shady, as if the sunlight was filtered through a thick material. I pressed my eye close to the gap, seeing only one part of the room – the left side. Piled on the floor were large leather bags, and above them on the wall was a long shelf on which sat some small felt mannequins. I knew immediately what they represented – they were crude effigies of Mongol deities such as I had seen in the yurt we had lived in while travelling to Xanadu. I remembered Khadakh calling the chief amongst them Itugen, the earth god. Craning my neck to see further into the room, I saw the edge of a metal pot in the centre of the room. I knew exactly the layout of the room, replicating as it did the interior of a Mongol yurt. It had to be Kubilai's inner sanctum.

The room would have a central fireplace, and travelling bags full of personal possessions lining the left-hand wall underneath the altar. It also meant that the bed, and whoever might be in it would be at the back of the room to the right, out of my line of vision.

Then I heard something. It was the lilting, soothing sound of someone quietly singing. I slid the dragon door right back, and stepped into the room. On the rumpled bed opposite sat a figure bundled up in a Mongol jacket. Whoever it was, wore a large Mongol cap covering their head, and was hunched over so that their face was invisible. The smoke rising in a column from the fire in the centre of the make-believe yurt further obscured the identity of the person, who was fiddling with a small bundle on their lap. It looked at first like another rag-doll effigy, but as I stepped round the side of the fire, the figure turned. I saw that the doll was a living baby, cradled in the arms of the Old Man.

The sight shot a picture of Caterina Dolfin back into my fevered brain. For the more I thought about my last days in Venice, the more obvious it became to me what her condition had been. Her pallor and sickness, the way she held back from me as though hiding her thoughts – something she had never done before – all now screamed the truth out to me. I could now almost envision Caterina cradling a baby – my baby – in her arms. I could almost convince myself that I had really seen it, and fondled it myself before I escaped my pursuers. I was nearly lost, but dragged myself back to my proper senses. Had I not resolved to forget all that and get on with my new life?

'Who are you? Why are you here?' The Old Man's voice was scratchy from little use – no more than a whisper.

'Because there is a murderer loose in this palace, who has killed twice and is bent on killing again.' I looked down at the gnarled, useless hands that could barely hold the baby. 'Why are you here? This is not your child.' I meant it as a statement, not a question, but the Old Man still replied.

'No!' He laughed nervelessly, and stared down with awe at the red-faced bundle in his lap. He held the baby as if it were finest Chinee porcelain – which in a way it was. It was certainly as precious, and I was terrified he might break it. 'This is the next Great Khan.'

It was just as I had guessed. Though it had been a surprise to see the Old Man himself here. His toothless mouth gaped open, as he sought to find the words to explain. But whatever he was about to say was cut off by another tongue.

'What is he doing here?'

I barely understood the words, but could tell the harsh tone of voice easily enough. I swung round to face the old woman, bundled up in a greasy jacket, her bandy legs poking out from below the ragged hem like two Mongol bows.

Bolgana had never looked so frightening.

Keeping my eyes on the Old Man, who was

standing beside me with the baby, I spoke to her.

'It's over, Lady Bolgana. Your father is free, and it doesn't look like he is seeking revenge. So why should you? I can see from the state of his hands that he could never have manipulated a knife so expertly as to cut the throats of Pisano and Yu Wan-Chu. But you could. It was you, wasn't it?'

Bolgana's ruddy face paled, and she opened her mouth and howled like a wolf. I was unnerved for a moment by the animalistic sound – transfixed like a startled coney. With surprising agility, Bolgana bowled past me, and snatched the precious baby from the Old Man's grasp. She held it threateningly by one arm like a careless girl with an unloved doll. The baby screwed up its face, and wailed. I knew I had to be careful, so I spoke clearly, making my tone of voice calm and reassuring.

'I should have realized from the start this was all to do with children – parents and children, and the debt they owe each other. Father to son – mother to daughter. And daughter to father. You must have nursed your hatred for Kubilai for a long, long time, Bolgana. How it must have shocked you to realize your father, presumed long dead, was still alive.'

Bolgana looked coldly up into my eyes, now cradling the baby lovingly in her arms.

'You know nothing. I loved Kubilai – and all his brothers – like the children I never had. My grandfather had fought against his grandfather and had lost. That was an end of it. My family swore allegiance to his, and I was happy to serve.'

'Then why turn against him suddenly?'

'Because you were right in one thing. I thought my father was long dead – killed in the battle or its aftermath that finished off my grandfather's ambitions. Imagine my shock, when I learned the old Christian priest had recently found him still alive. That Kubilai's father had tortured him by keeping him alive, and taking away his freedom. But what was even worse was that Kubilai and his brothers had forgotten about him. Simply forgotten about his existence. Lost him and his very name, leaving him to exist without life. For sixty years. I could not forgive him that. He had betrayed me and my family.'

'And Pisano, and Yu Wan-Chu? Why did you have to kill them?'

'It was Yu who got to know of my father's existence first. Only he didn't know who he was until he encountered the black priest. This Pisano was always creeping round the palace like a cur. Looking for his saviour. Kubilai took pity on him, and allowed him to go where he chose, like some favoured child-simpleton. Then Yu put two and two together and sold his secret to the black crow of a priest. Pisano had my father set in some role as saviour for his religion. Which was madness. Oh, yes, Father had toyed with your Western faith as much as grandfather had – out of curiosity. But it was always to the old ways that he returned. Anyway, the priest could not wait to tell me of my noble lineage. So I arranged to meet him in secret in the cane palace just before it was dismantled. I had only to come from Arik Boke's camp, and knew nobody else would be around. I suppose I already had some fear in my heart as to what he had to say.'

Bolgana paused, her head tilted to one side recalling how she felt on that fateful day. Her meeting with the black priest Pisano must have been a turning point in her life, and the end of his. The baby, unaware of the danger he was in, curled his little fist round one of Bolgana's callused fingers. She lifted him to her bosom, and cooed at him.

'What he told me – that my father was still alive, and imprisoned – took my breath away. I think I turned to stone in that moment, I felt so cold and dead like a rock high on the Altai mountains. I've been dead ever since.'

'Why did you kill him?'

'I had to. If he had let the secret out, then Kubilai would have got rid of my father to save his own embarrassment. And then me too probably.'

'And Yu Wan-Chu?'

'Unfortunately for him, he saw me at the cell door one night. I was trying to speak to my father through the slot in the door, as I hadn't laid my hands on the key to it then. Someone else did that for me only today. Yu saw me, heard me invoke my father's name, and that was that. He had to die then. I let him follow me, and led him to the pleasure grounds where it was out of the way of others. I was shocked to see the cane palace rebuilt. But it seemed a nice irony to kill Yu there too. So for the second time the building made a convenient and quiet slaughterhouse.'

'And now?'

Bolgana smiled, and hugged the baby close to her withered chest. I thought of my own child – saw it in Bolgana's arms – and shivered when she spoke.

'As you so wisely put it – this is all about parents and their children. And revenge. I would have killed Kubilai. But it's so much crueller to leave the father alive to mourn the loss of his son and heir.'

Her right hand snaked up to the long, thin pouch strung round her neck, and at first I thought she was merely touching it to invoke good luck. Then I heard the voice of the Old Man cackle behind me.

'It's a skinning knife she has in there. And she is expert with it too. I have seen her hold a beast with her teeth and strip it of its skin in seconds.'

I saw the glint of a slim, sharp blade appearing in Bolgana's hand, and did the first thing that came into my head.

'What's this in your ear?'

I gave a flourish with my fingers close to Bolgana's left ear, and produced a silver coin out of mid-air. The sleight of hand drew her attention for only a moment, but it was long enough. With my right hand I grabbed the hand in which Bolgana held the knife only inches away from the now wailing baby's throat, and twisted viciously. Bolgana squealed in agony as the cords in her wrist snapped audibly, but she still held on to her skinning knife. I marvelled at the strength and will power of the old woman, fighting on, and still hanging on to the baby. I too held on grimly as the blade weaved about in front of my eyes. Then I felt Bolgana's grip relax momentarily, and the woman leaned into my chest. I thought I had prevailed, only to feel a sharp, tearing pain at my throat.

The old woman was biting down on my neck for a second time, closing my airway like a wild beast throttling its prey. Just like when I had encountered her at the fire. This time I could not shake her off, and knew what it was like to be a deer held in a death grip by a wolf. I tried to gulp in air. I was blacking out. Then I heard a swishing sound, and felt the woman's jaws begin to relax. I looked down, not believing what I saw at first. The bloodied tip of a keen-edged sword blade forced its way out of Bolgana's chest. It stopped just short of my own, then slid back into the folds of the old woman's blood-stained jacket. I looked over her shoulder, and watched as Kubilai Khan withdrew his sword from her body. As it sucked out, Bolgana slumped to the floor, and I caught Kubilai's son and heir before his brains were dashed out on the stone floor.

A Beginning

It is later than you think

I looked down from the Inner City walls on to
the tented city below. It was surrounded by a
thousand horsemen, circling and recircling it,
raising clouds of dust. I thought my eyes were
deceiving me at first, for it looked as though
the whole of the city was on the move, sliding
gently eastwards. I grinned self-consciously,
peering round to see if anyone else had been
witness to my stupidity. How could a city
move?

Much had happened in the passage of the last
few days, and I would not have been surprised
to find the illusion to be caused by a spinning
head. As Bolgana slumped dead to the floor, I
had held the baby fondly in my arms for a time,
reluctant to give it up. I felt in some small way
what I had missed for ever by fleeing Venice. I
only reluctantly released it to the rotund Chabi,
who then returned the princeling to the care of
a wet nurse.

Ko Su-Tsung, who had unexpectedly appeared in the Khan's private chambers immediately

311

after my tussle, had arranged for Aunty Bolgana's body to be removed from Kubilai's sight. He also whisked away the Old Man.

I was of course promised a reward by the grateful Kubilai. It was left to Ko to grudgingly tell me that I could name my price, I had surprised myself by saying that I wanted nothing more than permission to leave. After despairing of being able to return to what I had left, after telling myself that I should not interfere, and remaining to all intents and purposes dead to Caterina and her child, I had finally stood with a baby in my arms. Only then had I known what I wanted. It was odd though to find myself forgoing the chance of worldly riches for a snotty child I had not even seen. Even now, I wondered if I should after all request some small trinket. Merely as a gift for Caterina, or an inheritance for the child, of course. My life had suddenly become more complicated than it had ever been, and I wasn't sure I liked the feeling.

I stared again from my perch atop the Inner City walls looking out over Camp Fields. Plumes of dust rose from the massive settlement, and it must have been these that had confused me. I could see churches, mosques and markets scattered around the valley, and could hear the sound of a million voices talking, arguing, and bargaining. It was too distant to make out the individual dramas being played out. So I failed to see the wagon provided by

312

the Khan for the heir to Prester John's legacy leaving Xanadu. The excitement and the crowds were probably bewildering for the Old Man. Kubilai would care for him, now he knew of his existence. The last thing the Old Man needed would be to be dragged westward as a saviour. Friar Alberoni would have to create some myths of his own for the Pope.

I called to mind again the history lesson Lin Chu-Tsai had given me about Kubilai's family, and more particularly about Aunty Bolgana. Family, which had meant different things to Lin and Ko, and finally myself, had been the key to the murders. Bolgana had got her nickname of aunty because it had been her cousin, Beki, who had wed Tolui, father of Kubilai. Poor drunken Tolui, spineless son of Chinghis, had been married off as part of a dynastic arranged marriage to ally Wang Khan's defeated tribe to Chinghis's dynasty. And yet that ill-starred alliance had produced four strong sons, two of whom had become Supreme Khan – Mongku and Kubilai; one who ruled over Persia – Hulegu; and Arik Boke, the runt of the litter. But the key was not Kubilai and his brothers. What mattered most was that Bolgana's grandfather had been Togrul – Wang Khan himself. And that her father had been so ill-treated. What did a daughter owe to her family other than a promise of revenge?

But in the end it was Kubilai who had extracted a gruesome revenge. That very morning, early, everyone had witnessed Bolgana's body being rolled in a carpet, and set beneath timbers over which everyone who entered the Inner City would walk. The carpet ensured that royal, albeit traitorous, blood was not spilled on the same earth that had so recently been propitiated with mares' milk. The body's location ensured that henceforth the House of Tolui would trample on Wang Khan's descendants. Of Bolgana's nameless father there would be no further sign – he would simply disappear.

I brooded on the woman's violent end, and a new dilemma. Instead of offering me freedom, Kubilai had sent word that I was appointed to the magistracy of the newly resurrected Lin Chu-Tsai. I was to be a sort of advocate or policeman to the Mongol court. It was intimated by Ko Su-Tsung, whose brow was thunderous as he conveyed the message, that I could refuse the privilege only at my peril. In fact, Ko looked as though he wished I would do just that. He knew that I suspected him of letting the Old Man loose to cause Kubilai mischief. But he also knew I could not prove it. Not yet, anyway. I told him I wanted to defer my decision, and still had not made my mind up even now. I felt further from Venice and Caterina than I had ever been.

I was distracted from my gloomy thoughts by the sound of peoples' voices drifting up to my eyrie. There was another sound too – a deeper sound, like the keening of shifting timbers, the groaning of a new ship on the slipway before it settles its weight in the comforting arms of the sea. I screwed my eyes up, and peered into the billowing cloud, trying to set my eye on some fixed point, some immutable yardstick. Seeing a cleft in the range of hills to the north of the city, I fixed on that and watched, my eyes swimming.

The city *was* moving!

Slowly but inexorably, landmarks and features in the settlement caught up with my hillside marker, and moved past. The troop of horsemen encircling the city were not the primary cause of the clouds of dust. Each building groaned and rumbled as it dragged itself west as if some monstrous giant cut off below the waist, and dragged along on his stumps. My eyes ached as I strove to make sense of the sight. Even the smoke from kitchen fires moved at its base as well as drifting in the breeze.

Then I saw it.

The whole city was on wheels. Wagons dragged the more substantial buildings along on massive wheels. Some carried the Mongol circular tents whole, while other, smaller carts were piled high with the dismantled black-felt yurts – a melange of tarry bundles and poles. Teams of horses and oxen strained against the massive burdens, pounding the earth, and raising dust with their hooves. Everyone and

315

everything was moving to the fabled east. Leaving the City of the Dead and its inhabitants behind.

Kubilai was leaving for his new capital without even giving me a chance to say what I thought of my appointment as *avogadore*. I would have to hurry if I was going to give the Khan my reply. I leapt down the wooden stairs, calling for my friends, Lin Chu-Tsai, Tadeusz Pyka and the beautiful Kungurat girl, Gurbesu.